# Dangerous Curves Ahead

Dionne Witt

Published by Sweet Pea Publications

ISBN: 0692632689

ISBN-13: 978-0692632680

Cover design by Dionne Witt

Author Photo by Deanna Harris

# Acknowledgements

If there is one thing I have learned in the past couple of years, it's that life is a journey, and it's definitely not a straight shot from Point A to Point B. Along the way, there are detours, bumps, (lots and lots of bumps!), some U-turns, even some changes in speed. I have found that the only way to handle all of this is with some good company along for the ride. And snacks. Don't forget the snacks.

This book began as a NaNoWriMo project many years ago. The first draft was completed, it went through editing and revision, and then it was locked away. Two people in the whole world have read it, and they told me it didn't suck. I took that as a good sign and decided maybe I should publish it. But not before sending it through several more rounds of editing and revision before I was satisfied. Here is the finished product.

Thank you to my parents, my sisters, my nieces and my great-nephew, for just being there for me and for Olivia.

Thank you to all of my incredible friends, Sarah, Jess, Jessie, Brenda, Renee, and Beth, for being some of the best gal pals I could ever ask for. Shout out to my LitChicks as well. We've had some fun times, and I'm sure there will be more in the future. And thanks to some new friends that have joined this crazy ride. You know who you are. :)

And as always, thank you, Olivia. My darling girl, I hope that one day you are as proud of me as I am of you. I love you, Sweet Pea.

# Chapter One

As a Driver's Education instructor for five years, I had seen plenty of bad drivers under the age of eighteen. One girl wrapped the back end of the car around a tree when she stomped on the gas while still in Reverse. Another boy took out four side mirrors of parked cars in one block before I was able to get him stopped. And my favorite disaster driver had to be the boy that thought it was best to turn the wheel almost half way around in order to change lanes, resulting in a near spin on the highway, and the two kids in the backseat throwing up in the car. It made for an interesting call home to the parents.

After three full semesters of uneventful student driving, I knew my luck was bound to run out. It was a blustery day in February, and I had one of my worst students ever sitting beside me at the wheel of the blue Chevy Lumina with the words "Student Driver" emblazoned down both sides in bright yellow. He was at least in the top ten. His name was Brandon, and he had transferred into George Washington High School at the start of the spring semester. I was assured that he'd had some practice driving, and that he would pass the test with flying colors in May. I really wanted all my students to pass, as this was the last semester that Driver's Education would be offered through the high school. This was my final time teaching young people to drive, and I wanted everyone to look at me and say, "Wow, all her kids passed. She was an excellent teacher," or something just as ego-raising.

I was having serious doubts about my teaching ability as we sailed through a red light at a busy downtown intersection, horns blaring at us, and tires squealing in near misses. In fact, I'm ashamed to admit that my first thought was that I was going to die on a Wednesday, and I was wearing underwear that read "Friday" on the front in gold, glittered lettering. Oh, how the paramedics and my mother would laugh.

I shook my head and focused on the situation at hand. I had to get the car stopped before the two girls in the backseat passed out or screamed themselves hoarse.

With a gentle yet firm grip, I reached over and grabbed the wheel, steering us down an empty side street, at the same time stepping on the special brake installed on the passenger side. We slowed to a stop and bumped the curb. Brandon's knuckles were white, as was his face, and he didn't appear to be breathing. I let go of the wheel with shaking fingers and put the car into Park, then removed the key from the ignition.

"So, um, that wasn't...bad," I said, trying to sound encouraging.

Brandon let out a breath that seemed to deflate him, and he went limp in his seat. I half-turned to check out the passengers in back. They had been holding onto their seat belts like lifelines for the past several blocks and seemed to have no intention of letting go.

"Would one of you like to drive us back to school?" I asked. "We need to be heading that way anyhow."

Lisa, the girl sitting behind Brandon, raised two fingers, still clutching her seatbelt. "I'll drive back, Miss Martin," she squeaked out.

I smiled at her and faced Brandon again. "You two can switch places," I said.

Brandon nodded and got out, his face now a bright shade of pink. His shaggy brown hair fell over his eyes, but I knew he wasn't looking at me anyway. I sighed a little as he took Lisa's place in back. Four weeks of driving with me, and he wasn't getting any better on the road. And from what I'd heard from Mr. Jenkins, the classroom instructor, he wasn't doing so hot there either. It was time for a call home.

Lisa drove us back to school and parked without any problems. I dismissed the kids to go onto their next period class, but asked Brandon to hang back for a moment. He stared at the ground, kicking pebbles with his sneakers, his hands shoved deep in the pockets of his coat. February in Iowa can be brutal, and today was no exception. The wind blew my hair all over the place, and I fought to control it while trying to talk to Brandon.

"How do you feel about your progress?" I asked. It was a safe question. Instead of coming right out and saying, "Kid, you suck," which would bruise his already fragile self-esteem; it was a way of letting him express his feelings.

Brandon shrugged and avoided my eyes. This was the response I'd been getting from him since day one, in both Driver's Ed and American History, which I also taught. His grade in that class was slightly better than in Driver's Ed.

"Have you been driving at home with your dad?" I asked.

"My uncle," he corrected me, muttering under his breath.

"Oh, yes, that's right. Your uncle." I gave myself a mental head slap. His father was a touchy subject. "Well, how are you doing with him?"

Another shrug. I grabbed my blowing hair into a messy ponytail and held it, once again cursing the fact that I didn't have the guts to just chop it all off.

"Well," I said, "how about I give your uncle a call and talk to him? See if he can help you out a little bit more?"

Brandon coughed and shrugged again. The bell rang, signaling the end of second period. The students began pouring out into the halls, heading toward their next class. We could hear them through the doors, it was so loud.

"You better get going. I'll give your uncle a call later," I said, forcing a smile. "Everything will be okay, and I'll see you seventh period."

Brandon spun on his heel and entered the building, leaving me to stand alone outside. I looked at my watch. Third period was my planning period, so I was free for fifty minutes. Making sure no one was watching, I edged away from the doors and around the corner, where I pulled out a pack of cigarettes and stared at it with longing.

What can I say? Teaching kids to maneuver through busy streets in two tons of metal made me antsy. I shook one out and held it between my fingers. I had officially quit on New Year's Day, and I hadn't caved yet, but if there was going to be a time to do it, now was that time.

"You know, smoking will kill you."

Thinking it was the principal about to reprimand me for smoking on school property, even though I wasn't, I jumped and tossed the cigarette to the cement, stomping on it until I ground it to smithereens. I whirled around to see my fellow teacher and my best friend since we were six years old, standing behind me, a smug smile on his face.

"Yeah? Well, so can driving with a bunch of sixteen-year-olds," I said, annoyed that he had scared me.

"That bad, huh?"

I nodded. "What are you doing out here anyway? You don't smoke," I said.

"Nope. But I knew you had just gotten back, and I wanted to make sure you were sticking to your promise to quit. Just trying to hold you accountable."

I scowled at him. Jeremy Lipton taught freshman Algebra and Advanced Calculus, something I could never do. I can't even balance my checkbook. In fact, he does it for me, something that embarrasses my mother, who is immaculate with hers, down to the penny.

Jeremy and I became friends in first grade, when we were sent to sit in the hallway for eating paste. We went through the rest of our school years together, even dated for a short while during senior year, until it became too weird. It was like dating a sibling, and that was just icky. So we remained friends. He was hired at George Washington the year before me and recommended me to the school board when an opening for a history teacher

6

occurred. The catch was that I would have to teach Driver's Ed as well, something I had thought would be no big deal, but boy oh boy, was I regretting it now.

"Which kid was it today?" Jeremy asked.

"Same one. Brandon Archer. I don't think he's a bad kid, just a bad driver."

"Have you talked to his parents?"

"He lives with his uncle, remember?"

Jeremy nodded. "Oh, yeah. How could I forget? So what are you going to do, Melinda?"

I blew out a breath and stomped my feet to keep warm. "Call his uncle I guess. See if he can work with Brandon more at home. The girls in his car are going to snap one day if he keeps driving like this."

"Good luck," Jeremy said. He knew that calling parents could be tricky. Either they wanted to work with you, or they wanted your head on a platter for daring suggest that their kid could use some improvement.

"You came out here just to make sure I wasn't smoking?" I asked, tilting my head to look at him. "Don't you have a class?"

"Study hall," he said, rolling his eyes. "I left one of the kids in charge while I took a potty break."

"Smithson would have your ass if he knew," I said, naming our hard-nosed and annoying principal.

"But who would ever tell him?" Jeremy asked, smiling. He checked his watch. "See you later."

I waved him away and stayed outside for another couple of minutes, letting the cold air wash away my craving for nicotine, then went inside and headed for my classroom. I passed the biology lab and caught a glimpse of Brandon sitting at his desk, his head resting in his arms on the table. He looked kind of sad, which made me feel bad for him.

In my room, I hung up my coat in the closet and pretended to be productive for the next half hour. This consisted of checking my email, reading the newspaper, and laughing at the comic strips. After I finished that, I dug out the guardian contact forms that each student filled out and found Brandon's.

I had first been told by the principal that Brandon was a special case, but capable of being in a public school. I wondered what that meant, and then I found out that Brandon Archer was the only son of the big-shot Hollywood actor, Garrett Archer. So what the hell was he doing in Cody, Iowa?

Not that Cody is a bad place. I was born and raised here. It's just different from Los Angeles, California. Located along the Mississippi River, Cody has a population of about 32,000 people, and isn't exactly well known. We experience all four seasons, sometimes within the same week, and while we're proud to put on our annual Fourth of July and Christmas parades, we don't host gala events like the Oscars.

Until a few weeks ago, Brandon had been enrolled in expensive private schools and tutored at home when necessary. When school wasn't in session, and sometimes even when it was, Garrett would haul Brandon around the world to promote his latest movies. But Brandon was shy and hated the publicity, and his grades suffered. Garrett had thought it would be best to get his son out of LA and into a more stable lifestyle. So he got in touch with his younger brother, Charlie, and foisted Brandon on him. Charlie Archer, single, never-been-married, had no children, and not expecting to gain a teenager. Charlie moved here to Cody, and so far, he hadn't set foot inside the school, but I had heard about the huge house he was renting and the big-ass black pickup truck he drove. The gossip going around among the single female teachers was that Charlie was quite attractive and an entrepreneur of some sort, something to do with restaurants, but since he never seemed to venture out, no one could find out anything more about him, like his favorite food or color or what he looked for in a woman. You know, the important stuff.

I picked up the phone and dialed the number Brandon had written down. After four rings, I got the answering machine.

"You've reached Charlie and Brandon. We're not home right now, so please leave a message and we might call you back. Ciao!"

I frowned at the "we might call you back" thing and muttered "Smartass!" right after the beep sounded. I froze and coughed.

"Um, hi, this is Melinda Martin, Brandon's Driver's Ed and history teacher. If you could please call me back at the school sometime today or tomorrow, I'd like to talk to you." I left him my direct number and hung up.

I could feel myself blushing. I had called a total stranger a smartass, and he had it on his answering machine. Sometimes I could be so smart. After I rolled my eyes at my blunder, I couldn't help but think that Charlie Archer had a pretty sexy voice for a smartass.

# Chapter Two

"You're late," I said as I opened the door to let my older sister Claire into my house.

She threw a paper bag at me and shrugged out of her coat. "The line at the grocery store was insane. The things I do for you and your stupid addictions."

"They're your addictions too, and they're not stupid," I said. I led the way to the kitchen and set the bag on the table, pulling out a nice, cold carton of Ben & Jerry's Cherry Garcia ice cream. "This is heaven."

"Heaven packed with a million calories," Claire said. She dug around in the silverware drawer for spoons. "Jeremy's not here yet?"

"No. He's picking up the pizza. What's up with you guys being late? Don't you remember you're not supposed to be late on TV night?"

Claire followed me into the living room where we took our usual seats; she on the couch, and me in the cushy armchair with my fuzzy blanket. Jeremy always sat on the floor, right in front of the TV so he could jump up, or wave his arms to block the screen until Claire or I screamed at him to move his fat butt out of the way. It was like this every Wednesday night, when we gathered at my house to eat a fattening dinner and watch our current favorite TV show, *Smallville*. Or as Jeremy referred to it, *Jailbaitville*, but whatever.

"It's about Clark Kent as a teenager, before he became Superman," I would say, and Jeremy would respond with, "Right, teenagers. Kids who could be our students. It's gross to lust after these people." And I would say, "But technically, the kids are being played by actors over the age of eighteen, so we're still okay."

Then Jeremy would pull my hair or give me a Wet Willie. We are so mature for being thirty-four years old.

Claire got sucked into the show the same way I did. The lead actor was hot, so we drooled over him and ate ice cream every week, which wasn't good for our hips, but we didn't care. At least not enough to stop doing it.

There were no longer any new episodes, but I had purchased all of the DVD boxed sets, and we had gone through them about four times so far. I was positive they would revolt at some point soon and want to watch something else, but until that happened, Clark Kent would continue to grace my television screen.

"So what's happening this week?" Claire asked, taking a big bite of ice cream.

"As long as Clark takes his shirt off, does it matter?"

"Not at all."

I licked my spoon clean and ignored the extra pound that I could feel attaching itself to my butt.

"I drove past the old movie theater on my way over," Claire said. "It's been bought."

I sat up straighter. "By whom?"

Claire shrugged. "Don't know. But the 'for sale' sign is gone, and it's been replaced with a new one that reads, 'Cinema – Coming Soon!'"

"No way would someone try to make it into a theater again. They'd never be able to compete with the Multi-Plex. It's why the place shut down in the first place," I said as I stabbed the carton of ice cream.

"I know, sweetie, I know," Claire said in a soothing voice.

The Cody Theater had been open since before I was born, and it introduced me to my first love: Superman. I have a slight obsession with Superman and Clark Kent, and it all stems from my first movie viewing experience at

13

the theater. I was five, and the theater was showing older movies in the afternoons at cheaper prices. My mom took me while Claire was in school, and I sat in the plush red seat, holding a container of buttered popcorn, mesmerized, as awkward and nerdy, but still cute, Clark Kent tried to keep secret from Lois Lane the fact that he was a superhero who could fly. The idea that such a man existed had ruined me romantically, since I was always on the lookout for a real-life Clark Kent to fly me away. So far, I had been unsuccessful, but I still held hope.

The single screen Cody Theater had closed its doors three years ago when the twelve screen Multi-Plex with stadium seating had been built on the other side of town. It just couldn't compete with that. And now, someone had bought it and was going to try to make it work?

I snorted. "Someone must have a lot of money to blow."

Claire channel surfed while we waited for Jeremy to arrive. He breezed in, just as we gave up on him and had started the DVD player, and took his place on the floor, opening the pizza box and digging in. His big head was already in my way. I threw a pillow at him, and he caught it and propped it under his butt.

"Thank you," he said. "So did you call Brandon's uncle?"

I reached down for a napkin and a slice of pepperoni pizza. "Left a message. I'm thinking he's not going to call me back."

"Why's that?"

"Aside from the fact that he's never set foot inside the school? His answering machine message was kind of snotty."

"So you'll just have to go visit him in person," Jeremy said.

"No way. You know I don't do home visits. It freaks out the kids more than it helps them."

Claire shushed us as the show started, and we were silent until about halfway through the episode when we saw skin. Then Claire and I started gushing over Clark Kent, and Jeremy got disgusted with us, hit the Pause button, and went to get a drink.

"Is Piper working tonight?" I asked, referring to Claire's eighteen year old daughter, my niece. She was a senior this year, and working part time as a counter clerk at the local dry cleaner's.

"She's closing, and then tutoring some middle school kids on their science."

"She's so smart. She's going to be number one in her class for sure," I gushed. I couldn't help it. My niece was pretty, popular, and a total brain. Everyone liked her.

"I hope so. She needs to get a good scholarship."

I paused in my ice cream eating and looked at my sister. "What's up? I thought Beau was going to help out with college."

Claire twirled her spoon in her hand, looking off into space. "He's worried about having money for his other kids now."

"That ass," I spat. "Piper's his kid too. His first, I might add."

Claire had been divorced for almost six years now, after she found out her husband Beau was cheating on her with the cleaning lady. Claire had the misfortune of coming home early to find them having sex on the just waxed kitchen floor. They were now married with three kids. Beau had been generous with helping out financially with Piper, and Claire made good money doing freelance writing for magazines, so I was surprised to hear she was concerned about paying for college.

"Does Piper know?" I asked.

"I haven't said anything."

"She'll catch on sometime. She's a smart kid."

Claire fiddled with her earrings, a frown crossing over her features. At that moment, Jeremy returned with a bottle of wine and three glasses, and we settled down to watch the rest of the episode, followed by one more. By the time it was over, I was giddy and horny as hell.

"No Clark Kent to help me tonight," I said and hiccupped.

"You need to find a boyfriend," Jeremy said, poking me in the side as I walked them to the door.

"Sure. Do you know of anyone?" I asked.

I kissed his cheek and hugged Claire tight. "Call me," she said. "We'll do something fun this weekend."

"Sure, give Piper a hug for me."

My two good friends waved goodbye and walked to their cars. I stood on the porch of my house and watched as their taillights disappeared in opposite directions. Then I went inside tried not to think about the depressing state of my love life.

* * *

Some teachers use the teacher's lounge as a place to unwind, relax, and have a can of Pepsi. Others use it as gossip central station. I've heard some of the craziest stuff while in the teacher's lounge. Most days I avoid it, only popping in to grab my mail or look for Jeremy. I'm not anti-social, but do I need to know that some kid's mom is boinking the basketball coach on alternate weekends? Nope, not at all.

So I spend my planning periods and lunch hours in my classroom. My desk sits by two big windows that face the football field, and I watch the kids during gym class when it's nice out. Sometimes, when it's warm and they're out there sweating themselves to death, I want to pass out cups of water as they stumble past my window. But the head gym teacher scares me, so I don't.

This semester, Jeremy and I had different lunch hours, so I was eating alone. I had brought in a dorm-sized refrigerator and a small microwave. The fridge was stocked with cans of Dr Pepper and Reese's Peanut Butter Cups.

That day, I had heated a bowl of my mom's special tomato soup for lunch. Mom worries that I don't eat well enough, so she'll make big batches of my favorite foods and give them to me in freezer ready containers. I swear I would starve if she didn't do that.

I was just bringing the spoon to my mouth when there was a knock at my door and in walked a man I'd never seen before. Trust me, I would have remembered. Holy smokes, he was gorgeous. Tall, over six feet, nice and muscled without being bulky, with dark brown hair, almost black, that curled at the nape of his neck. He wore wire rimmed glasses that framed bright blue eyes. And his lips. I could go on for a year about his lips, but I won't.

I froze and dropped the spoon. It sank into my bowl and disappeared in the soup, but I didn't care. A real-life Clark Kent had just stepped into my life.

"Are you Miss Martin?" he asked.

I nodded, thinking his voice sounded familiar.

"I'm Charlie Archer, Brandon's uncle," he said, coming toward me.

I squeaked and tried to stand up before pushing away from my desk, banging my hip against the edge. Biting back a curse word, I hobbled around to shake his hand, trying to remember what I'd decided to wear that day. But

I couldn't, so I sneaked a glance and saw black pants and a pink cashmere sweater. Good. I looked respectable.

And then I noticed the blob of soup down my front. Beautiful, just perfect.

"Nice to meet you," I said to my dream man, at the same time grabbing a napkin to blot at the soup. "You surprised me. I expected you to call first."

"Well, I wanted to see in person the teacher who thinks I'm a smartass," he said, rocking back on his heels a bit. An amused smile tugged at his lips.

My face flamed and I heard myself laugh. It came out somewhere between a bird twittering and a donkey braying. I snapped my mouth shut and took a moment to compose myself. It was almost impossible, with him standing so close. I could smell the faint scent of sawdust and paint, smells that reminded me of my dad's workshop.

"I'm sorry about that, I didn't mean it," I stammered.

He smiled, and I grabbed the desk to keep from falling over.

"Don't worry about it. I can be a smartass. But I'm here to talk about Brandon. He's having trouble?"

Good looks or no, when it came to a student's success, I was all business. I suggested we sit down and I watched as he squeezed his broad frame into a student desk.

"I swear these were bigger when I was in school," he mused. Then he looked at me with an expectant expression.

"Brandon seems to be having some trouble adjusting here. I was hoping you could tell me more about his background than I already know."

Charlie raised a hand to stop me. I faltered and stared at his hand. It was huge!

"I'm going to be honest with you," he said. "What my brother told your principal isn't one hundred percent true. Garrett didn't make the decision to send Brandon to me. Brandon did. To his father, he's an accessory, and he can't stand it. So he asked to live with me. The problem is, as soon as I had moved Brandon into my place, the financing came through on the new restaurant, and we had to come here."

"Restaurant?" I asked.

"I live in LA and own and run a very successful restaurant. I have one in New York City as well, and I was asked to bring that fine dining experience here, although tailored to suit the Midwest."

I almost laughed. Fine dining from LA?

"Our idea of a good place to eat is Red Lobster," I said.

"Ah, see? I'm here to change that."

"In Cody?"

"I bought the old theater. I'm in the process of converting it."

20

At that moment, I saw red.

"You? You bought the theater?"

He nodded. "It's in an excellent location, right along the river. The view is amazing. We start work on it this afternoon."

"A restaurant? You're turning the theater into a restaurant?"

He looked at me with a strange expression, and I realized I was almost wailing as well as sounding stupid and repetitive. I swallowed and coughed, disappointed to now find him unattractive, just on principle.

"Sorry. That place is very special to me," I said.

"Uh huh," he said, and the desk creaked as he edged away from me. "Well, um, back to Brandon?"

I sat up straighter. "Yes. He's having trouble in the Driver's Ed course, and he's not doing so hot in American History either. I was hoping you'd be able to work with him at home with the driving."

"Oh, well, what's his driving like?"

"In a word? Awful. He can't control the car, and I've had to grab the wheel. If that happens during the final test, it's an automatic failure. I was told he had some experience driving."

Charlie snorted, causing his nose to crinkle, and damn, he was cute again.

"Garrett let him sit behind the wheel of his Mercedes, but that's about as far as it got."

"Oh. What about his mother?" I asked, keeping my tone light. I had wondered about Brandon's mother, since Brandon never mentioned her.

Charlie pursed his lips. "She died not long after Brandon was born, complications from the delivery."

I nodded, feeling bad for asking.

"I'm surprised you don't know our family history. It's been major tabloid fodder for years."

"I don't pay much attention to that stuff," I said, and it was the honest truth. I didn't subscribe to or read entertainment magazines, follow the gossip websites, or watch those celebrity news shows. The extravagance turned me off. That and the fact that I could never keep up with who was hot or not.

"It's been a month, is it that bad?" Charlie asked, referring to Brandon's problems.

"It's not great," I admitted. "His other teachers have told me he's barely passing anything. I beat them to the punch by calling you about it. A month may not seem like very long, but if we don't make adjustments now, it won't get any better. He doesn't talk in class, and he hasn't turned in any homework."

Charlie frowned. My insides fluttered because he was so cute. I couldn't deny it.

"I see him doing homework all the time," he said.

"So why isn't he turning it in?"

"I don't know. I'll talk to him."

"Okay, and the driving?" I pressed. "He needs some practice."

Charlie scrubbed a hand over his face. "I'm so busy right now."

I shrugged. "If he doesn't pass, he'll have to go through the state program. Driver's Ed won't be offered in the school after this semester."

A smile crossed his lips, oh his lips, and he looked right at me. I gripped the sides of the desk to steady myself. That smile was dizzying.

"Could he work with you some more?" he asked. "Before or after school?"

"Me? Uh, um," I stuttered.

"Since you're teaching him anyway," Charlie went on. "I'm a terrible driver. I have so many speeding tickets on my record, and I'm not very patient when it comes to this kind of stuff. I can pay you for your time."

"Oh, well, uh, see, I can't use the school's car for after hours practice."

"You can use my car."

"You mean your truck?"

He tilted his head. "How do you know what I drive?"

I said nothing. It was better to remain silent than make an even bigger fool of myself.

"I have a car too," he said. "Brandon's familiar with it. Please."

I sighed because now I was being hit with puppy dog eyes, and I can't resist puppy dog eyes.

"Well…"

Charlie grinned. "Great! How about we start tomorrow? Drop by the theater around six or so. Brandon will be there, hanging out while I work." He paused for a moment and said, "That is, unless you're busy tomorrow night."

To which I shook my head and said, "No, not busy. No plans at all."

Wow, could I sound more pathetic?

He stood up, towering over me. I stood too, still staring up at him since he was at least a foot taller.

"Will you tell him or should I?" I asked.

"I will. And what about tutoring him with history?"

It was my turn to raise a hand. "He needs help in more than just history. Let me talk to some student tutors, see if anyone's available."

"All right, that sounds great. I'll see you tomorrow at six then."

He shook my hand, and I hoped mine wasn't too clammy or gross. After he left, I had to reheat my soup. While I waited for the microwave to ding, I realized that I had never said the word yes.

Charlie Archer was smooth, I decided. Had to be careful around him.

I took the soup from the microwave and looked around my desk for my spoon. Then I noticed it poking up from the soup. Of course, I reached in to grab it with my fingers, burning myself in the process.

I had to wait for the soup to cool before I could get the spoon, and then I had to reheat it again. By the time I was ready to eat, lunch hour was over. I sighed and put the lid on the bowl and stuck it in the fridge.

Charlie Archer owed me lunch.

# Chapter Three

After the final bell rang, the students rushed from my classroom. All except for Brandon. I could tell he wanted to talk to me, but he hesitated by stacking his books into a neat pile on his desk and casting nervous glances in my direction.

I tossed him an eraser. "Would you like to help me?" I asked.

He nodded and came to stand next to me at the dry erase board. We worked in silence for a moment until he worked up enough nerve to speak.

"I saw my uncle's truck here earlier. What did he say?"

I looked at Brandon, at his big blue eyes, and saw the family resemblance.

"We came up with a plan to help you out," I said. "You can talk with your uncle about it first and see if you want to go with it."

"Was he mad?"

I paused. "No, he was very helpful. He's concerned about your education."

Brandon breathed a sigh of relief. "Good. I don't want to upset him. I want to stay here because it's way better than being with my dad."

This was the most I'd ever heard Brandon speak. He seemed to realize it too, and hurried out, his sneakers squeaking on the tiled floor. He almost ran into Jeremy, who was on his way in.

"The scoop around school is that you talked with his uncle today," Jeremy said, setting his backpack by the door and going straight for the locked bottom drawer of my filing cabinet. It was where I kept my purse and my stash of candy bars and tampons. Jeremy ignored the tampons though, and he was the only other person in the world to have a key to that drawer.

"What do you mean, 'the scoop'?" I asked, setting down my eraser and going over to peer into the drawer.

Jeremy selected an Almond Joy. I grabbed a Snickers, and we pulled out two desks to face each other and sat down. It was our normal after school ritual. Our contracts required us to stay in the building for a half hour after dismissal. While others used this time to grade papers or get ready for the next day, Jeremy and I used the time to unwind and eat chocolate. We believed it was more beneficial to our sanity as teachers.

"I stopped in the lounge just a minute ago. Everyone's buzzing about Garrett Archer's baby brother being here," Jeremy said.

"You know, I hadn't even thought of it like that. I guess because I don't think Garrett Archer is a very good actor."

Jeremy almost choked. "Are you kidding? He's Oscar-nominated! Everyone in Hollywood loves him, and he's in the tabloids every other day."

"I fell asleep during his last movie," I pointed out.

"You had pneumonia," Jeremy said.

"Still. I'm not intrigued by him. His brother on the other hand..." I let my voice trail off, and Jeremy sat up straighter and looked at me.

"You like his brother? Brandon's uncle? So when's the wedding?" he teased.

I growled and bit off another piece of my candy bar. "He's the guy that bought the Cody Theater. He's turning it into a restaurant!"

"Good. This town needs something nice. It sucks having to drive to the cities all the time for crab legs or good fettuccine."

"But you know what that theater means to me."

Jeremy rolled his eyes. "I know. It's where you fell in love with Superman. That movie has messed with your head. Guys like him don't exist."

"Charlie Archer looks just like Clark Kent. It's eerie."

"Is he the reason you're wearing your lunch?" Jeremy asked, motioning to my soup stain.

"This isn't going to come out, is it?" I asked, staring at my sweater.

"You know, I just realized something," Jeremy said, balling up his wrapper and tossing it toward my trash can. He missed and got up to get it. "You always spill food on yourself whenever you see a hot guy, especially one that looks like Clark Kent."

"I do not!" I cried. "I'd have to be eating all the time."

He tapped my head with the wrapper before throwing it away. "You are always eating, silly. I can't believe you're not five hundred pounds."

I chewed on my candy and thought about what he'd said. After a moment, I sighed. He was right. Every guy I'd ever been attracted to was tall and dark-haired with glasses, and I'd ruined almost three entire wardrobes with food since I was fourteen years old.

"I'm so pathetic," I muttered.

Jeremy's response was to log onto my computer and check his email.

"You have your own classroom too, you know," I said, a bit miffed that he hadn't told me I wasn't pathetic. I packed my black messenger bag with some papers I needed to grade and got my purse out from the filing cabinet.

"Your classroom is so much brighter," he said without looking up from the screen. "I don't have any windows. It's like a dungeon. Plus, you've got the chocolate." He snatched another candy bar before I slammed the drawer closed.

He hopped around the Internet for a few minutes while I tapped my foot and waited. I needed to stop at the dry cleaner's on the way home to drop off my sweater and talk to my niece.

"Wow, Charlie Archer *is* cute," Jeremy said, wiggling his eyebrows at me.

"What? Where?" I asked, dropping my stuff on the desk and hurrying around it.

"Wow, you want this guy bad."

I slapped his shoulder and looked at the screen. Jeremy had done an image search for Charlie Archer and to my surprise, there were hundreds of photos of him.

"He looks good in a tux," I said, staring at a picture of him on the red carpet. The caption read, "Garrett Archer attends the Academy Awards with his brother."

"Yeah, not bad," Jeremy said. "I'd even go so far as to say he's better looking than Garrett."

"Are you sure you're straight?" I asked him, ducking away from his swatting hand.

He shut down my computer, and we headed out. We said goodbye to other teachers and walked to our cars.

"So what are you doing about Brandon? We kind of got sidetracked with his uncle," Jeremy said.

"Well, I guess I'm going to work with him after school with his driving, and I'm going to ask Piper to tutor him with the other stuff. She's excellent at tutoring, and I think she'd get along with Brandon."

"Whoa, wait a sec. You're giving the kid after school lessons? Whose bright idea was this?"

I could feel myself blushing. "Well, it was Charlie's suggestion."

"And you said yes because?" Jeremy asked, rolling his head in my direction.

"Because it was a good idea?" I squeaked.

"Not because you want to pounce the uncle?"

I glanced around the half full parking lot. "Shut up! I do not need the school gossips hearing you say stuff like that. Pounce the uncle, what is *that*?"

"Mel, every female teacher here wants to pounce the uncle after seeing him today. The guy's good looking, and he was charming to everyone he talked to."

"He was charming to everyone?" I asked, feeling rejected.

Jeremy patted my shoulder. "Don't be disappointed. If you like him, go for it. I just don't think using his nephew to do it is a good idea."

"I'm not using Brandon. He needs my help," I said, wishing I didn't sound quite so pitiful.

"And you need to get laid, I know."

I screwed up my face at him and unlocked the door to my little blue VW Beetle, my baby. "Go home, Jeremy. Go home to your one bedroom apartment you share with, oh that's right, no one."

"I can't even be insulted by that, since you're not going home to anyone either."

"But I have a house. I win."

"Love you, Melinda," he said, blowing kisses at me as he got into his car. "And you're not pathetic."

"Love you too," I said, smiling.

Our friendship is strange like that, probably because we're both a bit strange ourselves. But I could never understand why he was still single. Sure, he dated. Bimbos that I could never remember the names of, but there was never any one woman that he called me up about and said, "Hey, this is the one." I do remember one ex-girlfriend that dumped him because she thought *I* was weird. She was a psycho bitch anyway.

I stopped at a red light on the way to the dry cleaner's and began doing a little jig in my seat, taking off my sweater while still wearing my wool coat. I'm an expert at making it look like I'm just bopping along to the radio so people don't flag down the nearest cop to arrest me for indecent exposure. I made it to the dry cleaner's and was greeted by my niece, Piper. She worked three days a week, going there right after school let out.

"Hey, Piper," I said. I placed my sweater on the counter. "Had a little accident with some tomato soup."

"This is cashmere," she said, taking in the stain with a critical eye.

"Yes."

She sighed, her "Aunt Melinda is such a lost cause" sigh, and marked the spot with tape, then wrote out a special tag for it.

"Monday okay to get this back?" she asked.

"No hurry."

She looked at me. "You did this today, didn't you?"

"Uh."

"So you're not wearing anything under the coat?"

"I've still got my bra on," I sniffed.

Piper laughed.

"Do you have any extra time to tutor another student?" I asked.

She worked on tagging some clothes and shrugged. "I could make time. Who are we talking about?"

"His name's Brandon Archer. He's in my history class, and he needs some help."

"Garrett Archer's son?" she asked, perking up a little.

"Yeah. Don't tell me you like Garrett Archer."

"I don't think he can act his way out of a wet paper sack, but his brother's cute."

"You mean Charlie?"

Piper raised a brow and grinned. "Oh, Charlie is it? I heard he stopped in to see you today."

I cursed myself for blushing and gave her my best teacher stare. "So will you do it?"

"Just let me know when it's best to get together with him."

"Piper, you are a saint," I said.

"I know," she said and waved goodbye as I left.

On the way home, I drove past the Cody Theater and spotted the sign Claire had said was there. I felt my nostrils flare a bit at the thought of the place being turned into an overpriced restaurant.

There were a few guys working on the outside of the building, pulling down the boards that covered the windows. I was all set to flip everyone the bird, when I saw him, pulling up in a monstrous black truck. He got out holding two cardboard cup carriers filled with coffee.

"Aw man, he's hot and nice!" I said aloud, watching him pass out the coffee to the workers.

He looked up and saw me just as I was going by. He smiled and waved at me, and I did the most mature thing I could think of.

I ducked down behind my steering wheel. After all, I wasn't properly dressed.

*Wow*, I thought. *I really do need to get laid.*

# Chapter Four

Fridays suck, I decided, dragging my tired self up the front steps to my house and pausing on the porch to check the mailbox.

"Bill, bill, junk, junk, bill," I muttered, rolling my eyes.

Holding my mail, my purse, and my school bag, I fell inside the house and tossed everything on the couch. Then I collapsed next to it all, still wearing my coat. I closed my eyes and tried not to think about the events of the day, but everything came rushing back in a tidal wave of agony.

First, I forgot to set my alarm the night before, so I overslept. I had to rush around to get ready for school, which I hate. My outfit matched, but I had chosen two different colored shoes of the same style, one black, one dark brown, which Jeremy took great pleasure in pointing out to me the second he saw me. In my haste to get out of the house, I also forgot to grab my lunch and the assignments I was supposed to hand back to my students. I had to eat the hockey-puck on a bun that the school insists is a hamburger, and of course, my students couldn't help but hassle me a bit, since I always have their homework ready to give back the next day. In exchange for their forgiveness, I extended them a day on the paper that was due next week.

And then Brandon hung around after class again to talk to me. He told me he was excited that I was going to be helping him, and that his uncle hadn't stopped talking about me. I should have been pleased about that last statement, but I was mortified instead, especially when Brandon grinned at me before he left.

I rubbed my eyes and took off my coat, then went to look for some food. It was 4:30, and I had to be at the theater, ready to drive with Brandon, at six. I popped a frozen dinner in the microwave, then went to change clothes, kicking off my mismatched shoes in disgust.

I stared at the inside of my closet, unimpressed with the selection. Sure, it was fine for teaching, but I owned nothing that screamed, "Look at me! I'm sexy!"

I chose a pair of dark jeans and a bright red sweater. I thought about wearing a skirt, and decided against it. Skirts didn't work well when it came to having to hit the brakes fast. And then I realized I'd made a huge mistake.

Any car that Charlie owned didn't have the special brakes on the passenger side. Gaaaah. Okay, maybe we'd just work in an empty parking lot and start from the beginning. *Yes, I can do that*, I thought as I dressed.

I tucked two paper towels under my chin and wolfed down my dinner, proud for not spilling all over myself, then thinking that I could have made it a lot easier if I'd just eaten first, and then changed clothes. But ah well. I wasn't all there at the moment.

I was nervous.

It was that weird, fluttery feeling that I always got before the first day of school, or a first date. If Brandon were being honest with me, Charlie had talked about me. I could ignore it and tell myself duh, I'm Brandon's teacher, after all. But something was telling me it was more than that. Just a little.

I refreshed my makeup, grabbed my coat and purse and headed out. While I drove, I rehearsed what I was going to say.

"Hi, Charlie, nice to see you again. Beautiful day isn't it? Even though it's all cloudy and cold." I shook my head. "No, err. Hello, Charlie. Um, how are you? How's Brandon? Um, how's the theater going?"

I let out a sigh and rolled my eyes. No matter what I came up with, I was going to sound stupid because I was nervous. All coherent thought flies out of my head when I'm nervous. It's a curse.

I stopped my car in the theater parking lot and took a moment to calm my racing heart.

"Hi, Charlie," I said to my steering wheel. "Nice to see you again. How are you? Yes, yes, that's what I'll say."

Feeling confident now, I got out of the car. Walking around the building to the main entrance, I was hit with a feeling of nostalgia. My mom used to bring Claire and me here every Saturday afternoon when we were little. She loved seeing the matinees, and Claire loved the popcorn. I could almost picture us standing in the lobby, bouncing around as we waited for Mom to buy the tickets that would take us on some grand, new adventure.

I was standing near the door, staring at the empty frames that had once held the posters for upcoming movies, when it opened and out stepped Charlie.

"Miss Martin," he said. "I wasn't expecting you just yet. I'm sorry, I haven't cleaned up. But Brandon's inside waiting. Come on in."

He motioned for me to follow, and I found myself gaping at his jeans, jeans that were well worn in all the right places and hugged his hips and butt like they were made for him. I swallowed hard and went after him.

"How are you?" he asked.

"Um, good. I wore shoes that didn't match today to school." I heard myself say it, I saw the expression on his face, and I wanted to die.

"Oh, okay. Brandon's in the office," he said.

I walked behind him, wishing I could just turn around and run away. He paused outside the door of the office and turned to me. I wasn't paying attention and ran right into him. His hands gripped my upper arms to steady me.

"Whoa, sorry," he said.

I blinked. "Huh?"

*Oh brilliant, Melinda,* I thought. *Moron!*

Charlie dipped his head a little, giving me a look over the rims of his glasses. "Are you okay? You seem distracted, Miss Martin."

"Melinda," I blurted out.

"Pardon me?"

I tried not to think about his hands still on my arms and said, "My name. It's Melinda. You can use my first name."

He smiled, that damned dazzling smile that took my breath away, and nodded.

"Okay then, are you ready?"

"Well, there's a problem with the car," I said. "You don't have brakes on the passenger side, so we'll have to stick to light driving."

"That's fine. Brandon said he'd like to start over. And about your payment?"

I shook my head. "I can't take money from you. I'm his teacher."

"Okay. Well, can I offer you a free meal when I get the restaurant opened? I feel like I should be giving you something for using up your personal time."

I looked him square in the eye, feeling some of my spunk returning. "What makes you think I'll want to eat here?"

He dropped his hands from my arms and tucked them into the back pockets of his jeans, grinning. "Still bitter about that, eh?"

"Yes, very. Now, let's get Brandon and start driving."

"Sure."

Brandon was hunched over the desk of the manager's office, reading his history textbook and taking notes. He looked up when we entered and smiled.

"Hi, Miss Martin."

"Hey, how's the paper coming?"

"Fine. It'll be better now that we have that extra day."

I coughed, not wanting him to mention my fashion faux pas and said, "Okay, you ready to drive?"

He stood up to put on his coat. I leaned against one wall and watched as Charlie handed over a set of keys.

"Take it easy on her, she's old," Charlie said, and I blinked before realizing he wasn't talking about me. "But she's yours once you pass your driving test.

Brandon nodded and took the keys. "Thanks, I'll be careful."

Charlie gave him a pat on the shoulder, then looked to me. He saluted me and said, "Good luck. I'll be here when you guys get back."

Brandon scooted out of the office, and I turned to go after him.

"Oh, and Miss Martin?" Charlie asked, catching my attention.

"Melinda, you can call me Melinda -"

"You look very nice tonight," he interrupted.

I gulped and stuttered, "Oh. Sure, I do." I slapped both hands to my forehead, embarrassed by what I'd said. "I mean, thank you. You look nice too."

He chuckled and sat down at the desk. I sucked in a hard breath and left before I could make a bigger dumbass out of myself.

\* \* \*

Brandon did very well during our drive together in his uncle's car, a Toyota Camry. I was expecting something flashier, like a Mercedes or a Jaguar since Charlie was a rich Hollywood type. Brandon was more relaxed, and he even laughed a couple of times. I was shocked. Who was this kid? I hardly recognized him. He parked the car next to mine and turned to me, all goofy grin and smiling eyes.

"How did I do?" he asked.

"Pretty darn well, I'm impressed."

"I'm just so nervous with the girls," he said, running his hands over the steering wheel. "And I'm more comfortable in this car. Charlie has taken me driving in this one, I know it better. We drove this out here when we moved. The truck is a new purchase, and I can't see myself driving that."

"All it takes is practice. If we keep up this progress, you'll pass the test, no problem."

"Cool." Brandon nodded and looked at me. "So what do you think of him?"

"Who?"

"My uncle. I can see the way you look at him."

I was thankful for the darkness in the car since I could feel my face getting hot again. "That's not something I should be talking to you about, Brandon. I'm your teacher."

"I know. But can I say that I think my uncle likes my teacher?"

I giggled a little, then stopped myself. "Let's go inside. We need to discuss your tutoring so you can catch up."

Brandon walked ahead of me, and I took my time this trip to take in the lobby of the old theater. The concession stand still stood there, although the cases were empty. The carpeting hadn't been changed yet, so it was still the lush burgundy shag that I remembered, just worn in some places. All the poster frames were empty, some frames gone, leaving blank spaces behind, and the wood paneling had been torn down.

I sighed and headed to the office.

"Brandon says you think he did an awesome job," Charlie said, standing as soon as I saw him. He was beaming with pride.

"He's an awesome kid," I said, winking at Brandon. "I think this extra practice will help him."

"So what about his other classes? Oh, I'm sorry, please, have a seat."

He motioned to the chairs across from where he was behind the desk. Brandon already occupied one, so I took the other and unbuttoned my coat.

"My niece, Piper Nichols, is a senior," I said. "She already tutors four other high school students, plus a group of eighth graders on their science."

"So she's smart like her aunt," Charlie said.

"Uh, so anyway," I said, trying to remember to breathe, "she can work with Brandon's schedule and meet him for study sessions."

"Anytime after school is fine," Brandon said. "I'm not involved in anything, so I've got lots of free time."

"Can she meet him here?" Charlie asked.

"I think that would be fine. I'll tell her and she can call Brandon with times."

Charlie placed his hands on the desk and stood up. "Now that business is taken care of, would you like a tour of the place?"

"Oh, well, sure," I said. "But I bet I won't like what you've done so far."

"Stubborn, aren't you?" he asked, then guided me out of the office. Brandon moved to sit behind the desk and work on some of his homework. I caught a trace of a smirk on his face as he waved at us.

Charlie gave me a very detailed tour, telling me how everything was going to be changed, and I found myself becoming more and more saddened by the whole idea. This was like a second home to me, and even though I knew the building crew he'd hired to do the work and trusted them to do a great job, listening to him talk about tearing down walls and expanding the building just seemed horrible to me.

"And of course, a state of the art kitchen," he said, waving his hands in the air. "What's your favorite dish? I'll add it to the menu."

"Movie theater popcorn and Twizzlers," I answered. I ran a hand over the empty candy case.

"Done."

I looked at him, and he was grinning. "Don't try to win me over that way," I said.

"I have a feeling men will do pretty much anything to win you over."

I snorted, something I have a habit of doing, and that my mother just hates. "Please. Men aren't exactly falling over themselves for me."

"I can't imagine why."

He was making me giddy, and I realized that I liked it. I turned away so he wouldn't see me smile and spotted

44

the doors to the theater. He followed my gaze and walked over to them.

"This of course will be the main dining area," he said.

I strode past him into the huge room that had housed all of my adventures and let out a disappointed gasp. All of the plush, red seats had been removed. The dark carpeting had been pulled up, and the floor was bare. Even the screen was gone.

"What did you do with the seats?" I asked.

"They're all sitting in a storage shed. I'm not sure what to do with them yet."

I sighed, resigning myself to the fact that there was nothing I could do to stop what was happening. I was just going to have to live with it. But that didn't mean I'd ever eat in this place. Charlie Archer wasn't getting any of my business! So ha!

"I'll have you know that the only reason I'm still speaking to you is because you're Brandon's uncle," I said as we left the theater and went back into the main lobby.

"Not because I'm cute, huh?" he asked, adjusting his glasses.

Guuuuuh. I'm such a sucker for a guy in glasses.

"That's not even a factor," I lied.

Charlie laughed. "I like you, Miss Martin," he said. "You intrigue me."

"Ahh, intrigue is code speak for 'freak me out', I get it."

He glanced over his shoulder at the office. I could see the door was open, and I would swear I saw a shadow moving closer, like Brandon was inching forward to be able to hear better.

"If you could put aside your hatred of me for one night, do you think I could take you to dinner?" Charlie asked.

Okay, first off, I'm not accustomed to being asked out. I've always been the one to do the asking. Second, inside I was freaking out. My inner teenager was screaming, "Oh my God, oh my God, oh my GOD! He's asking you out on a date!"

I tried not to let her out and pretended to think it over. "Hmm, I don't know if I could be civil for one whole night."

He grinned at me, and I admitted defeat.

"All right. Sure. I think it might be fun."

"Excellent. How about tomorrow night?"

"Tomorrow night?" I cried. "Wow, that's soon."

"I'll take you anywhere you want to go."

The crazy side of me was trying to pick the most expensive, elegant restaurant within an hour's drive, while the logical side of me was worried we'd be seen. A Saturday night in this area was primetime for any teacher or parent to spot us on a date.

"You know what? How about you come over to my place?" I heard myself saying.

*Gah! What are you doing?!* my brain screamed. And then my mouth said, "I'll cook!" and my brain had a conniption. What in hell was I saying? I don't cook!

"That sounds wonderful. I've been so busy since we moved here, Brandon and I have almost every takeout place memorized."

"What will Brandon do?"

Charlie shrugged. "He'll be fine. He's been bugging me to get out of the house anyway, says I work too hard. What time should I come over?"

"Seven?"

"Seven works for me."

I nodded. "Okay then. I'll see you tomorrow, my place, seven." I needed to get out of there. I needed to call Claire. I needed to become Julia-fucking-Child overnight!

"So, where is your place?" Charlie asked, and I wanted to die.

"Duh, yeah. You need my address. And my phone number. Not that you'll need to call me, but hey, you might if you're running late."

I was babbling like an idiot. Shut up, Melinda, just shut up.

I pulled a scrap of paper from my purse, checked to see there was nothing embarrassing written on it, like tampons, or laxatives, and wrote down my home and cell phone numbers and address.

"I guess I'll go now," I said, thrusting the paper into his hand.

We both heard the mad scramble as Brandon lurched from the doorway where he'd been eavesdropping and hopped into the chair behind the desk. He was blushing when I popped in to say goodbye.

Charlie walked me to my car, insisting on it since it was dark out, and I squealed out of the parking lot like my ass was on fire.

"What have I done?" I wailed, driving away. I dug around my purse for my cell phone and dialed Claire.

She was all breathless when she answered, and I figured she'd been working out on her treadmill.

"Hey, sorry, are you busy?" I asked, propping the phone between my neck and shoulder, steering the car, and searching for a cigarette at the same time.

Pretty good for a Driver's Ed teacher, eh?

"What? No, I'm fine. What's up?"

"I need to come over there. Now."

"What?" she asked, alarmed. "What for?"

"I just got asked out by Charlie Archer, and I offered to cook for him!" I cried. I slammed on the brakes at a red light, losing my grip on the cigarette. It fell to the floor, and I left it and started digging for another one.

"What made you say that? You can't cook."

"No shit, Sherlock. I panicked, I flipped out, I don't know. But he's coming over to my house tomorrow night and I need something fabulous to wear, and something edible."

"You're hopeless, aren't you?"

"I'll be there in ten," I said and hung up. I tossed my phone onto the passenger seat and put the cigarette in my mouth. Then I screamed in frustration because I was trying so hard to be good. I spit the thing out and drove faster.

Claire met me at her front door, shaking her head. "You said you'd cook for him?"

I pushed past her and went straight to the freezer, snatching the Cherry Garcia and digging in with my fingers.

"Jesus, calm down," Claire said, handing me a spoon.

"I'm so stupid!" I cried with my mouth full. I swallowed and regretted that, as I suffered an instant brain freeze.

Claire passed me a glass of warm water. I sipped it and then let my head drop to the counter.

"Are you on crack? What were you thinking?" Claire asked, sneaking in and taking away the ice cream.

"I wasn't. He was showing me around, telling me his grand plans for the new restaurant -"

"Oooh, how is it? What's it going to be like?"

I raised my head and glared at my sister. "Hello? I have a crisis, remember? Let's focus on me here."

"You're such a drama queen," Claire said. She pulled out a well-used cookbook from her kitchen island and flipped through it.

Unlike me, my sister could cook. She enjoyed cooking. Hell, she and my mother exchanged recipes three times a week. And then there's me. For the first semester I was in college and living away from home, I existed on macaroni and cheese and microwave popcorn.

"You need something easy, something that can't fail," she mused. Her eyes roved over page after page, and I began to get worried. She was almost halfway through the book and kept saying, "Oh, maybe this. Wait, no. Not for you, hmmm."

"All right already! Just pick something!" I cried.

She finally smiled and turned the book around to show me a picture of a beautiful oven-roasted chicken. "This isn't too hard, and you can serve it with a salad, some cooked vegetables, and a fancy dessert."

I studied the recipe. It seemed easy enough.

"Okay, let's go," I said, pointing to the door.

"Go? Go where?"

"The grocery store," I said. "What, you think I have this stuff at my house? Then *you're* the one on crack."

# Chapter Five

Saturday morning, I was lucky to get into the best salon in town to have my hair trimmed and my eyebrows waxed. I wasn't brave enough to do my legs, since I always screamed bloody murder when I had my eyebrows done. And I suffered through the eyebrows because there have been too many times when I'd plucked them myself and one was arched up into my hairline while the other was non-existent.

The rest of the afternoon was spent cleaning my house. It's small, a good starter house, and it seemed to have accumulated enough dust and dirt to choke a horse. I scrubbed the floors, dusted, vacuumed, and did several loads of laundry. This included the sheets from my bed, because, you know. Just in case.

I bought this house three years ago, and it was a real fixer-upper. But my dad is a retired carpenter, so he offered to help me, for which I am forever grateful. We had to tear down the entire porch and build it again because it was about two steps away from collapsing. The living room is pretty spacious and opens into the kitchen. I put in new cabinets, painted the walls a neutral beige, I think the official name was Earthenware, and installed all new appliances, except for the oven. It was old, but still worked fine. My dad kept telling me it would burn the place down, but since I was't much of a cook, I had no fear of that.

The dining room is small, but held a table for four and my grandmother's antique china cabinet with her china tucked inside. Down the hallway from the living room were my office and a bathroom. But the entire reason I bought this house was the second floor. Upstairs was the master bedroom and bath, and a second bedroom. My room was huge, with enormous closets and tall picture windows that let in plenty of sunlight and a bench seat under one of the windows. I curled up there many nights to grade papers or read. The bathroom was connected, with a step down to go inside. There was a separate shower and a whirlpool bathtub that came with the house. I'm not kidding.

The place was old and had needed work, but the bathroom was gorgeous, with white tiled walls and floors, and brass fixtures. I fell in love with this bathroom. I had no garage, which sucked during the winter months, but I dealt with it because I had a designer bathroom.

Yes, my logic is skewed.

Standing in the living room, a dust rag tucked in the back pocket of my jeans and my hair tied back with a bandanna, I thought I'd done a pretty good job. Everything was in order, and while I knew it wasn't a fancy condo like Charlie and Brandon lived in at the north end or town, it was home to me.

I checked my fridge and saw the food that Claire had helped me prepare the night before. She'd left me strict instructions on how to cook the chicken to the appropriate temperature, no need for food poisoning to happen on a first date, and how long to bake the corn casserole and scalloped potatoes.

While we were at the grocery store, I received a call from Brandon on my cell phone. He said, "My uncle loves blueberry cheesecake," and hung up. I talked Claire into making one for me, since there was no way in hell I could have managed that.

Now I just needed to shower and dress.

"And put on some makeup," Claire had reminded me.

Makeup. Check.

I stared at my closet for the second time in two days, wondering what I was going to wear. While I stared, I called Claire and asked her opinion.

"I can't see what you have," she said.

"Then come over."

"No, you can do this. You're an adult."

"I'm merely a child masquerading as an adult. Tonight is going to be a disaster!" I fell face first onto my bed, inhaling the clean scent of Mountain Breeze fabric softener.

"It won't be a disaster. Just remember to breathe, and don't burn anything."

I hung up on her and continued to glare at my selection of clothing. Charlie hadn't given me enough time to go and buy a new outfit, and for that I was irked. But then the small, sane part of my brain pushed through and reminded me that he'd asked me out after I'd spilled tomato soup down my front, so he had to like me for me.

This made me feel better, and I chose a blue cashmere sweater and nice jeans, laying them out on the bed. This was supposed to be a casual date, so I felt jeans were appropriate. I decided not to go with the pajama pants, even though we'd be at my house. I would save those for the third or fourth date, if we had a third or fourth date. My fears of mucking this up were front and center, and I tried to ignore them.

I popped downstairs, preheated the oven, and pulled all of the food out. The chicken needed to go in first, and then the corn and potatoes could follow thirty minutes later. If I timed it right, everything would be ready by seven. We could eat right away, or it could sit and warm in the oven for a little while.

I busied myself setting the table in the dining room and slid the chicken in the oven. I then ran upstairs to shower, making sure to shave my legs. I dressed and ran downstairs with my hair wrapped in a towel. I checked on the chicken and saw that it was turning out quite nice. I patted myself on the back and put the corn and potatoes in beside the chicken.

I was curling my hair when I heard the smoke detector go off in the kitchen. I raced down the stairs two at a time and screamed when I saw black smoke seeping out of the oven. I grabbed oven mitts and opened the door and was engulfed in smoke. I waved it away and tried to see my perfect dinner.

And my perfect dinner was on fire!

I turned off the oven, coughing at the smoke, and wondering where I had put the fire extinguisher. The smoke alarm was blaring and flames covered my food.

Before I could do anything else, I was pushed aside and Charlie was there, aiming my fire extinguisher at the oven and dousing it with white foam. I found my broom and knocked the smoke alarm from the ceiling.

Still wearing the oven mitts, I tried to fan away the burnt stench, and Charlie opened the back door and windows, letting in the cool night air.

"What was it?" Charlie asked, swinging the door back and forth.

"Chicken, potatoes, and corn," I coughed out. "I guess my old oven decided to make something more interesting."

"Flaming poultry," he said. "Never had that before. Is that an Iowa specialty?"

I stopped waving my arms and looked at Charlie. He wasn't laughing at me, and he wasn't mad. He was smiling. I looked at that smile and I burst into giggles. Charlie stepped away from the door and came right for me. He set my oven mitts on the counter and took me into his arms for a big hug, and we laughed together.

At that moment, I knew he was going to be different than all the others.

Charlie called for Chinese takeout while I ran upstairs to change clothes and calm down. So far, I had screwed up the meal. What else could go wrong?

When I came back to the living room, I found Charlie bent over, stoking the fire he'd built in the fireplace. He'd also pushed aside the couch and spread out a blanket on the floor, with the place settings from the dining room set up there.

I took a moment to admire his rear, then went over to sit on the stone hearth.

"That feels so nice," I said.

"It's a perfect night for curling up by a fire," he said, and I felt a shiver race up my spine. Then he added, "As long as it's not shooting from the oven."

I laughed. He put the poker back in the stand and faced me.

"The oven is toast," he said. "How long have you had it?"

"It came with the house. My dad said I should pitch it, but I thought it had character. "

Charlie smiled. "I hope you don't mind," he said, motioning to the blanket. "I thought we could eat here, picnic style."

"It's fine. I'm just sorry you won't get a home-cooked meal."

"Don't worry about it. I'm more interested in the cook than the meal anyway."

I pulled my knees up to my chin and said, "So, Charlie Archer, tell me about yourself."

He shrugged and reached for the wine bottle and glasses. "What do you want to know?"

"I don't know, surprise me," I said, taking the glass he handed to me.

"Did you know I have an older brother who's an actor?" he asked, a hint of sarcasm in his voice.

"Yes. Not interested in him. Move on."

"Well, that's refreshing. Most people want to know about him and nothing else."

"That must be rough. I can't imagine having a famous sibling. My sister, Claire, and I are good friends."

"I can't say that about Garrett and me. It seems our lives have been nothing but one big competition." Charlie drank some wine and looked at me. "It's okay though. I gave up hoping for a brotherly relationship years ago."

"Ouch. That hurts."

He shrugged.

"Okay, have you ever been married?" I asked, switching topics.

He blinked at me. "You get right to it, don't you?"

"Sorry. My sister says I'm blunt like a post."

"No, I like it. In Hollywood, everyone dances in circles. You spend most of your time trying to separate the bullshit from the even bigger bullshit. And no, I've never been married. Or engaged. And I don't have any children. I don't trust myself to raise kids."

"What about Brandon?"

"Brandon's different. He came to me almost an adult. He's got some issues with his dad, but that's not his fault. Garrett's not the best father in the world."

"He always seems so loving whenever he does an interview with Brandon."

"That's because he's always on when there's a camera aimed at him. The real Garrett is a self-centered asshole." He paused and blinked. "Wow, that came out more bitter than I intended."

I scooted closer, wanting to hug him. "No, you can go on. I won't tell anyone."

"Why are we talking about me and my family?" he asked with a small smile.

"Because I'm utterly dull. Continue."

"Wait. Tell me a bit about your family, and then we can keep talking about me."

I tapped my lip with my index finger. "Hmm, well my dad is a retired carpenter. He used to work on houses, and he still builds furniture for fun. My mom is a retired art teacher. She used to work in the elementary schools. She's very crafty and organized, and I gained none of those skills. My older sister Claire is a freelance writer for magazines, and her daughter is Piper." I shrugged. "Oh, and then there's Jeremy, my best friend."

"Your best friend is a guy?"

"Uh huh. He works at the school with me. He's not gay, and he hates all things girly, but he's my best bud. I would trust him with my life."

"Did you ever date?"

I blushed and Charlie laughed. "Briefly!" I said. "We realized dating wasn't a good thing for us, so we just stayed friends."

"Hmm. Interesting. All right. What else?"

"What do you mean, what else?"

"I don't know. An interesting fact."

"My New Year's resolution was to quit smoking, and I haven't smoked since," I said. "This is huge for me, because when you're trying to teach kids history and how to drive, it can be pretty hard not to smoke."

"Well, that's great," Charlie said, nodding. "How do you feel?"

"It's getting better. Jeremy will tell you the first few days were pretty ugly. Okay, now your turn. Why is Garrett a self-centered asshole?"

Charlie took a sip of wine and I watched him swallow, thinking how sexy that simple motion was.

"I hate the way he treats people like objects. Women, his family, even his own son. Brandon's so reserved, and he can't get close to people. Garrett made him that way. I think Garrett got it from our father. He was never very tender with us either."

"But Brandon seems to be opening up a little under your care. I think he looks up to you."

Charlie looked at me out of the corner of his eye. "You think so?"

"I do. He's very concerned about your opinion of him, and he worships the ground you walk on."

"Hero worship?"

I nodded and sat up. "I happen to know a lot about that."

"Oh yeah?"

"Uh huh. Eventually, you'll get to know that about me."

Charlie set his wine glass down and turned to face me. "I hope I do," he said.

I sensed more than felt us moving closer. Before I knew it, our lips were just millimeters apart. I could feel his breath, warm and feathery against my skin, could smell the wine, and I became intoxicated with sensation. I realized I wanted him to kiss me, more than I'd ever wanted to be kissed before.

"Melinda," he whispered, right as his lips touched mine.

To say that I saw fireworks would be an understatement. It was as if my whole body was on fire, and for a brief second I feared I had gotten too close to the fireplace. I pulled him closer, running my hands through his hair.

And then the doorbell rang. I was so surprised I jerked away and fell off the hearth. Charlie took a breath and smiled.

"Hold that thought," he said, tapping my nose.

He paid for the food and brought the bags inside. My stomach rumbled at the delicious smells.

"Hungry?" he asked.

I tilted my head and sighed. "Yes," I growled, annoyed we'd been interrupted.

He laughed and unpacked the cartons, opening each one and passing me a set of chopsticks. We dished up the food and settled side by side to eat.

"I'm not a slut," I said a moment later, and Charlie choked on his cashew chicken. He coughed and took a sip of wine to clear his throat.

"Why would I think you were?"

"Well, uh, I think we might be pretty close to…you know."

"Having sex?" he prompted, holding out a bite of noodles to me.

I took them and nodded as I chewed. "This is our first date. I met you two days ago. And now I'm considering jumping into bed with you. I just wanted you to know that doesn't always happen. Okay, it never happens. I'm not a slut."

"Melinda, you're the first woman I've even entertained thoughts of sleeping with in the past two years."

"Two years? What kind of man are you?"

He laughed and looked at me from behind those glasses, and I had to take another bite of chicken to keep from jumping him right there.

Once we were finished with dinner, we packed the leftovers into the fridge. Then I took his hand and led him up the stairs to my bedroom. My heart was pounding like a freight train against my chest. Sure, I always did the asking out, but when it came to sex, the guy would make the first move. And yet, here I was, pulling Charlie to my bed, begging him to take me.

I turned on the light on my nightstand and sat down on the bed, my mouth dry and my hands shaking.

"So, this is my room," I said.

"It's very nice," Charlie said, sitting beside me. He pushed aside my hair and planted soft kisses along my collarbone, making me gasp.

"Yeah, uh, my mom helped me decorate," I said.

"Uh huh."

More kisses, up my neck, my ear. I was quivering, and all I could do was talk about my room? No wonder I couldn't get laid.

"I'm sorry," I said, turning my head. "I'm a little nervous. It's been awhile, and I don't think I'm very good."

Charlie tilted his head at me. "Maybe you haven't been with the right guy yet."

That declaration made my stomach turn to complete jelly. He tugged at my sweater, and I raised my arms so he could lift it off. He tossed it somewhere behind him, then turned all of his attention to me. I gulped as I stared into his deep blue eyes, praying I remembered how to do this with a real live man.

He kissed me then, and we slid down on the bed until he was lying on top of me. He kept one hand behind my neck, and the other moved across my stomach and then headed for my breasts. His hands were big and slightly rough from working, but it just added to my pleasure. He unhooked my bra and eased the straps down my shoulders, removing it and dropping it to the floor beside the bed.

"Is that a tattoo?" he asked, looking down at my left breast.

I shook my head. "No, it's a birthmark."

"It's in the shape of a heart."

"Weird, huh?"

He dropped a feathery kiss right on it, and I felt my breath hitch. He trailed kisses down my chest, across my belly, moving south, and I wiggled beneath him, biting my lip to keep from moaning out loud.

"Do you want me to stop?" he asked.

I shook my head, gripping the sheets. "No, don't you dare stop."

He grinned and continued on his way, licking and nipping the inside of my thighs. Before I knew it, we were both naked and he was leaning over me with a questioning expression. I nodded and wrapped my legs around his waist, my arms around his neck.

He stared me straight in the eye, gauging my response to his movements, speeding up, slowing down, until my nails dug into his shoulders as he buried his face between my breasts, making noises of pleasure that rumbled against my ribcage and shook me to the core. We tumbled over the edge together, a sweaty, tangled mess of limbs that had gone boneless.

I brought my breathing under control and lay under him, satisfied and exhausted. He raised his head and kissed my nose.

"Are you all right?" he asked, brushing a stray lock of hair from his sweaty forehead.

I exhaled and grinned. "I'm wonderful."

"I don't know what you were talking about before, Melinda, you were excellent."

I blushed beneath his intense gaze, and buried my face against his shoulder.

"Did I say something wrong?" he whispered, nudging me a little.

I looked up at him and blinked away tears. "No, you said something right."

He kissed me until I was dizzy and then we curled up under the blankets. He held me and we drifted off to sleep.

When I woke up, his side of the bed was empty, and I felt a flare of disappointment, but then I spotted his clothes sitting on the floor. So unless he had driven home bare-ass naked, he was still there. I grabbed a blanket from the chair in the corner and wrapped myself in it, toga style. As I passed my dresser mirror, I caught a glimpse of myself and paused.

My lips were swollen, my hair was a mess, and my cheeks were flushed.

I looked like a woman who had just had the most incredible sex of her life. I was giddy as I went downstairs. Then I shot to very horny when I saw Charlie standing at the open fridge, his boxer shorts sitting low on his hips, his body outlined by the bright light. He was all lean muscle and I couldn't help but giggle into my hands as I honed in on the dimples just above his rear. He heard me and turned his head.

"Are you checking out my ass, Miss Martin?" he asked.

I sidled up to him to peer into the fridge myself. "It's quite nice."

He reached around and patted my butt. "So's yours."

"You're hungry?" I asked.

"A little. I see you have blueberry cheesecake. It's my favorite. How did you know?"

I feigned innocence as I pulled it out, balancing it in one hand while I held onto my blanket.

"I better take that from you," he said, setting it on the counter. "Don't want you to drop it. Drop the blanket if you want though. I wouldn't mind."

I stuck my tongue out at him and flashed him. He growled low in his throat and pulled me close.

"Don't tease me unless you intend to use that."

"Cheesecake first, you later," I said.

He cut two slices and we carried our dessert to the living room. As we passed the hall, he nodded toward it.

"What's down there?" he asked.

"A bathroom, my office, and a linen closet."

"You have an office?"

"Yes," I said, trying to pull him back to the living room. "It's where I plan lessons and stuff."

"Cool. Can I see?"

"Um, no."

"Why not?"

"I have things in there."

"Like what?" He was curious now and heading down the hall. I couldn't catch him because I was trying to hang onto my blanket and my plate without dropping them. He stood in the doorway and waited for me. The door was open and the light from the streetlamp outside on the corner was bouncing off my framed movie posters when I got to him.

I sighed and tried not to blush too much. "It's my office slash Superman museum," I said, flipping on the light switch.

Charlie nibbled on his cheesecake as he took in all my collectibles. I held my breath and watched his eyes scan everything from my Superman lunchbox to my *Smallville* action figures. Would he think I was weird?

"So you're a Superman fan, huh?" he asked a moment later, and there was no trace of disapproval or disgust in his voice.

I exhaled and nodded. "Since I was a kid. I saw the first movie in the Cody Theater. I'm kind of attached to it."

"Ah, so that's why you hate my turning it into a restaurant."

"It'll take some time to get used to. I still don't know if I'll eat there though."

Charlie laughed and shook his head at me. "So tell me why you love Superman so much."

"I just adored the idea of a real hero, someone who believed in the good of all people. And of course, the fact that he could fly was pretty awesome too."

Charlie eyed me sideways. "You like a guy that can fly?"

I nodded. "Sure. The thought of soaring above the clouds, free like a bird?" I shrugged. "It's sexy."

Charlie set his plate down on my desk and enveloped me in his strong arms. I put down my plate too, and ran my fingers up his biceps.

"I can fly, Melinda," he said.

"What?"

"I can fly," he repeated, dipping his head to kiss my neck.

"Like, stick your arms out and flap, or what?"

He chuckled. "No, not like that. I have a private pilot's license."

"Are you serious?" I asked. "You've probably got a plane stashed somewhere too, right?"

"Hangar 12 at the Cody Municipal Airport," he said.

I gaped at him. Was this guy for real?

"Would you want to go flying sometime?" he asked.

I couldn't speak for a second. "You're going to take me flying? You?"

"Yes, me, Melinda. I'll fly you wherever you want to go."

I squeaked out a yes, and then we made love on my office floor.

It was almost 2am when Charlie left my house. He hadn't expected to stay so late, and he wanted to get home before Brandon got worried.

"When can I see you again?" he asked as he held me on the porch.

"I don't know. When are you free?"

He sighed, and I could feel his breath rustle against my hair. "I should get some more done at the restaurant. The carpenters are just getting into the real work."

"I'm coming over Monday night to drive with Brandon. My niece is going to tutor him on Tuesday night. We can be alone then."

"Tuesday seems so far away."

"We can make it. Just think happy thoughts."

Charlie smiled and kissed me. I was getting used to all this attention. He drove away, and I went back inside. I curled up in bed again, but it didn't feel right without him there. I wondered what it would be like to wake up next to him day after day.

That thought struck me as quite odd. I'd never felt so emotionally close to any man before. I could count the number of serious boyfriends I'd had on one hand, and I had never imagined a future with any of them. What was going on? Was this...love? No, it couldn't be.

I debated on whether or not to call Jeremy at this time, and decided, yes, I should. He was awake, which didn't surprise me. He's a night owl.

"Jeremy, I think, I think Charlie, Charlie and I," I stammered.

"Oh God, you slept with him, didn't you?" he asked.

I paused for a moment, chewing on my lower lip. "Is that a bad thing?"

"I don't know," he said, and I could hear the smile in his voice. "Was it?"

I stretched out on my bed, remembering the feel of Charlie against me, the grin on my face bigger than a Cheshire cat's.

"It was fucking fantastic," I said, and Jeremy laughed.

"Good for you. You deserve some good sex."

"It was more than that though," I said, sitting up. I propped two pillows behind me and smoothed the blankets over my legs. "He's so smart, and kind, and super hot. I can't believe he likes me."

"You sound like a teenager. Mel, you always underestimate yourself. You're a beautiful woman."

I took this in and shook my head. "It doesn't sound the same coming from you."

"Hey, I told you this years ago when we were dating," he said, sounding offended.

"I know, but it's different now. I'm not sleeping with you."

"Anymore."

I blew air from my mouth and said, "One time. And admit it, it was disastrous."

"Like sleeping with my sister," he said and shuddered. "Okay, I get what you mean."

I picked at a loose thread on my blanket. "Jeremy, what if he's, you know?"

"Are you going to say the words I think you're going to say?" he asked, his voice dropping. "Because if you are, this is more serious than I thought."

"Maybe I'll hold off. I'm not sure where this is going to go, but the ride so far has been highly satisfying."

"All right, that's enough. If you go into details, I may have to scour my brain with bleach."

I blew a raspberry into the phone. "G'night, Jeremy."

We hung up and I fell asleep, dreaming of Charlie.

# Chapter Six

Sunday was spent searching the ads for sales on ovens, but even with the sale prices, I just couldn't see myself forking over $700 or more for a new one that I would use maybe twice a year. I sat at my kitchen table and cast scrutinizing glances at my old oven. I wondered if my dad could fix it since he's a genius at fixing things. I called him, and he and my mom came over for lunch, which meant Dad brought his toolbox and Mom brought the food.

"It smells in here," my mom said as soon as she stepped inside the house. "Did you open the windows?"

"Yes, and then I had to close them because it's the middle of February."

Mom handed me the Tupperware containers that held chicken noodle soup, ham and cheese sandwiches, and a Caesar salad, reached into her purse, which wasn't really a purse, but a freaking huge tote bag, and pulled out a can of spray air freshener. She began spraying every room.

Dad hugged me and we headed for the kitchen with his trusty toolbox. "Let's see what you've got here," he said.

"You were cooking?" Mom asked when she returned to join us in the kitchen.

"Yeah, just simple stuff."

"Why?" she asked, her voice a bit suspicious.

"Uh, becauseIhadadate," I blurted out so fast I hoped she wouldn't make it out. But my mother had incredible hearing and the ability to decipher gibberish, a trait that came in handy while she taught art in the elementary schools. Her eyes lit up. I groaned as she pulled me to the living room and sat me down on the couch.

"With whom? Anyone I know?"

So maybe inviting my folks over was a bad idea.

"A guy named Charlie Archer -"

"Garrett Archer's brother?!"

Her screech was so loud, my dad hollered at us to know what was wrong.

"Melinda's dating a movie star's brother!" she hollered back. Dad just grunted and went back to work.

"Just one date so far," I said. And mind blowing sex, but we weren't going there.

"How did you meet him?"

I looked at my mom and sighed. "Mom, please don't go spreading this around all over the place. It's no big deal."

"What are you talking about? He's converting the old theater into a restaurant, right?"

"You knew about that?" I asked, my tone accusing. "Why didn't you tell me?"

But she waved my questions away and said, "So what's he like? Is he as handsome as he is on TV?"

"Charlie's never been on TV. He's not an actor."

"But he's been shown on TV with his brother. He's very nice-looking, dear. And rich, too, from what I've heard."

She nodded her approval, and I shoved a throw pillow in front of my face to muffle my screams. Mom sniffed in disgust, and I peered over the pillow at her.

"I don't know why you get like this, Melinda," she said. "I'm just anxious to see you married and happy."

"I don't have to be married to be happy," I said, sighing. "I'm young yet."

"You're over thirty."

"Claire's single," I threw in.

"Yes, and we all know how sad that is."

I growled and stood up. "I'm going to go see if Dad needs any help."

I left her in the living room and sat down on the floor next to the oven, where my dad was tinkering with his tools.

"She pushing you to get married again?" he asked without looking up.

"I had one date with the guy. We're not picking out the wedding colors just yet."

"She's just afraid she'll be too old to play with grandkids."

"She's got Piper."

Dad looked at me and smiled. "But Piper's a grownup now, going to be heading off to college soon. She wants babies to bounce on her knees."

"So get her a dog."

Dad chuckled and shook his head. "Mel, she loves you, you know that."

I glanced over my shoulder, saw her dusting my furniture with her own rag and polish.

"I know. But she needs to lay off the pushing. I'll find the right guy, and when I do, I'll be sure to invite her to the wedding."

Dad wiped his hands on an oil-stained cloth and looked at me. "I think this thing is toast," he said.

A chill ran up my spine at those words. Charlie had said the same thing. How eerie was that?

"Um, okay," I said.

"You all right?" Dad asked, looking at me funny.

I stood up. "Yeah, I'll just go talk to Mom now. Thanks."

When I was a little girl, I decided that I wanted a man just like my father, and not in the gross way. I wanted someone I could trust and depend on. Someone who was strong, smart, attractive, and good with his hands. The fact that Charlie and my dad had used the same phrase to describe the state of my oven had freaked me out. Maybe it was some kind of sign.

* * *

I arrived at school the next morning, still wondering if I needed a new oven, maybe I could just get by with a toaster oven instead, when I was greeted by Gloria Milner, the school gossip. I tried to hurry past her to get to my room, but she kept up, chattering away. She was like a little yappy dog that you couldn't shake off your ankle no matter how hard you tried.

"I heard you had Charlie Archer over at your house this weekend," she said, a huge smile on her bird-like face.

"Oh yeah? Where did you hear that?" I asked.

"I heard that your oven caught fire. I heard that his big black truck was parked outside your house until after two in the morning."

What the hell? Who was out driving past my house in the wee hours of the morning? And what if Gloria ever lost her hearing? She'd be totally screwed.

"Wow, that's interesting, Gloria. I have to finish grading some papers," I said, unlocking my door and stepping inside. I closed the door in her face and went to sit at my desk. My cell phone rang and I answered it.

"Good morning, beautiful," Charlie said, and I couldn't help but smile.

"Hey, how are you?"

"Lonely. I tried to catch you before you left this morning, but I was a little slow. How's your oven?"

"Still dead."

"Sorry to hear that. I just wanted to let you know that I was thinking of you."

"Thinking of me, or thinking of running away from me?"

"Thinking of you and your perfect body that I want to hold against me again."

My heart skipped a beat, and I felt tingly all over, remembering his touch.

"You're stopping by tonight, to drive with Brandon?" he asked, interrupting my lust-filled thoughts.

"Yes."

"I guess I'll have to wait until then to see you. Bye, Melinda."

I spent the rest of the day in a great mood, and even Gloria couldn't put a damper on my day. She tried though, with her wheedling questions and sly looks. Even the other teachers were whispering behind their hands.

Brandon did much better during Driver's Ed. He was more relaxed, and either didn't catch any of the gossip floating around about me and his uncle, or he didn't care. Brandon had enough sly looks for me of his own.

After we got back to school, he just grinned at me and said, "I've never seen my uncle so happy."

I glanced around to make sure we were alone and said, "You know, maybe we shouldn't talk about this at school. The relationship between your uncle and me is private."

"Oh, yeah. I get it. I just wanted you to know. He thinks you're pretty neat."

Then he ran off, leaving me alone with my thoughts. Until Jeremy showed up.

"You're the number one topic around here today," he said.

"Just goes to show how boring everyone else is."

"Small town, not much else to talk about."

I brushed hair from my eyes. "They're just interested because he's Garrett Archer's brother."

"Of course. And he's rich. Have you realized how rich this man is?"

My stomach rolled. "How rich is he?"

Jeremy rubbed his gloved hands together. "You don't know?"

"I don't know his entire history, no."

"But you slept with him."

I rolled my eyes. "Do you get the life history of every woman you sleep with, before you sleep with her?"

"All right, all right. True."

"So," I said, nudging Jeremy. "Dish."

Jeremy took a deep breath and launched into what he'd found on the Internet about the Archer family. Garrett and Charlie were the sons of Hollywood legend Jackson Archer. Their mother died when Charlie was six, and Garrett was twelve, and Jackson raised them himself, along with an army of nannies. Garrett went into acting, and Charlie chose a different path, but still connected to Hollywood. He enjoyed food and studied cuisine in Europe before coming back to LA and starting his own restaurant. It was an instant success, and he launched another in New York City. Not only had he made a fortune on his own, but when Jackson Archer died a few years ago of cancer, Charlie and Garrett inherited his estate as well.

"He's worth, like, millions, Mel. You're dating an honest-to-God millionaire," Jeremy finished, a huge grin on his face.

I wasn't smiling though. The thought of how wealthy and sophisticated Charlie was had made me queasy.

"Mel, are you okay?"

I nodded and waved a hand at him.

"You don't look so good."

"I just need to think."

"About what?"

"About why a guy like him would want a woman like me."

"Oh geez," Jeremy said, leaning against the building. "Enter self-doubt, right on cue."

"What are you talking about?"

"You're moving into your self-doubt stage, where you try to talk yourself out of a good relationship by telling yourself you're not pretty enough, or smart enough, or blah, blah, blah!" Jeremy exclaimed, startling me. "If you like this guy, don't do it."

"I don't do that."

"I'm calling bullshit."

I glared at him and crossed my arms.

"You are good enough for him, Mel," Jeremy said. "You're worth it."

I said nothing. He reached out and poked me in the ribs.

"Say it!" he cried.

I giggled and sputtered, "I'm worth it!"

"That sounded like a bad L'Oreal commercial, but I'll take it."

I went inside to my classroom to eat my lunch and do a little research of my own. What Jeremy had said was true. Charlie was a very wealthy man. I found pictures of him hobnobbing with A-list celebrities at his restaurants and at parties with his brother. There were several articles in food magazines about his success and some recipes from his menus.

There wasn't much news about his past relationships, although he had dated a Victoria's Secret supermodel for almost two years. I clicked on the link for her official website, immediately sucking in my stomach when I saw her in skimpy lingerie. I decided I was going to need to start working out. As I scrolled through more pictures, I realized it was going to take something along the lines of plastic surgery before I'd ever get her figure.

I turned off the computer and focused on my lunch, a very healthy grilled cheese sandwich with bacon. I shrugged and dug in, trying not to think about Charlie's Hollywood life. As much as I didn't want to admit that I had self-esteem issues, deep down, I did, and it wasn't easy to just push them all aside. But with Charlie, I vowed to try.

When I arrived at the theater that night at six, I was nervous about seeing him. The guy was a millionaire, and just thinking about that made me dizzy. I got out of the car and wobbled to the door. My senses were assaulted by the sights, sounds, and smells of a crew of construction workers. The concession stand was gone, and the walls were being painted. My shoulders sagged again at the thought of my beloved theater being changed to a restaurant.

Charlie came up behind me and put his hands on my arms. "You've got them working late, don't you?" I asked.

"I have a deadline to meet, and they agreed to the extra hours in exchange for a healthy bonus. How's it looking?"

"Oh, uh, it's nice."

"You don't seem enthused."

I turned and looked up at him, at his Clark Kent-like appearance as he stared at me over his glasses, and I tried to see the millionaire in him, but all I saw was Charlie. I relaxed into his arms.

"Sorry, I just have a hard time believing this place is changing so much."

"I'm thinking of putting popcorn and Twizzlers on the menu, as a special entrée," he said, kissing my cheek.

I laughed. "Well then, maybe I will eat here."

"Brandon's waiting in the office. I'm sorry I can't hang out with you more, but I've got an important business call coming in."

"No problem. Are we still on for our date tomorrow?"

"It's supposed to rain, so I figured we would hold off on flying. How about you come to my place? I'll cook you dinner."

I nodded. "That sounds good, and I'll bet your dinner is way better than mine ever would have been."

"Cooking just takes practice, that's all. Maybe I'll teach you."

"I'll bet you can teach me a lot of things," I said, smiling.

He tipped my head up and kissed me, and I didn't want to go driving anymore. When we heard applause break out around us, we moved apart. Embarrassed, I raised both hands to cover my face.

"Thank you, thank you," Charlie said, bowing a little.

I ducked my head, ran to get Brandon from the office, and left the theater. I wasn't big on public displays of affection, which just showed me how attracted I was to Charlie. I'd kissed him in front of all his workers.

Charlie Archer was having an effect on me, and I was enjoying it.

# Chapter Seven

It was drizzling and the sky was a dark gray when I stopped at the dry cleaner's after school on Tuesday, to pick up my pink sweater and drop off my blue smoke-scented one. Piper was working the front counter, and there were two other customers ahead of me. I peered around them and took a look at my niece, then cringed. She was wearing what her mother and I called her "happy face" which was a huge smile and wide eyes. The bigger her smile, and the wider her eyes got, the more annoyed and pissed off she was. It was kind of scary.

The customer she was waiting on was a man dressed in an expensive suit, holding a bag of clothing in one arm and waving the other in the air. Piper just nodded and listened to him with the smile plastered on her face.

"I need these clothes today! In an hour! I have to be in Chicago for the last flight out," the suit man cried.

"I'm sorry, sir, but we don't offer one hour cleaning. There's a Quik Clean on First Street though —"

"That place is a pit. I want my things cleaned here. I demand immediate service and satisfaction."

I made a face and shook my head. What an asshole.

"I'm sorry, sir," Piper repeated, her voice level and calm, but also a bit dangerous. "It's just not possible."

"My clothes have food stains on them!" the man shouted. "What the hell am I supposed to do?"

I was two steps away from going up there and pounding his face against the countertop, but then I stopped. I knew my niece. She was feisty and didn't take crap from anyone. She leaned back and crossed her arms over her chest and stared at the man, still smiling.

"Hello?" the man said, waving his hand in her face. "I have food on my clothes. What am I supposed to do?"

Piper tilted her head and said, "I'd suggest wearing a bib, sir." Her delivery was perfect, her expression sugary sweet.

I clamped a hand over my mouth and stifled a giggle. The man gaped for a second, then turned around and stomped past me and out of the store.

"Next!" Piper said, and the next customer, also a man, stepped forward.

He dropped a bag on the counter and said, "You take hangers back, right?"

Piper nodded and the man turned around to leave.

"Hey, Piper," I said, approaching with caution. "How are you?"

She opened the bag and pulled out a wad of hangers and said, "Fine. I'd be even better if people read the sign out front that said we only *take back our OWN hangers!*" Her voice rose and was aimed in the direction of the leaving man, who hunched his shoulders and bolted from the store.

I jumped back a step. "Uh, is today a bad day?"

Piper blew her bangs out of her face and ground her teeth together, dumping the hangers in a nearby trash bin. Then she turned to me and sighed.

"Sorry. Yeah, bad day."

"What's going on?"

She busied herself by spinning the rack to retrieve my pink sweater and checking in my blue one. She sniffed the blue sweater and made a face.

"This reeks of smoke. You didn't light your hair on fire again, did you?"

My face flushed at the memory of a cigarette gone very wrong, and I shook my head. "No. My oven died."

"You were cooking?" she asked, wrinkling her nose in disgust.

86

"Hey, this isn't about me. What's up with you? What's wrong?"

"I got an early acceptance letter from Michigan State."

I blinked. "Isn't this good news? You wanted Michigan State, right?"

"Yes."

"Piper, this is fabulous," I said, and then I saw the tears gathering in her eyes and asked, "Isn't it?"

"Yeah, it's great. If I could afford it. I don't know if I'll be able to get a scholarship there because they're so competitive. Mom makes too much money on her own for me to qualify for much in financial aid, and Dad's decided not to help me at all."

I felt a sudden urge to hold my former brother-in-law's head down in a toilet bowl and flush a few times. I remembered Claire mentioning he was worried about the money, but she hadn't said anything about his backing out completely.

"Uh, what does your mom say about this?"

"I haven't told her."

"Which part?"

Piper sighed. "I told her I got into Michigan State. She was thrilled. Then I called Dad and told him." Her lower lip trembled.

"Not so thrilled," I finished for her. "Why isn't he going to help?"

"Sharon thinks he should save his money for their kids. College will be more expensive when it's their turn, and my mom makes plenty of money. After all, I'm just one kid. Sharon has three." She sounded like she was reciting a practiced speech, which was probably what Beau had done.

"Sharon has her head shoved so far up her ass she can't see straight," I spat out. Then I calmed myself and reached across the counter to take Piper's hands in mine. "Sorry. Forget I said that. I'll talk to your mom about this. We'll get it taken care of."

"What do you mean?"

"I mean, if it comes down to it, I'll fork over some money to help you."

Piper opened her mouth to object, but I shushed her. "You can think of it as a loan, and you can pay me back when you're a hotshot attorney."

"Out of state tuition is high until I establish residency," Piper threw in.

I shrugged. "So what? It'll work out."

She smiled, a genuine smile, and came around the counter to give me a hug. "You're awesome, Mel."

"I try."

She sniffed and wiped her eyes, then went back to her post. Within seconds, she was composed again.

"I'm tutoring Brandon tonight," she said. "We're meeting at the library once I'm off work. He said he gets distracted by all the noise at the theater."

I nodded. "That's good. You'll like him. He's a great kid."

"So what's on your agenda for the evening?" she asked, all innocence and sweetness.

I narrowed my eyes and looked at her. "What have you heard?"

She tapped her fingernails on the counter. "You're the talk of the town."

"Oh God," I said, putting my head down.

I could hear the mischievous grin in Piper's voice as she said, "He's a gorgeous, wealthy man -"

"Why does everyone point out the wealthy part?" I asked, my voice muffled.

"-and he likes you a lot," Piper finished. "At least that's what I've heard."

I raised my head. "Yeah? From whom?"

"Well, Mom ran into Mrs. Larson at the grocery store, and Mrs. Larson said Charlie's truck was parked outside your house until two am."

"Mrs. Larson!" I cried. Of course. She was my neighbor two houses down, and also Gloria Milner's mother-in-law. I was going to have to be careful from now on.

Piper gave me a claim check for my blue sweater, lowered her voice and asked, "Did you sleep with him?"

I jerked and grabbed the paper from her. "I am so not having this conversation with you. Goodbye."

I could hear her giggling behind me as I left, and while I was embarrassed that everyone was so quick to assume that Charlie and I had done the deed – which we had, but whose business was that but ours anyway? – I was glad that Piper was in a better mood than when I showed up.

I was driving home when Claire called me to talk about Piper's birthday party.

"Are you bringing Charlie?" she asked, her voice super sweet, and I could almost see her batting her eyelashes.

"Isn't it a little soon to be introducing him to the family?"

"Isn't the first date a little soon to be jumping into bed?" she countered.

"What? Jeremy told you?"

"Aha! So you did. You little ho, you," Claire giggled.

"Shut up."

"Anyhow, enough about your sex life. Bring him. Mom's dying to meet him, and I think he's pretty amazing."

"You haven't even met him. How would you know if he's amazing?"

"He's dating you, isn't he? That takes a special kind of man."

"Very funny," I said.

"Next Friday night, seven pm, Mom's house."

I promised her I'd be there, and that I'd think about asking Charlie to come. I didn't want to scare him away too soon.

"By next Friday, you'll have known him for two weeks," Claire said. "Plenty of time to brief him on the workings of our family."

I hung up and shook my head. I couldn't remember my family being so interested in who I was dating. It was a little unnerving. When I got home, I noticed I had a missed call on my phone, and that annoying little message icon. I hated that icon with a passion, so I hurried to listen to the message to get rid of it, squealing a bit when I heard Charlie's voice.

"Hey there, just wanted to let you know I'm still thinking about you. See you later tonight, around seven-thirty? I've got an important call coming in at six, and then I'm dropping Brandon at the library after that. Call me if that doesn't work for you."

I did a dance around my living room. Charlie was so amazing, I felt like I was dreaming. I had to force myself to grade papers and do my teacher duties before getting ready for my date.

By the time I left my house, the drizzle had turned into a full-fledged downpour. I was soaked before I got into my car.

"Great, just perfect," I muttered, shaking my head. Raindrops splattered my dashboard, and I ran a hand through my hair. It caught in some tangles, and I groaned.

So much for wanting to look nice.

I drove to the north end of town where the houses were newer and bigger. This was a nicer neighborhood than mine, with tree lined streets and large yards. A few years ago, the area had been flat and bare. Then a rich developer had decided to build monstrous houses, and like flies to shit, the doctors and lawyers moved in. The area was called Cherry Orchard, although as far as I knew, there had never been an orchard there, let alone a cherry one.

I had my heat going full blast, so my hair was drying, but in frizzy poofs. So much for the smooth curls I'd worked on for a half hour.

I made a mad dash to the front door, just as Charlie opened it. I slid inside, out of the rain.

"Whoa, you're like a wet puppy," he said, taking my coat and laughing. "Hold on, I'll get you a towel."

He hung my coat in a closet and took off down a hallway. I slipped out of my shoes and left them on the rug near the door, then I just stood there shivering in the foyer. To my left was the living room, to my right a large dining room. A staircase was in front of me, leading up to the second floor.

Charlie returned with a fluffy white towel and handed it to me. I began scrubbing at my hair.

"Do you want some dry clothes?" he asked.

"Nah, I'm fine."

I finished toweling my hair and looked at Charlie. My knees started to knock together at the sight of him. Dressed in jeans and a nice blue button down shirt with the sleeves rolled up to just below the elbows, he was grinning at me and swiping at the wet spots I'd left on his front.

He reached out and pulled me against him, his lips descending on mine for a kiss. My body went limp against him, and the towel dropped to the floor.

"Well, hello," I breathed when we broke apart.

"Yeah," he said. "God, I've missed you."

"You saw me yesterday."

He shrugged. "That was yesterday."

I snuggled against him, then I sniffed the air. "Something smells good."

"Dinner's almost ready. How about a tour of the place first?"

"Sure. I like the decorating."

He took my hand and guided me from room to room. "It came like this, so much homier than my place in LA."

"Oh yeah? What's that like?"

He wrinkled his nose a bit. "Sterile. It's a penthouse apartment. I didn't have time to decorate it myself, so I hired someone. Unfortunately, she turned it into a museum. It's full of antiques and expensive art pieces that scare the crap out of me. I keep meaning to change it, but I never get around to it."

I was surprised at how clean the house was. Not a speck of dust anywhere. My mother would have been so proud. Charlie told me he had a cleaning lady come once a week.

"The stupid thing is that I work my butt off the night before to pick up the place."

"Wait, so you clean before the cleaning lady comes?"

"Yeah, isn't that ridiculous?"

I thought about it for a minute before deciding I would do the same thing. Who wants a stranger to find your dirty socks and crumbs in the couch?

We went upstairs and Charlie pointed to a closed door. "Brandon's room is the messiest place in the house. He's got two clothes hampers, but the clothes don't quite make it in."

"Can I take a peek?" I asked.

Charlie nodded. Brandon's room was messy, but not in that, "I'm never taking my shoes off in this room because I might step in something gross," kind of way. He was more cluttered than anything. Posters of movies and musicians hung on the walls, and stacks of magazines covered the desk, along with a few empty soda cans. As Charlie had said, two clothes hampers stood near the closet, with a pile of clothes surrounding them.

"Typical teenage boy's room," I said.

Charlie grinned. "He'd love to hear you say that."

"Why?"

"Because this is the first room that he's ever made his own. He's got a room at my apartment, but he wasn't there long enough to change anything. And any place he's lived with Garrett wasn't supposed to be typical."

"That's sad."

"It's the way Garrett and I were brought up. Our rooms never reflected who we were. They were always picture perfect, like in magazines."

I put my arm around his waist. "I'm glad Brandon gets to be himself with you."

"Me too."

"Okay. So where's your room?" I asked, poking him in the side.

Charlie tapped my nose and pulled me further down the hall. His room held a big king-sized bed with a navy blue down comforter and lots of fluffy pillows. A sturdy oak dresser stood against one wall and two matching nightstands were on either side of the bed. His closet door was open, and I glimpsed a rack of expensive suits.

"It's very masculine," I said in a low voice.

I ran my hand over the comforter, marveling at the softness.

"Needs a woman's touch," he said, hugging me from behind and nuzzling my neck.

I shivered and leaned against him.

"We should…eat," I gasped. "Before it burns and we end up ordering takeout again."

Charlie let out a soft moan. "Later?"

"Oh, God yes."

We went back downstairs where Charlie poured me a glass of wine and ordered me to go sit in the living room while he got the food ready. I refused, wanting to be close to him. So I hovered around the kitchen while he checked and tested everything. It smelled wonderful, but I was embarrassed to admit that, aside from the obvious vegetables, I had no idea what he was cooking.

When everything was done, he pushed me out to the dining room.

"I'll serve you," he said.

"Well, can't beat that." I took my wine glass and sat down at the table, feeling like a princess.

He came from the kitchen carrying plate after plate. When he was done, he refilled my glass and sat across from me.

"Dig in," he said, motioning to my food.

I picked up my fork, studying everything. "Uh, not to sound ignorant, but, can you tell me what it all is?"

Charlie smiled and pointed to each plate. "This is chicken piccata with an arugula and goat cheese salad. Roasted broccoli and green beans. For dessert, I've got ricotta with honey and raspberries."

I frowned and poked at the salad. "What's arugula?"

"It's a plant. It's good. Try it."

I took a bite and chewed. "Leafy." I swallowed, and my taste buds were hit all at once. I sat back. "Whoa."

"Good whoa?" Charlie asked, cutting into his chicken.

"Wow. This is amazing."

I dug into the chicken and savored the taste. "You need to cook for my mother. She would die."

"I'd love to."

After a few moments of trying a bit of each dish, I hunched my shoulders and said, "I guess you may have something here with your restaurant thing."

"Are you admitting I may be a success?"

"Maybe. Is everything you make this good?"

"I'd like to think so. I studied with some excellent chefs in Italy, France, and Germany."

"I can't wait for dessert," I said, licking sauce from my lower lip.

"Me neither."

His tone was deep, with a slight growl behind it that made me look up. He was giving me a heated stare from across the table, and I could feel my stomach flipping.

"Oh."

He shook himself and took a drink of wine. "So tell me about school. Why did you decide to become a teacher?"

"Changing the subject, huh?"

"It's the only way we'll get through the meal. Otherwise I'm liable to jump across the table and take you right now."

I blinked. "Okay, well then. School. Teaching. I could give you that same old excuse about wanting to make an impact on a child's life, but I won't."

"That's not how you saw it?"

I shook my head. "Kids today are different. They're educated about so many other things, outside of the classroom, so I didn't go into this profession with visions of hugs and perfect grades and valedictorians all lined up. The truth is, I didn't know what I wanted to do, but suddenly I was in my second year of college and I needed a major. I guess I just followed after Jeremy."

"Your guy friend."

"My best friend," I corrected. "We went to the same college. He's always known he wanted to teach. There's something good and bubbly about him. God, he makes me sick."

Charlie smiled.

"Jeremy is everyone's favorite teacher at school. Mr. Cool. He's tough, but in a way that the kids don't hate him, and he's involved in everything. This year he's in charge of Prom decorations, so he's got tons of planning to do for that. I think he's also signed up for something with graduation."

"And you're not?"

"Me? Yeah right. I'm lucky if I can find two shoes that match, let alone plan a big to-do like Prom or graduation." I finished my wine and Charlie poured me some more. "Jeremy was hired right out of college, but I bummed around for awhile, substituting here and there, trying to get a feel for the profession. My first year as a full-time teacher, I took on everything, trying to be like Jeremy. But I burned out, couldn't keep up. My second year, I found my niche, which is as the smartass teacher that kids can talk to. I think it also helped that I taught Driver's Ed. I got to see all the kids at their worst."

"Oh yeah? What do you mean?"

"Even the smartest kids can suck at driving," I said.

Charlie nodded and swallowed a bite of chicken. "Garrett sucked at driving, still does. That's why he's chauffeured everywhere now."

"Wouldn't that get boring?"

"It makes him feel important. Ever since he was in that Tom Cruise movie and got nominated for an Oscar, his ego has gotten a million times bigger."

"No offense, but I don't much care for his acting."

Charlie grinned and pointed his fork at me. "That makes two of us. My dad was a brilliant character actor. He could play a bad guy just as well as the romantic hero. He always thought I could do that, and in high school I was in drama, but I didn't find the work appealing. I hate being in the spotlight. Brandon's like me in that way. We're both kind of shy."

"I find it sweet and endearing," I said.

After a few minutes, I wiped my lips with my napkin, then placed it beside my plate and stood up.

"Well, I'm done eating," I said, raising a brow.

"Where are you going?"

I tipped my head toward the direction of the stairs.

"Dessert," I said, then took off.

I heard Charlie's chair tip over and hit the floor as he raced after me.

# Chapter Eight

"One container of cashew chicken, one of sesame chicken, two pints of fried rice, an order of crab rangoons, an order of pan-fried noodles," I rattled off into the phone, pacing my kitchen.

"Mushu pork," Claire yelled from the living room.

"Gross, that shit is so disgusting," Jeremy groaned. "Get an order of almond cookies!"

"Mushu pork and an order of almond cookies," I said. "Yup, that should be all, thank you."

I hung up and joined them. "Food will be here in forty minutes," I said.

"Did you ask for extra soy sauce? Last time they didn't send enough," Claire said, channel surfing. We were waiting to watch *Smallville* until the food arrived, so she stopped on the Food Network and studied the dish being made.

Jeremy nudged her foot from where he sat. "They send plenty of sauce. You just drown all your food in it."

She kicked his hand and shushed him.

I looked at the TV and watched a skinny blond prepare a chicken dish.

"Charlie made an excellent chicken piccolo last night," I said.

Claire looked at me and giggled. "Do you mean chicken piccata?"

I frowned. "Okay, yeah. That's it. It was fantastic. He's a great cook."

Jeremy leaned back against the couch. "So tell us all about him. You've been kind of mum about him."

"What am I supposed to say?"

"Well, so far we know he's gorgeous, wealthy, a great cook, and good in bed. Am I missing anything else?"

I smiled and stretched out in my chair. "He's excellent in bed. Best lover I've ever had."

"Ah see, now this isn't fair. You're having sex again and we're not," Jeremy said.

"Yeah, well, it's been a lifetime since I had sex, so I deserve it. You said so yourself."

"I did. Doesn't mean I can't be jealous."

Claire thwapped him on the back of the head. Jeremy glared at her, and just before I could step in to break them up, the phone rang.

"Hey, beautiful," Charlie said in a deep voice when I answered. I curled around the phone in my chair, a huge grin taking over my face.

"What are you doing?" I asked.

"Trying not to die by paper cuts," he said. "I'm buried in three feet of paperwork here, and I'm starting to get cranky. What are you doing?"

"Waiting with Claire and Jeremy for our food to arrive so we can watch *Smallville*."

"Oh, sorry. Didn't mean to interrupt."

"You didn't," I assured him, while giving Jeremy the finger as he made faces and kissing noises at me. Claire thwapped him again.

"I'm swamped for the rest of the week," he groaned. "But I'm free again Tuesday night."

"So Tuesday's become our official date night?"

"I guess so. Wanna go flying?"

"If the weather's good, yeah. I'd love to."

"You driving with Brandon tomorrow night?"

"Sure am."

"I'll break away from my desk for a few minutes to see you."

"Good," I said. We chatted about a few other non important things until the doorbell rang and Claire jumped up to answer it. "Our food's here."

"I'll let you go then. Just wanted to tell you I'm thinking about you. Bye."

We hung up and Jeremy grinned at me.

"You're in love," he said.

"Huh? We haven't said it."

"Ah, but I can see it in your face, and I can hear it." He nodded. "It suits you, Mel."

Claire came back with three bags of food and we dished it up and started the show, but I couldn't pay attention.

I was too busy wondering if I was in love with Charlie.

* * *

The rest of the week was uneventful, except for the thrills I got from talking with Charlie every day, and the kisses we shared when I went to the theater to drive with Brandon.

On Saturday, I was enjoying sleeping in when Jeremy burst into my house and pulled me out of bed.

"Gaah, what the hell?" I cried, grabbing at the blankets.

"Let's go," he said.

"Go where? What are you doing here?"

"There's an estate sale in Davenport. Some little old lady died and all her stuff's up for sale. Including a nearly new oven. We gotta go. Start's in an hour."

"We'll never make it." I crawled back into bed, but Jeremy stole my blankets.

"Get your ass up. You want an oven, you need one, and here's one for under fifty bucks."

That woke me up right away. "Give me ten minutes," I said and bolted for the bathroom. I showered and dressed and we ran out of the house to his truck parked in the driveway. He sped toward Davenport while I bounced along to a song on the radio.

"You're awesome, you know that?" I asked, leaning over to kiss his cheek.

"I know," he said. "So how's Charlie doing?"

"He's fine. Busy getting the restaurant put together."

"When does it open?"

"He wants to have it open by graduation, so he can have a special party for the seniors."

"That sounds neat."

"Yeah."

Jeremy glanced at me sideways. "You're still bummed about the theater."

I sighed. "I guess so. I know it's not going to change back into the place I knew, but it still makes me feel like I've lost something."

"But you've gained an excellent boyfriend. Isn't that a fair exchange?"

I giggled. "I suppose so." I poked his side. "You need to start dating again. When's the last time you went out?"

"Oh, I think it was before the last presidential election," he mused.

"Come on, I haven't seen you out with anyone in ages."

He shrugged and stared out the windshield. "No one I'm interested in."

"What about that new substitute math teacher? Kelly? She's cute."

"She's married."

I wrinkled my nose. "Oops."

"I'm not worried, Mel. I'll find someone. You did, so that gives me hope."

I slapped his arm, and he laughed.

We arrived at the house, a big old rambling thing that looked stuffed to the gills with loot. We hurried inside and took seats near the back of the huge living room. There were so many good things up for sale that when we left an hour and a half later, I had my new oven, a bookcase, two Tiffany-style lamps, and a gorgeous Crystal vase, and Jeremy walked off with an antique silver jewelry box and a crystal decanter.

"What do you need a jewelry box for?" I asked.

Jeremy tightened the straps that held my oven in place in the bed of his truck and just smiled.

"I may get a girlfriend someday and want to give her something nice," he said.

"Well, she'll certainly appreciate it. It's beautiful."

We drove back to Cody, to my house, and I jerked in surprise when I saw Charlie's truck parked in front by the curb. He was sitting on the steps leading to the porch, a bouquet of flowers in his lap. He stood up and waved as Jeremy backed into the driveway.

"Prince Charming," Jeremy said.

"Be nice," I warned.

"Am I ever anything but?" he asked.

I ran up to the steps and Charlie hugged me.

"What are you doing here?" I asked.

"I decided to take a break from work and come see my girl," he said, kissing my nose. He handed me the flowers.

I sniffed them and smiled. "They're beautiful, thank you."

Jeremy came up behind me then, and I turned around to make the official introduction. I realized I was a little nervous. Jeremy was like family to me, so having him meeting my boyfriend, my heart fluttered at the thought, was a bit serious.

Jeremy stuck out his hand and Charlie shook it. They eyed each other for a moment and I hopped from foot to foot.

"Nice to meet you, Jeremy, I've heard a lot about you."

"Same here."

Jeremy stuffed his hands in his pockets and jerked his head toward his truck. "So you gonna help me unload this stuff or what?"

Charlie grinned and followed him. I let out a great sigh of relief and hurried to unlock and prop open the door. Then I watched with amusement as they heaved and huffed and lugged in first the bookcase, and then the oven. Charlie's cheeks were pink by the time they shoved the old oven aside and got the new one in place. Then I giggled out loud as Jeremy collapsed on the tiled floor.

"But you can't stop now," I said, prodding him with my foot. "You have to take my old one to the dump."

He turned his left hand palm up and curled all the fingers inward except for the middle one.

"Wimp," I muttered.

I sat down at the table and Charlie hooked up my new appliance in a few minutes. By the time he was done, Jeremy was rested enough to lift his whole head from the floor.

"It costs fifteen bucks to leave that thing at the dump," he complained.

"Well, what else am I supposed to do?" I asked.

He sat up and held out his hand. "Gimme fifteen bucks, and I'll do it."

I rolled my eyes and dug around in my purse. "All I have left is a twenty." I held it out to him.

"That'll work," he said, snatching it from my fingers.

"I get change."

"Nope. I don't carry change."

He stood up and brushed himself off. He and Charlie removed the dead oven and loaded it onto Jeremy's truck.

"You want a cup of coffee or cocoa?" I asked, stomping my feet on the porch to keep my toes warm.

"Cocoa sounds good," Jeremy said, and Charlie agreed.

They draped their coats over kitchen chairs and sat down while I busied myself making homemade cocoa.

"Guess we'll see if this baby works," I said, setting a saucepan on the front burner.

I mixed sugar, hot water, cocoa powder, and salt together and brought the mixture to a boil. Then I stirred in milk and let it heat.

Jeremy got up and grabbed three mugs from the cupboard. "You got any marshmallows?" he asked.

I pointed to the pantry and he went to get them.

"I take it he's here often?" Charlie asked with a slight smirk.

"At least once a week. He and my sister Claire come over for dinner and we watch *Smallville*."

"That's neat that you have such close friends."

Jeremy gave a short laugh as he returned with a bag of mini-marshmallows. "She forces us to come over here every week under threat of death or self-mutilation."

I swatted at him with an oven mitt, but he danced out of reach.

"See what I put up with? You sure you want to go out with her?" Jeremy asked.

Charlie just grinned.

I turned off the stove and added vanilla, then stirred it all together.

"That smells great," Charlie said, sniffing the air.

"It is great," Jeremy said, holding the mugs while I poured. "It's one of the few things she can cook."

"If I wasn't holding a hot pan, I'd bash you with it," I said.

"You two are kind of violent," Charlie said with a laugh.

"Just her. I'm a lover, not a fighter."

"You're a pain in the ass," I muttered. I set the pan in the sink. Jeremy dropped a handful of marshmallows and a spoon in each mug and handed them out.

I sat down beside Jeremy and stirred the marshmallows, letting them melt a little bit.

Charlie blew on his and took a sip. "This is good, Mel," he said, and I sat up straighter.

"Someone who has studied at the culinary schools in Europe has just complimented my cocoa," I said, nudging Jeremy.

"Big deal. It's when he starts complimenting your sexual prowess that it's serious."

Charlie choked and set his mug down. I reached over and smacked his back. Jeremy just snort-giggled and drained his mug, wincing a little as the hot liquid seared a path down his throat.

"Well, gotta go," he said, his voice husky. He saluted us both and took off running out the door.

I listened to his truck roar away and hoped he'd at least make it to the dump before fate kicked his ass.

"You okay?" I asked Charlie.

He nodded and wiped his mouth with the back of his hand. "He's quite a character."

"You don't know the half of it."

Charlie chuckled a little bit. "Maybe if I'd had a friend like him growing up, I'd be a more sociable person."

"You didn't have friends?"

"Not many. I was always a bit of a loner. It's why Pamela and I got along so well."

"Pamela?"

His features contorted for a moment. "Brandon's mother, my ex," he said softly.

"Oh."

"I haven't mentioned her?"

I shook my head. "I thought you said you didn't have any children."

"It's a long, complicated story. High drama," he said with a sigh.

I wrapped my hands around my warm mug and leaned on the table. "I like drama."

"You sure you want to hear it?"

I nodded. "Spill."

He took a deep breath and focused on a point on the kitchen wall.

"I met Pamela when I was studying in Paris. I was twenty. We met in a little cafe, and it was instant," he said. "I loved her. She didn't have any family, and I felt like I didn't, and we connected. I told my dad about her and he wanted to meet her for himself, find out what she was after." He snorted and his voice became heavy with sarcasm. "Because everyone was after the Archer fortune. So I brought her home over Thanksgiving break, and Garrett took an immediate liking to her. I didn't know it until later, but he seduced her right away."

I gasped and frowned. "Why would he do that?"

Charlie shrugged. "He was between movies, he was probably bored."

"Or jealous."

"Nah. I was nothing to be jealous of."

I stayed quiet. Sibling rivalries were a thing of my past, so I wouldn't cross them out of his. Claire and I had plenty of fights and did things just to spite each other when we were young and stupid.

"We went back to Paris, she was an art student, and he continued to keep in contact with her. By Christmas, she had dumped me and moved back to the States to be with him. They got married a month later."

"Ouch. What did you do?"

"It hurt a lot back then, knowing that Garrett had won a game I didn't even know we were playing. And then it got worse when he told me Pamela was pregnant. When Brandon was born, I hated him."

"What? You hated Brandon? Why?" I asked, shocked that Charlie could say that.

"I was angry. And then Brandon turned three months old and Pamela died. Some kind of complication from the delivery, and I felt bad and went home to see him. I was jealous of Garrett for a long time, but not anymore. Brandon's my nephew, and I love him. It's not his fault his parents screwed up."

I shook my head. "Nope, it's not, and at least he's got you to help him out. He likes you, Charlie. I'll bet he wishes things had turned out different."

He took my hand and kissed it. "I just hope he doesn't regret staying with me."

"He won't. If anything, he'll be a better man because of it. I haven't met your brother, but he doesn't sound like the best role model for a teenage boy." I picked at some lint on my sweater and coughed. "So what did your father say about everything?"

Charlie stared into his cup, and I knew whatever had happened wasn't good.

"You know what? Nevermind. I was just being nosy," I said quickly.

"That was when he stopped talking to me," Charlie said, and I sucked in a breath.

"Your father?"

"I was overreacting. I was jealous of Garrett. I was a sad, pathetic boy who was easily fooled," Charlie said without emotion.

I just sat there, stunned into silence.

Charlie shook his head. "Well, that was a depressing conversation. Shall we move on?"

I finished my cocoa and looked at him. "Did you have plans for the rest of the day?" I checked my watch. It was 12:30.

"Unfortunately, yes. I have people coming at one to work on the kitchen. I just wanted to stop by and say hello."

"Bummer. I'm horny," I said.

Charlie blinked, then growled and pulled me into his lap. We slid to the floor together and made love beside my new oven.

# Chapter Nine

It was the last week of classes before Spring Break, so no one wanted to focus, least of all the Driver's Ed class. Brandon was doing better, and the girls in his car had even told him so, which made him grin and blush at the same time. Then they giggled and nudged each other. It was cute and a little sickening.

On Monday, we did a destination drive to a bakery downtown where we all got gooey brownies, and the kids promised not to tell the principal on me. Brandon told me that Piper was an awesome tutor. He even asked if she was seeing anyone.

"Not that I'm interested in her or anything," he added, then hurried away before I could say anything.

On Tuesday, Charlie called me during my lunch hour and asked if I'd like to go flying that night.

"The weather's perfect, and it'll be clear skies," he said in such a low voice that I felt like purring.

I agreed and he told me he'd pick me up around 7:30.

When the school day ended, Jeremy came and hung out in my classroom for awhile.

"So you guys going out tonight?" he asked, propping his feet up on a desk and grabbing a candy bar.

"He's taking me flying," I said. "My boyfriend's a pilot."

"Hmmm. He's more like Clark Kent than I originally thought."

"Oh shut up."

"If he wants to fly you to Paris for some real French food, I'm going to have to smack you."

"You're just jealous."

"Maybe."

I studied him for a moment. "Do you have any plans for tonight?" I asked.

He smiled. "I have a date."

I sat up. "What? With whom?"

"Some guy from the cable company. He's coming to hook up my new digital box between four and eight pm."

116

I groaned and threw my candy wrapper at him.

Charlie picked me up at 7:30, and we drove to the small airport. I was excited to go flying, but nervous at the same time.

"Piper's a sweet girl," he said, breaking into my thoughts.

"What?"

"She stopped by to pick up Brandon. They were headed for the library for a study session. She seems really smart."

"Oh she is. She's going to be a kick-ass lawyer someday. She can argue the stripes off a zebra."

He chuckled. "I'd like to see that. Brandon was blushing a million shades of red when I left them."

"She has that effect on boys."

"Like her aunt."

I snorted. "Yeah, sure. That's why I've been single for so long."

"Well, does Piper have a boyfriend?"

I paused. "No. She thinks high school boys are a waste of time. I think she's waiting until college."

"See? Smart."

We parked and walked through the small airport lobby, then out through the sliding glass doors.

"That's it?" I asked.

"What's it?"

I waved toward the doors. "No metal detectors? No x-ray scanning where I have to stand with my hands over

117

my head and look like Bullwinkle? You can just walk out to the planes?"

"This is a little different than a commercial airport. I've called ahead to have the plane pulled out," Charlie said. "It's all ready to go."

He was beaming with pride as he took me to his plane, a small four-passenger Cessna that was gleaming white with a blue stripe down the sides. He did a pre-flight check and then helped me inside. He handed me a set of headphones and told me to buckle up.

"This is going to be fun," he said.

He started the plane and the engine roared to life. I could feel my heart racing as we started moving. He talked to me the entire time, explaining what he was doing. Soon we were heading off down a runway, and I bit my tongue as the plane left the ground. We climbed steadily to about 3500 feet, and then leveled off.

It was the most magnificent thing I'd ever done. We circled the town of Cody and went out over the river for a bit. The view was incredible, and I turned to Charlie and gave him two thumbs up. He laughed and pointed out the high school to me. We flew for about forty-five minutes, and then he landed us back at the airport.

I jumped from the plane and bounced around the ground for a few moments, sticking my arms out and zooming around.

"That was awesome!" I cried, running right into Charlie's open arms. He picked me up and swung me around. "It was perfect!"

"So you approve?"

"Oh, I approve. You can fly me anywhere you want to. I'll go."

We walked back inside the small terminal, and Charlie chatted with one of the workers about putting the plane away. I watched him interact, smiling and shaking the man's hand. I had noticed that he treated people with respect, no matter their position, and I admired that.

We left and drove back to my house. I wanted to ask him to go to Piper's birthday party, but it was on Friday night. Kind of short notice.

Charlie started a fire, poured two glasses of red wine and we curled up on the couch under a blanket. He ran his hands along my knees, making me giggle.

"You're amazing," he said, his voice soft and husky.

I felt my body temperature rise, though from the wine, the fire, or my emotions, I wasn't sure.

"You are," he said, scooting closer. "You're not afraid to express your opinion, even if it doesn't agree with others."

"Oh yeah?"

"Yeah. You hate the idea of my turning the theater into a restaurant, and yet you still go out with me. You're a riddle, Melinda Martin."

"I'm not that difficult to figure out. I'm pretty shallow, to be honest."

"I think you're beautiful."

He leaned in to kiss me, and I closed my eyes, allowing myself to get swept away in the moment. Soon we were lying down, and the clothes were being peeled away when my cell phone gave a loud ring, jolting us both out of our lustful hazes.

"Ignore it," I said, kissing his chin. It stopped ringing, and then a second later started up again. "Damn it!" I groaned, letting my head fall back on the cushions.

Charlie got up and walked over to the end table where the phone sat. I watched him answer, shirtless, with his jeans unbuttoned and his muscles glistening in the firelight, and I had to grin. He sauntered over and handed me the phone.

"Whoever this is, this better be good," I growled.

"Did I catch you at a bad time?" my mother asked.

I clutched at the throw hanging over the back of the couch and pulled it up to my chin.

"Mom! Um, no, I was just, we were just," I stuttered.

Charlie sat down in the armchair and just smiled at me, drumming his fingers on his thighs. Mmm. Thighs.

"Melinda, are you listening to me?"

"Ah, uh, what?"

"Are you going to invite Charlie to Piper's birthday party?" Mom asked, sounding exasperated but amused at the same time.

God, was she picturing us having sex? Ewwwww!

"I was thinking about it, yes."

"What's to think about? We all want to meet him. Your dad even did a Google search on him."

"He did what? Dad knows how to do that?"

"Of course he does. We were curious, dear. He's very handsome."

I could almost see her wiggling her eyebrows in a suggestive manner.

"So are you bringing him?"

"God, yes! Fine!" I yelled. I dropped the phone to my chest and said, "Charlie, will you go to Piper's birthday party? It's on Friday."

"And Brandon! Invite his nephew, too!" my mom yelled.

"And Brandon," I said.

Charlie blinked and then nodded. "Sure, we'll come."

I raised the phone to my ear and told Mom we would all be there.

"Thank you, dear. We'll see you Friday."

I hung up and pulled the blanket over my head. "That was so embarrassing."

I heard Charlie get up and felt him sit beside me. He massaged my shoulders and tugged at the blanket.

"Hey, we weren't having sex yet," he said, emphasizing the *yet*.

"If you don't want to go, that's fine," I said, peeking up at him.

"Why wouldn't we want to go? I'd love to meet your family. Piper's great, so the rest of them must be great too."

I snorted. "Oh, and Jeremy will be there as well."

"Jeremy?"

"Yes."

"Hmm."

I sat up fast, bumping my forehead against his arm.

"What's that? That hmm?"

"Nothing." He smirked, and I knew he was teasing me.

"My mom likes him. He's been coming to family stuff since we were kids."

"Hmm."

"Hey!" I cried, swatting his chest. "You have nothing to worry about. Jeremy and I only had sex once –"

"What?"

"– a long time ago, and it was gross, so we never did it again."

Charlie laughed and grabbed at me. "It's fine. I just like giving you a hard time. It makes your nostrils flare like a bull's."

"Oh, that's romantic."

"It's cute as hell."

He climbed on top of me and held me down so he could kiss me all over. I wrapped my arms around him and we rolled. We rolled right off the damn couch. He landed on top of me, knocking the wind out of me.

"Oh Jesus, are you all right?" he asked, scrambling off.

As soon as I could breathe again, I let out a wheezy laugh. Soon Charlie was laughing with me. It felt wonderful, and I loved it.

# Chapter Ten

We arrived at my parents' house and I hesitated before getting out of the truck. In the backseat, Brandon picked up the gift he and Charlie had chosen for Piper and nudged me with it.

"What're we waiting for?" he asked in a stage whisper.

Charlie shrugged. "I'm not sure. You okay, Mel?"

"I just don't know if this is a good idea. Meeting my parents so soon?"

Charlie took my hand and smiled. "Okay, so what's so bad about meeting your parents? Are they scary? Rabid? Will they kill me and bury me in the backyard?"

I laughed. "No. At least I don't think so. It's just, I haven't had a serious boyfriend in so long, and I'm not sure how my family will react. And is a birthday party the best place to do introductions?"

"It's perfect," Brandon said. "If there's a problem, your folks won't want to cause a scene in front of Piper. It would ruin her birthday party, and I'm sure they won't want to do that."

I considered this and decided Brandon was right. Sixteen years old, and he was the voice of reason to my immature brain? Yikes.

"What's not to love about me?" Charlie asked. He dipped his head and peered over the rims of his glasses at me. "I'm smart, polite, very well-mannered –"

"Not to mention handsome and charming and disgustingly rich," Brandon said with a little too much cheer.

I reached behind me and swatted his head. "Those are all valid reasons, so I think I'm okay now, thank you. We can go inside."

I reached for the door handle, but Charlie and Brandon screamed at me to stop. I jumped and screamed back.

"What's the big idea?"

"You can't get out yourself," Brandon said, scrambling to hop out of the truck.

"I have to make a good impression by opening your door for you," Charlie added.

"Huh?"

Brandon poked me in the shoulder. "Your mom's watching from the window."

I looked up and sure enough, Mom was peeking out through the curtains. Charlie opened my door and took my hand to help me out. Brandon hopped out of the backseat, holding Piper's present. I still didn't know what it was. Brandon and Charlie had gone on a super secret shopping trip to find the perfect gift for Piper, and they wouldn't let me know what it was. Mom opened the front door with a huge grin on her face and welcomed us inside.

Actually, she pushed me aside and went right to Charlie, giving him a huge hug. I sniffed like I was offended, but I felt myself smiling.

"You must be Charlie," Mom said. "It's so nice to finally meet you. I feel like Melinda's been hiding you away forever."

"Mother," I said, breaking between them. "We haven't been together that long."

"Well, we can't remember the last time you brought anyone home to meet us. Your father and I were beginning to think you were a lesbian."

"Mother!" I screamed, wanting to die.

126

Charlie laughed and patted my arm. "No, no, she's definitely not a lesbian."

"God, please take me now," I muttered, and Brandon just chuckled.

"And you're Brandon, the boy that Piper's tutoring?" Mom asked, guiding him toward the kitchen. She took the gift from him and set it on an end table with the others. "Claire's putting the finishing touches on the cake," she called back to us. "Your father is outside working on the deck."

"What's wrong with the deck?" I asked. She didn't hear me because she and Brandon were already through the swinging door.

I took Charlie's hand and led him into the kitchen to get to the back door. Claire was placing frosted flowers on the cake and looked up when we entered.

"Charlie, this is my sister Claire, Piper's mom," I said.

Claire wiped her hands on a dishtowel and came over to shake his hand. "I've heard so much about you," she gushed, giggling a little.

"I hope it's been good."

Claire glanced sideways at me with a glint in her eye, and said, "Oh, I've heard it's been very good."

I coughed and elbowed her in the stomach. "Gee, the cake looks good," I said, while throwing up a prayer for instant death. "Where's Piper?"

"Upstairs on the phone with her father."

"He's not coming?" I asked.

127

Claire shook her head and began sticking candles into the cake with renewed fervor. "Sharon won't let him," she said.

"Why not?"

"She says they have to take their kids to her mom and dad's house this weekend."

"Is this a new development?"

"Of course. Especially since her parents have been dead for fifteen years."

I winced. "Ouch."

"Sharon hates Piper, and she has Beau's balls in a jar somewhere," Claire said. She shoved a candle so hard into the cake, it disappeared.

Mom had already put Brandon to work pulling food from the refrigerator, and he threw a questioning glance at me. I just shook my head and hugged my sister.

"It's his fault for not realizing he's missing out on a crucial part of his daughter's life," I said. "I wouldn't feel too sorry for him."

"No, but I do feel bad for Piper."

I had to agree there. Claire retrieved the candle and cleaned it off, and I led Charlie outside.

"Beau?" he asked.

"Claire's ex-husband. He had an affair with the cleaning lady and now they have three kids together, and Sharon won't let him outside without a leash. I bet she's afraid he'll cheat on her too."

"She has a good point," Charlie said.

"Except that means she won't let him near Piper either. He doesn't see her often, and he's missed every birthday since the divorce. I'm willing to bet money he won't even show up to her graduation."

Charlie rubbed my back. "From what I've seen of your niece, she's pretty well adjusted. He'll regret it later in life, and hopefully, Piper will see fit to forgive him."

"You speaking from experience here?"

He shrugged. "My dad wasn't around much either. Unless he was trying to push us into the acting business. I rebelled, and he didn't like it, which distanced him further from me. Garrett was always the golden child anyway."

"So both our families are dysfunctional."

"Can you show me one that isn't?"

"Very true. Hey, you have a cleaning lady," I said, raising a brow. "Should I be worried?"

"She's in her sixties, and I don't go for cougars. I prefer neurotic, horny, teachers."

I laughed, then processed what he'd said and frowned. He rolled his eyes at me, kissed my forehead, and we stepped out onto the deck and looked around for my dad. I saw his tool box sitting on the steps and a pair of work gloves resting on the covered picnic table.

"Dad?" I asked.

A hammer tapping was my response, and then he said, "Under here."

I smiled and hopped down onto the ground and peered under the deck. Dad was lying on his back, pounding at a loose board.

"Thought I'd get this done," he said.

"You're going to get all dirty," I said, helping him out.

He brushed himself off and dropped the hammer in the tool box with a clang. "Little dirt never hurt anyone. You must be Charlie. Nice to meet you," he said, extending his hand.

"Pleasure to meet you, sir," Charlie said. He nodded to the deck. "Did you build this yourself?"

"Last summer. Do you know much about carpentry?"

Charlie smiled. "A little." He stepped forward, and he and my dad began discussing the intricacies of woodworking.

They began talking in a language I didn't understand. Something about saws and sanding and wood types. Charlie examined the railing and nodded, impressed.

"Very nice work."

Dad grinned and clapped his hand on Charlie's shoulder as he stood.

"Would you like to see my tool shed?"

"Certainly, sir."

"Ah, enough of that. Call me Brian."

They walked past me down the deck steps. I wasn't even invited along, but that was okay. This was the first time Dad had ever offered to let one of my boyfriends see his shed. I went back inside the kitchen, shaking off the cold air.

"Going well?" Mom asked, blinking like an innocent owl.

I took off my coat and draped it over the back of a chair. "You should know. You left the door open a crack, just enough to eavesdrop."

Mom had the grace to blush. "Charlie's very nice," she said. "And handsome."

"I know," I said, snatching a carrot stick. My face hurt from smiling so much. My parents approved!

We heard the front door open and close and then Jeremy made his way into the kitchen, pulling off his gloves.

"Sorry I'm late," he said.

Mom gave him a hug. "You're right on time, sweetie. We haven't started eating yet."

I introduced Jeremy to Brandon, even though they'd seen each other around school. They became engrossed in arranging carrot sticks on a platter.

Piper came into the kitchen then, and we wished her a happy birthday. She was smiling, but there was still sadness in her eyes. Mom, Claire, and I exchanged glances, and Brandon just stood still, not saying anything. I could tell he was uncomfortable, and if Jeremy hadn't been blocking his way, I'm sure he would have bolted from the room.

I clapped my hands together and said, "I'm hungry. Anyone else want to eat?"

Everyone agreed, and we brought the food out to the dining room. I went outside to get Charlie and my dad. I found them hovering over a new saw that Dad had gotten. I could almost see the drool hanging from their chins.

"Time to eat," I announced.

Charlie tore his eyes away from Dad's workbench and nodded. "Well, look's like it's time to go inside."

Dad nodded and gave the saw a loving pat. "It's a beautiful thing."

"It is," Charlie agreed.

We walked inside and Dad whispered in my ear, "He's a keeper, Mel," as he passed me on his way to the dining room.

Everyone sat down and Mom served the food. Piper always chose the same thing as her birthday meal. Butterfly shrimp, homemade French fries, onion rings, fruit salad, and raw vegetables with Mom's special dip.

"This looks wonderful," Charlie said, eyeing the food.

"I'm sure you've had better, owning restaurants and all," Mom said, ducking her head a little.

"We have plenty of good food, but there's something about a home-cooked meal that's ten thousand times better," Charlie said.

Claire smirked. "Yes, how was the home-cooked meal?"

I kicked my sister under the table, hard enough to make her wince, but not hard enough to wipe the smile from her face.

"Oh, well, Melinda makes excellent Chinese food," Charlie said with a straight face.

Dad coughed behind his napkin.

"This fruit salad is good, Mom," I said.

"Not as good, I'm sure, as the famous cranberry salad that Cinema serves," Mom said, looking at Charlie.

"Cranberry salad?" I asked.

"It's award-winning, Mel. Charlie created it himself," Brandon said.

"I'd love to taste it," Mom said.

"Mother," I hissed. "You can't expect Charlie to just give up a special reci –"

"I'll make some for you," Charlie said, putting his hand on my knee. I jumped and bumped the table. "It'll be my pleasure."

Mom just beamed.

"They like you, you don't have to impress them," I muttered.

"I like them. I want to impress them," he muttered back.

Piper snorted.

After dinner, Claire and I lit the candles and carried out the cake. Piper made a wish and blew them out, then we served it while she gathered her presents and began opening them. My parents gave her a Visa gift card.

"To buy stuff for college," Mom said. "You'll need to decorate your dorm room and buy books and supplies."

Jeremy gave her a pair of diamond stud earrings. Piper squealed so loud that Brandon jumped a foot in the air and dropped his fork. She bolted from her chair and almost knocked Jeremy off his own seat.

"Oh my God, these are gorgeous! Where? How?"

"Why?" Claire asked, throwing a pointed look in Jeremy's direction.

"Hey, why not? She's eighteen. A woman going into the real world. She should have some bling," he said.

I giggled but stopped when Claire glared at me. Piper put the earrings on right away and twirled around the table. When she sat down again, she was out of breath and her cheeks were pink.

"My gift won't compare to that," I said, shoving my present towards her.

"I'm sure it's awesome," she said.

I had worked on this gift with Claire for the past eighteen years. Every picture that Claire had ever taken of Piper, I had a copy of, and I put together a scrapbook. In the past several years, scrapbooking had taken on a life of its own, and I jumped on the bandwagon, buying special books, papers, stamps, and stickers. It was an easy craft, one that couldn't be messed up, and I was pretty damn impressed with my work.

Piper flipped through the pages, her eyes filling up with tears, her mouth curling into a smile. I had even included pictures of her with her father, which I knew was going to be emotional for her. But he was her dad. Even if he was a jerkoff.

She reached the last page and closed the book. "Thank you," she said. "It's wonderful."

She sniffed and Mom passed her a clean napkin, and she blew her nose. I even caught my dad wiping his eyes. After we all composed ourselves, Piper reached for Brandon and Charlie's gift. The box was huge and wrapped in bright paper.

"You didn't have to get me anything," she said, peeling back the paper.

"I wanted to," Brandon said.

We all leaned forward a bit, wondering what was in the box.

Piper gasped and pulled out a black leather briefcase. It was engraved with Piper's initials on the edge.

"Oh wow. I was looking at this exact same one!" she exclaimed. She popped open the latches, her eyes rounding with pleasure. The interior was lined in calfskin.

"How much did that cost?" I asked Charlie.

He shook his head. "It's rude to ask that about a gift."

"This is amazing. All the big hotshot lawyers are carrying these," Piper said. "I can't believe I have one!"

"You'll be a great lawyer," Brandon said with a grin.

Claire's gift was wrapped in a simple white envelope. Piper eyed her mother with curiosity before opening it.

Then she let out another ear popping squeal that I'm positive the neighbors heard.

"Can you quit with the screaming?" my dad asked, covering his ears, but he was grinning.

"What is it?" Mom asked, trying to see.

Piper waved the single sheet of paper in the air, and I saw it was the title to a car.

"Well, you do need a way to get from here to school, right?" Claire asked, laughing as Piper hopped into her lap and kissed her cheek.

Charlie and Brandon offered to do the dishes, and Mom didn't even object. She poured coffee and served it in the living room.

"Melinda, he's wonderful," she said, stirring cream into her cup. "Is it too soon to talk about marriage?"

I jerked, spilling hot coffee down the front of me. "Aarrggh! Mother, please, stop talking about marriage." I dabbed at my sweater. That was three pieces of clothing stained since meeting Charlie. I was on a roll.

Charlie drove Brandon home then took me back to my house. We curled up in a blanket in front of the fireplace. I was warm and toasty, and not from the blanket or the fire, or even the arms that held me.

In the pit of my stomach, there was a stirring going on. An unfamiliar feeling that I wasn't sure how to decipher.

"What are you thinking?" Charlie whispered in my ear.

I smiled and snuggled closer. "That you were perfect tonight with my family. They want to adopt you."

"I think they'd rather have me marry you."

"Oh, not you too."

"Don't worry. I'm not thinking about it yet."

"Good. I was about to kick you out."

"Why? I'm comfy."

We sat there and watched the fire burn, and I took the time to reassess my situation. I'd never been in love before, so I wasn't sure of how it felt.

"I have butterflies in my stomach," Charlie said, breaking into my thoughts.

"Sorry. Sometimes the shrimp isn't so good."

He chuckled and poked my side, making me giggle. "I've never been in love, Mel," he said, and I froze.

"Okay, quit reading my thoughts."

"What?"

"I was just thinking that same thing."

Charlie buried his nose in my hair and inhaled. "I love the way you smell. The way you feel against me. It feels right."

"Isn't it too soon?" I breathed.

"What are the rules on love?"

"I don't know."

I tilted my head up and kissed his chin. "Can I ask a favor?"

"Anything."

"Let's not say it until we're both absolutely sure."

Charlie looked down at me, his glasses slipping down his nose. "All right. But how will I know when you feel it?"

I took a deep breath and said, "Oh, don't worry. You'll know."

# Chapter Eleven

It had become my tradition over the years to hibernate during Spring Break. For one week during the cold and dreariness of that time before the sun decided to make its presence permanent, I would burrow beneath the warmth of my blankets, only emerging for the necessities, like food and the bathroom.

When I was in college, my friends and classmates would jet off to warmer climates and lots of beer. I tried it once. Jeremy and I hit the beaches of Cancun. I was exhausted by the second day and stayed in our hotel room for the rest of the trip. Jeremy got sunburned and drunk, and ended up bringing back some floozy, but I slept through the entire thing. Thank GOD.

I had originally planned for this Spring Break to follow in the sluggish footsteps of those before it, but there was something different this year.

I had a boyfriend.

It made me grin like a fool just to say it or think it. What was better was that everyone liked him. I wasn't getting lectures from my mom about what a loser he was, or offers from Jeremy to hire a hit man. I didn't need to sleep all week because I was hyper enough on the pure joy of having found Charlie. I couldn't say I was in love, not quite yet, but I was in lust, that was for sure. We had both proven this already.

Sunday morning I was up with the birds and waiting outside Bebe's Sweet Shop. She was more than a little shocked to see me stroll in at seven a.m.

Bebe is my mother's best friend, so she knows all about my Spring Break routine.

"What the hell are you doing here at this hour?" she asked, eyeing me with suspicion. "Are you sleepwalking?"

I laughed. "No, I'm awake."

"You seem almost...giddy."

"I am. I have a boyfriend," I said, enjoying the way the word just rolled from my lips.

Bebe grinned. "Your mom's told me all about him. That hunk Charlie Archer, right?"

"That's him."

"If I were twenty years younger, Mel, I'd be chasing after him myself. Anyway, what can I get you?"

I studied the display case and pointed. "A dozen of your honey-glazed doughnuts and a half dozen cherry chocolate éclairs, please."

Bebe pulled out a pastry box and filled it up, adding a couple of cream-filled doughnuts as well.

"Ten dollars," she said, ringing up the sale and winking at me.

I handed over the money, knowing full well I was getting a great deal on a sugar induced high. I left with my purple box and drove to the gourmet coffee shop for a bag of hazel-nut cream coffee beans. Charlie had mentioned being surprised at finding his favorite coffee bean here in Cody.

I headed north toward Cherry Orchard. I read the street signs as I drove to Charlie's house, wondering how much crack the city developers had ingested when it came time to name the streets.

Windtail Lane, (does wind have a tail?) and Charmin Circle, (like the toilet paper?) were a couple that I passed.

Just as I was contemplating what must look better on an address label, Road Apple Lane or Cheddar Twist Drive, a black and white blur darted out in front of my car and froze. I hit the brakes and swerved, coming to a stop by the curb, just inches away from a post that held a mailbox shaped like a whale.

I hadn't felt a thump, so I was pretty sure I'd missed it, but I got out to check anyway. The blur was still sitting in the middle of the street, and I could see it was a small animal, but not a skunk or a raccoon. As I approached, it looked up at me with tear-filled eyes and began to quiver like a tiny earthquake.

"You're a puppy," I said, crouching down. I extended my hand and smiled in what I hoped was a non-threatening manner.

Although my dad would be screaming at me about rabies and whatnot, I wasn't afraid. The dog whimpered and sniffed my fingers, then trotted over and rubbed its head against my hand. I scooped it up, and it curled against my arm and sighed.

"Aww, poor little," I paused to check, "guy. Who do you belong to?"

He didn't have any tags and he wasn't very old. A couple of months at best. He was skinny and dirty, and I assumed he didn't belong to anyone in this neighborhood, where pets were treated better than children, with a fancier wardrobe than mine.

He'd been dumped somewhere and had wandered around looking for a home. My heart melted when he closed his eyes and sighed again. I tucked him inside my coat and ran for the car. Driving one-handed while holding him was a bit of a challenge, but I pulled into Charlie's driveway without incident.

As I got out of the car, the front door opened and Brandon stepped out, fully dressed and wide awake.

"Hey, Mel. Whatcha got there?" he asked, jogging over to see.

His eyes widened and his face broke into a grin as he looked at the puppy resting in the crook of my arm.

"Oh wow," he breathed.

"Grab that pastry box and the bag of coffee beans, would you please?" I asked.

Brandon picked up the things and closed my car door, then followed me into the house.

"Charlie's still sleeping," he said.

"What are you doing up so early?" I asked.

"I'm always up early, even on the weekends. I've never been good at sleeping in."

We went into the kitchen. Brandon placed the stuff on the kitchen island and filled a small bowl with water. We hunkered down around the puppy to watch him drink. His little pink tongue lapped at the water, causing us both to giggle.

"How come he's all dirty?"

"He ran out in front of me on my way here," I said. "He's a stray."

Brandon nodded, and I could see it in his eyes. He wanted this dog.

"I'll go wake your uncle," I said, straightening up.

"All right. If you're not back in five minutes, I'm not coming to get you."

I blinked. "Yeah, right. Not going there."

Brandon just waved at me as I made my way up the carpeted stairs. I found Charlie passed out on his bed facedown, one leg hanging over the side. His hair was standing up in places and he was drooling onto his pillow.

It wiped any last thoughts of him being the perfect man from my mind. Yick.

I stood over him, staring down at his face, hoping my mere presence would wake him.

He snored and continued to drool.

Just for kicks, I picked up his glasses from the nightstand and peered through them.

"Holy shit, you're fucking blind," I exclaimed as my eyes crossed and did a little dance as they tried to focus.

Charlie jerked awake, snorting and spitting and sucking in drool at the same time. He squinted around, clutching his pillow like a life preserver.

"What? Mel? Is that you?"

I handed him his glasses and he put them on.

"What are you doing here? What time is it?" He reached for the clock, looked at it, then looked at me.

"I wanted to surprise you with doughnuts and coffee," I said.

"It's seven-thirty on a Sunday."

"Uh huh. I wanted to see you."

He smiled at that and tugged at my arm. I kicked off my shoes and crawled beneath the covers with him. He pulled me close and kissed my head.

"Brandon's awake," I said. "He's downstairs, and if we're not down there in five minutes, he's going to assume we're having sex."

Charlie grimaced. "Well, there goes that idea."

"Plus? You need to brush your teeth first," I added.

"Fussy, aren't you?"

I sat up. "I'll go and start the coffee."

He sighed and ran a hand through his hair. "All right. What kind of doughnuts did you bring?"

I told him and got out of bed, edging for the door. "Oh, and there's a puppy too," I said.

Charlie narrowed his eyes at me, but I took off running before he could ask any questions.

Brandon was busy giving the puppy a bath in the huge kitchen sink. He was scrubbing with his hands, lathering up the little guy's fur. The puppy seemed to be enjoying it.

"Charlie's awake," I said, searching the cabinets for the coffee grinder.

"Did you tell him?"

"I said there was a puppy here."

"And then you ran."

"Of course."

Brandon used the sprayer, washing away all the soap. "Should I just towel him off, or should I use a hair dryer?"

I looked at the little dog, shivering from the cold. "Just towel him off. Use a hair dryer and you'll blow him into the next county."

Brandon carried him into the laundry room and returned with him wrapped in a clean towel. The dog was getting his fur fluffed when Charlie came in, freshly showered himself.

"Hmm," was all he said.

"Isn't he cute?" Brandon asked. "I'm gonna name him Whip."

"Why Whip?" I asked.

"Look at his tail. It's like a little whip."

Charlie crossed his arms and tried to appear stern, but he just couldn't pull it off.

"I don't know if we can have a dog in this house, Brandon," he said. "We're just renting."

"You could check. I'm sure it'd be okay."

"Where did he come from?" Charlie asked me.

"I almost hit him. He was just trotting around in the street. I couldn't leave him out there. It's cold," I said.

"Why don't you keep him?"

I laughed. "I killed a cactus. No way in hell could I manage a dog."

"Please," Brandon said, holding Whip up for Charlie to see. "Look, he's clean now. And we can get him checked out by a vet."

The bath seemed to have reenergized him. Whip wiggled his legs and licked Brandon's hands.

"You're going to be responsible for him?" Charlie asked.

Brandon nodded. "I will. I'll feed him and bathe him and walk him." He paused and looked down at Whip. "He'll be my first pet."

I watched Charlie's resolve take a flying leap out the nearest window. He bent to pet Whip.

"All right," he sighed. "I don't know how your dad will like it —"

"Dad's not here," Brandon said.

Charlie nodded. "Okay. You can keep him."

Brandon's grin was huge as he leaned over to hug his uncle. I choked up a little at that. Most boys at that age weren't too big on public affection.

"Thanks, Mel," he said.

"For what?"

"For not running this little guy over."

I smiled and passed him a doughnut. We ate breakfast and then all piled into Charlie's truck to hit the Wal-Mart for pet supplies. Against Charlie's protests, Brandon tucked Whip into his coat and we walked inside.

We filled a cart full of food, treats, toys, and bath essentials. As we were unloading it all onto the conveyer belt, Whip let out a tiny, muffled bark. The three of us froze, until Brandon coughed. Then Whip barked again, and the bottom of Brandon's coat started to move.

Charlie, Brandon, and I started to hack. The lady at the cash register just smiled and rang up our stuff. We hurried out of there, giggling like crazy people.

And as we drove back to their house, we came to a stop at a red light next to a store with big glass windows. I looked over and caught our reflection. Charlie behind the wheel, me sitting beside him, and Brandon in the backseat holding Whip. We looked like we belonged together.

A warm feeling tickled my heart and I turned to look at Charlie. He smiled at me and reached out, taking my hand.

Okay. It was official. I was in love. But being the insecure, stubborn woman that my mother raised, I didn't want to say it first.

As we were hauling all the doggy goodies inside, my cell phone rang. I dug around my purse and found it, saw that it was my mother, and answered it.

"Why were you buying dog food with Charlie and Brandon?" she asked after I said hello.

Standing in the middle of Charlie's driveway, I threw hesitant glances over both shoulders then up and down the street.

"Where the hell are you? Hiding in the bushes?" I asked.

"Melinda, there's no need to curse. I'm at home with your father."

"How did you know we were buying dog stuff?"

"Well, first Bebe called and told me you had stopped in at seven a.m. Then Meg Pritchard was out at Wal-Mart and called to say she saw you there. Did Charlie get a dog?"

I smacked my forehead. Cody wasn't a huge town, but it was big enough to make me forget that my mother had a network of gossips all over the place. Of *course* she'd know we were out shopping at Wal-Mart.

"I found a stray this morning on the way over here. Brandon decided to keep him."

"Make sure you get it checked out," Mom said. "You never know what kind of diseases it may have. Did you touch it?"

"Yes. But Brandon gave him a bath. His name is Whip."

Mom paused a moment and then said, "Your father wants you to be very careful until you get it checked out. He doesn't want you to get rabies."

I considered driving over there and collapsing on their front porch with an Alka-Seltzer in my mouth just to freak them out, but decided against it. My mother was not above spankings.

"I'm sure the dog is fine. Charlie's going to make an appointment with the vet first thing tomorrow," I said.

"Good idea. Now," Mom said, and I could tell she was getting to the real purpose of her call. "Did you spend the night at Charlie's?"

I resisted throwing my phone into the street and said, "No, Mother. I did not spend the night. I'm hanging up now."

"Because people will talk, you know," Mom said, oblivious to my annoyance. "You've been spotted together, but you haven't come out as a couple."

"What kind of nonsense are you babbling about now?" I asked. "We have to make an announcement?"

I pictured myself taking out a front page ad of the *Cody Herald* declaring that I was A) not a lesbian, and B) Charlie Archer's official girlfriend.

"Mom, I'm hanging up now. For real. I'll call you later," I said as I walked inside the house.

I clicked off the phone just as I heard the words, "...special party to celebrate..." and walked right into Charlie's arms.

"What's up?" he asked.

"My mother is insane," I said against his chest.

He chuckled and hugged me. "I like insane."

We went into the living room where Brandon was lying on the floor with Whip running around in circles chasing a toy.

"What kind of breed do you think he is?" Brandon asked. "I think he looks like a Chihuahua mixed with something else, like a miniature pinscher."

"Could be. We can ask the vet. I'll make an appointment in the morning," Charlie said. He yawned and shook his head.

"Aww, you're sleepy," I said.

He yawned again and smiled. "I was up late last night."

"Oh yeah? It wasn't with me."

Brandon reached over and covered Whip's ears. "Please, not in front of the puppy."

I threw a sofa pillow at him. He batted it aside with his hand, and Whip ran after it.

"I was trying to figure out how I'm going to be open by graduation," Charlie said. "There's still a lot of work to do. You'd think it'd be easier the third time."

"Not necessarily. You said you were tailoring it to fit the Midwest. There are bound to be changes."

"When did you get to be so smart?"

"Hey, what are you talking about? I've always been smart."

The phone rang, and Brandon got up to answer it. I could hear him talking in the kitchen, his voice starting out loud and excited, then turning low and a little bit gloomy.

"Must be Garrett," Charlie said. He patted the cushion next to him and Whip struggled to hop up. Charlie picked him up and plopped him on the couch where he began to burrow his nose between the cushions.

"How do you know?" I asked.

"Only his dad can make him revert to a five-year-old."

I looked towards the kitchen. I couldn't hear Brandon talking at all now.

"Why doesn't Garrett seem to like him?"

Charlie shrugged and scratched Whip behind the ears. "I don't know for sure. I do know that Brandon doesn't want to be an actor, but Garrett keeps pushing. It's caused quite a few arguments between them."

"What does Brandon want to do?"

"He's always been interested in being a doctor. I think he'd be good at it. But Garrett doesn't think there's any glory in helping others."

"Sounds kind of like a jerk."

Charlie raised a brow. "I'm neither confirming nor denying that."

Brandon returned, and I noticed a definite droop in his shoulders.

"That your dad?" Charlie asked.

"Yeah."

"What's he know?"

Brandon shrugged. "I'm gonna go upstairs, okay?"

Charlie nodded. Brandon picked up Whip and headed up the steps. A moment later we heard his door close.

"Remind me to hoof Garrett in the nuts if I ever see him in person," I muttered.

Charlie laughed and pulled me on top of him. We lay curled up on the couch just holding each other. Eventually we both dozed off, but just before I drifted into LaLa Land I thought I heard Charlie whisper, "I love you."

# Chapter Twelve

Brandon and I got in some extra driving during the week off from school. We even drove to Davenport and hung out at the mall for a day after Charlie got mad at us and kicked us out. I had teased him by telling him I'd spotted three new gray hairs, and he freaked out and bought hair dye, which he tried to hide, but failed miserably. Whip found the box in the trash and dragged it out for all to see.

I still hadn't told Charlie how I felt, and I wasn't 100% sure I'd heard him correctly that Sunday morning. I called Jeremy to discuss it and he came over with ice cream.

We positioned ourselves on the couch, each taking a stab at the pint, often times attacking the other with our spoons.

"Are you going to tell him or wait for him to say it?" he asked.

"We both said we'd wait until it was for real. But what if he's not ready to say it?"

"Not to sound obnoxious -"

"That's never stopped you before."

"Har har. No, really. I think he's in love with you. I think he's been in love with you since day one."

"So how come he said it before he fell asleep?"

Jeremy shrugged and grabbed for the ice cream. "Maybe he was practicing. He might have thought you were asleep already." He paused with the spoon halfway to his mouth and looked at me. "Are you pouting?"

I shook my head.

"You are. You're pouting!" Jeremy exclaimed. The ice cream fell from his spoon and splattered on his lap, but he didn't even notice. "You're pissed you didn't get some great, grand declaration of his undying adoration for you!"

"You've been studying Shakespeare again," I said. "I'm not pouting."

Jeremy cackled. "You're expecting something big, aren't you? Like, he'll attach a banner to the tail of his plane and fly around town with it. Or, or he'll hold a huge press conference and announce it to the world."

I smacked him hard in the shoulder. "Shut up! I do not expect that. It's mushy and sentimental and -"

"What Clark Kent would do for Lois Lane?"

I was blushing by this time. "Maybe."

Jeremy poked me in the leg with his spoon, leaving a stain on my jeans.

"For the record, I think he will do something big." He smiled at me. "Because, God help him, he's as crazy as you are."

"What's that supposed to mean?"

"I just think that you two are well suited for each other. You're like the cheese to his macaroni. The peanut butter to his jelly."

"Why do those all have a sexual connotation to them?"

"Because you have a dirty mind, you horn ball."

I couldn't argue with him there.

After Jeremy left, I dropped by Claire's house to see if she'd let me borrow a cookbook. I wanted to try to make Charlie a special dinner since I'd failed the first time.

Claire was on the phone when I arrived and waved me in. I went poking around her kitchen cabinets while she finished her call.

"What are you looking for?" she asked, joining me.

"Something to snack on. You need to go grocery shopping."

"I just went yesterday."

"And it's all healthy stuff," I said, holding up a box of gluten free crackers. "Where's the junk?"

"I'm trying to eat better."

"What for?"

She shrugged and looked at her hands. "No reason."

"You're such a crappy liar. Are you dating someone?" I asked, getting excited. My sister hadn't been on a date in quite a long time, longer than me.

"Maybe I want to," she said.

"Good for you. You deserve to be happy again."

"I'm happy. I just…Piper's leaving in the fall."

"Yeah." I frowned. "Don't tell me you've been staying single because of her."

"I don't want her to think I'm not here for her."

"She knows you'll always be there for her, even when she doesn't want you. It's the beauty of motherhood. Half the time I don't want Mom around at all, but she's always nearby, and I guess that's comforting in some strange way."

"Just wait until you have kids of your own," Claire said. "You'll change. Hell, you may even grow up."

I snorted. "Not likely."

She had to agree with me. "But you're so good with Brandon," she said.

"That's different. I didn't have to change his diapers or anything like that."

"Motherhood is fun."

"Okay, why are we talking about this? Charlie and I may be serious, but we're not that serious. No babies will be produced in our near future."

Claire smiled sadly. "Too bad. I'd like a few nieces and nephews."

"You could always have another kid."

"Are you kidding me? Now?"

"A lot of women have kids later in life."

"I am not one of those women." She tapped her chin with her fingers. "You, on the other hand, are in the prime of your fertile years."

I giggled. "Heh, you said fertile." I found a package of cheese cubes in the refrigerator and started in on those. "So who was on the phone?"

"I've got a food magazine interested in a piece about Charlie's restaurant."

"Cool. You gonna do it?"

"Of course. I can't wait to see what he's done with the place. If it's anything like his other two, it'll be fabulous."

"He told me he was toning it down just a bit," I said. "I don't think too many folks around here will be ordering Cristal."

Claire waved a hand and said, "Okay, why are you really here?"

I took a deep breath. "I want to cook for Charlie."

"Fourth word sounds like cook…"

158

"Shut up. Yes, I messed up last time, but it wasn't entirely my fault."

"What's the occasion?"

I bit my lip. "I, uh, want to tell him I love him."

Claire squealed and hugged me. "I've got the perfect menu."

* * *

To pull this off, I'd enlisted the help of Brandon. I wanted to have dinner ready for Charlie, but at his house. I was going to surprise him when he came home.

Brandon helped me buy all the ingredients, and on Monday night while we were supposed to be driving, we were at my house instead, preparing the dishes. It turned out Brandon had picked up a few tricks from his uncle on cooking. He was a natural in the kitchen, and I envied him a little bit.

On Tuesday, while Charlie was still at the restaurant working, I hurried over with the food. Brandon made sure I was set before Piper picked him up for a study session at the library. We put Whip in the laundry room where he curled up in his special doggy bed and went to sleep.

I had the table all prepared when Charlie staggered in an hour later. He was tired, with his shirt half tucked in and his hair sticking up in places, and I felt my heart lurch in my chest. I loved this man, plain and simple.

"Wow, what's all this?" he asked, coming over to kiss me. "You look beautiful by the way. That color pink suits you."

I was wearing the same sweater I'd had on when he first met me at school. I hoped I wouldn't stain it tonight.

"I cooked," I said proudly.

"I see that. It looks great!"

He moved to pull out my chair for me, but I stopped him. "No, I'm serving you tonight."

"I could get used to this."

He sat down, and I dropped a linen napkin in his lap, then poured him a glass of wine. We both noticed my hands were shaking.

"What's going on?" he asked. "Are you okay?"

He looked up at me with those blue eyes and my entire prepared speech flitted away like dust.

"Shit," I muttered. "Shit, I love you. Oh, fuck, damn it!"

He blinked and sat back. "Somewhere amid all the cursing, I think I heard you say you loved me."

I fell into my chair and buried my face in my hands. "Argh, this is coming out all wrong."

"Mel?"

I looked up to see him smiling at me, his eyes crinkling at the corners. "I love you too."

"Really?"

"Really."

He stood up and pulled me into his arms. "I was going to tell you, but I wanted to make it special," he said. "I think I may have said it in my sleep, but I'm not sure."

I took a shaky breath. "You did."

He hugged me close and kissed me, and I went limp against him. "Can I show you?"

"You can."

We turned off the oven, blew out the candles and made sure nothing else would start on fire. Then we ran up to his bedroom where he proceeded to show me just how he felt.

We lay in bed, the sheets tangled around us and the comforter half hanging off. I trailed my fingers up and down his chest, loving the feel of him, so solid and strong.

"You're a wonderful woman, Mel," he said, and I beamed. "Now, let's see if you can cook."

I laughed and got up, wrapping a blanket around me. Dinner was reheated, and we ate with Whip hovering under the table for scraps, which we gave him. Then it was back to bed.

Brandon came home and went right to his room with Whip. Charlie checked in on him, and I listened from behind the door.

"How'd dinner go?" Brandon asked, a smile in his voice.

"It was good. Mel tells me you're quite a chef."

"I've learned from you. So you liked it?"

161

"I did. I was wondering if you'd like to put something on the menu."

I peeked around the door and caught the grin that spread across Brandon's face. "Wow, for real?"

"Sure, why not?"

Brandon nodded. "Yeah, that'd be cool. Dad would never let me have a say in anything he was working on."

"I'm not like him."

"I know," Brandon said. "You're better."

At that, I slipped back into Charlie's room before I started crying. Charlie came back a moment later and I could tell he was a little shaken up.

"You're a better father than Garrett ever hopes to be," I said as he crawled into bed.

"He's a good kid. He deserves better than my brother."

I wrapped my arms around him. "He's got you now. I know you won't let Garrett hurt him anymore."

We talked some more about the restaurant, Brandon, and us before we fell asleep. It was still early, before ten, so I felt safe napping for a little while before I went home.

Hours later, I stretched out on the soft cotton sheets and rolled onto my side, snuggling against Charlie who made a small noise. I cracked open one eyelid, thinking I'd better get going before it got too late, and let out an ear piercing shriek that even scared me.

"What is it? What's going on?" Charlie cried, sitting up and rubbing at his eyes.

"It's morning!" I cried, hopping out of bed.

"Uh huh," Charlie said slowly. Then he got it. "Oh, shit."

I had stayed overnight and it was now 6:55 in the morning, and I had to be at school in twenty minutes. I didn't have time to run home, shower and change. I was screwed.

"Call in sick," Charlie said. He lay back against the pillows, folding his arms behind his head as he watched me run around his bedroom naked.

"I can't do that."

"Why not?"

"Because I'm not sick!"

I scooped up my clothes and ran for the bathroom for the quickest shower of my life. When I emerged, Charlie was standing by the sink, holding out one of his white shirts.

"What am I supposed to do with this?" I asked. I pulled on my pants and zipped them up.

"Wear it, dork."

"It's huge."

"So tuck it in and roll up the sleeves," Charlie said, putting the shirt on me and doing up the buttons. "You can't wear that pink sweater, it's covered in dog hair and everyone knows you don't have a dog. Everyone will suspect something."

"They will anyway. Teachers are smart."

He picked up a comb from the counter and ran it through my wet hair. Then he got my coat and purse and shoved me down the stairs and out the door.

"Wait, where's Brandon?" I asked.

"Took the bus to school."

My face flamed. "Oh God. He knows we're having sex."

"He already knew that. Now go!"

I hauled ass to school, zipping into my parking spot just a few minutes later than when I was supposed to be there. Gloria popped her head up from the trunk of her car three spaces down where she was lifting some boxes of books. I ignored her knowing smirk and ran inside, colliding with Jeremy.

"Whoa, whoa," he said, catching me. "New shampoo?" He looked down and raised a brow. "New shirt?"

I let out a cry of annoyance and went to my classroom. Since it was Wednesday and a driving day, I had to see Brandon twice. He was trying hard not to smile, and I was trying not to blush. I could feel myself sweating, probably staining Charlie's size Ginormous shirt as I taught seventh period.

"Okay, everybody remember that the third quarter ends next Tuesday, less than a week. All makeup work must be in by no later than Monday by the final bell," I said. "Your test over this unit will be Tuesday, but it will go on next quarter's grade."

The class breathed a collective sigh of relief. The bell rang and everyone scattered. I tugged at the collar of my shirt, Charlie's shirt, and smoothed my hair back. Since I hadn't had time to style it that morning, it had dried crinkly instead of straight. I'm positive I looked like some kind of 80s reject.

Brandon took his time before leaving and I went over to stand beside him.

"Why didn't you wake us up last night or this morning?" I hissed.

"I fell asleep around 10:30. I didn't know you were still there until I came outside and your car was in the driveway. I figured you guys had made plans to play hooky or something."

I sighed. "No hooky."

Brandon reached out and patted my arm. "Don't worry about it. And hey, I just wanted you to know that even if it seems like everyone else knows you stayed over, I didn't say a word to anyone."

I rolled my eyes. "Oh yeah, that makes me feel much better."

"So you two are in love, huh?" he asked, lifting his backpack onto his shoulder.

"Yes, we are," I said, turning to look at him. "Um, are you all right with that?"

He beamed. "Are you kidding? I'm more than all right with that!"

He hugged me then and took off running. I stood there and stared after him, wondering why this gave me a funny feeling in the pit of my stomach.

# Chapter Thirteen

Two things I loved about Brandon were his innocence and his smile, and by the beginning of April, it seemed I wasn't the only one. Many times I'd catch him surrounded by a group of girls at his locker, all talking and giggling and making him blush. Charlie said that Brandon didn't know how good looking he was, even though everyone else thought so. The reason he was clueless was because he'd been told by so many people a million times in Hollywood. It had become redundant.

Brandon had girls calling him at home, and while he was always polite, he turned them down if they asked him out. I had heard that a group of junior boys hated him because of who his dad was, but I couldn't pinpoint exactly who. I knew he had friends, but it seemed that he hung out mostly with Piper, which I thought was nice. I didn't see any romantic sparks between them; just a good solid friendship. Kind of like what I had with Jeremy.

One day, after classes had ended, Brandon was met by three girls, all seniors, who were curious to know if he was going to prom. At George Washington, you were only allowed to go to prom if you were a junior or a senior, unless you were attending with one. I knew these girls had gone every year since 9th grade because they always snagged older guys. It seemed this year, they were going for younger.

I heard them talking and peeked outside my door and into the hall. Brandon was cornered against a row of lockers, and his face was bright red. At six feet, he towered over them, but he seemed very uncomfortable to have all their attention.

Charlie had told me that Brandon's first serious girlfriend had dumped him right before they'd moved here to Cody. She just couldn't see herself associating with a boy who lived anywhere but Los Angeles. Brandon had been crushed and hadn't dated at all since then.

I would have been amused by the scene in the hallway, except I knew that none of these girls liked him for himself. They were turned on by his dad.

"So who will it be, Brandon?" one girl asked, putting her hand on his arm.

"Be?" he asked.

"Who will you take to prom?" another giggled. "Any of us will go with you."

"Oh, um, well, I," Brandon stammered. "I already have a date, actually."

"Oh yeah? Who?"

I watched Brandon's eyes scan the crowded hallway. He focused on someone, and I turned to look.

Piper was heading toward us, dressed in skinny jeans with dark gray ankle boots, a gray fitted blazer, and a white cashmere scarf. Her long hair was flowing behind her. She looked like an ad for the GAP, and I hated to admit I was jealous of her fashion sense.

"Piper!" he said, just a little too loudly.

She stopped and smiled. "Hey, Brandon. What's up?"

The girls took a step back, and I stifled a giggle. They may have been up there on the popular list, but Piper topped it.

"Her? You're going with her?" one girl asked.

"Yes. I'm going to prom with Piper," Brandon said, his eyes wide.

Piper didn't even blink, just smiled and nodded. "He asked me a week ago," she said.

"Are you guys together then?"

Brandon shook his head. "Piper's my friend. That's all."

"Is this why you keep turning down Ray Smithson?"

I gagged. Ray Smithson was the principal's son and Piper's male equal when it came to popularity, but not in brains.

"No. I keep turning down Ray because he's an idiot," Piper said. Then she looked at Brandon. "Don't forget. You have to call for a limo by Saturday."

He sagged against the lockers, relief all over his face.

"Yeah, sure."

The girls sniffed and walked away. Piper moved to stand by Brandon, who wiped his brow.

"Thanks," he said. "Sorry about that. I panicked. You don't have to go if you don't want to."

"Hey, why not? It'll be fun," Piper said, nudging his arm. "And I was serious about the limo."

Brandon laughed. "Yeah?"

"Oh yes," Piper said, a huge grin on her face. "I'm gonna milk this for all it's worth, bud."

"I can't believe you don't already have a date."

She shrugged and tucked a stray strand of hair behind her ear. "I've been asked by a dozen guys, but there's no one here that even remotely interests me. I'd rather go with a good friend anyway."

Brandon beamed, and I ducked back inside my classroom. High school dynamics were always so interesting.

# Chapter Fourteen

"So, Garrett's birthday is coming up," Charlie said, scooping out a spoonful of ice cream and offering it to me.

We were cuddled up in his bed. An old black and white movie was on TV, but we weren't watching it.

"Uh huh," I said, taking the bite.

"He's having a party in LA at my restaurant and he wants Brandon and me to be there."

"Uh huh," I repeated, taking another bite. It melted on my tongue and I savored the rich cherry taste, praising Ben and Jerry once again.

"I'd like you to come with us."

My eyes widened, and I choked. Charlie had to smack me on the back for a few seconds until I caught my breath.

"You what?" I asked.

"I want you to come with us. You could meet Garrett, see LA, my first restaurant. I still have an apartment there, so we'd stay there. I would pay for your airfare and -"

I sat up and held my hands up to stop him. "Wait a sec. You want me to come to LA with you."

"That's what I said."

"Isn't this a little sudden?"

He set the ice cream down on his nightstand and took my hands. They were cold, the first time I'd ever touched his hands and they weren't warm. I knew it was just from the ice cream, but it still threw me.

"Melinda, we've been together for over a month. I know it doesn't seem like a long time -"

"Forty-two days," I said.

He sighed. "All right, forty-two days, but they've just flown by." He paused and tilted his head to look at me. "I thought we were good together."

"No, I mean, yes, we are." I leaned closer. "I just don't know if I'm ready to enter your spotlight."

"What spotlight? Garrett has that. I'm just his nobody brother."

"Right. Who happens to own two of the hottest restaurants in the country, and is the brother of a famous movie star. Charlie, you said yourself you're something of a minor celebrity. I'd do nothing but make a fool of you in public. I can't handle that kind of humiliation."

"You won't make a fool of yourself because that's just impossible. Brandon and I would love to show you around LA, our hometown."

I chewed on my lower lip for a moment. "When is it?"

Charlie's expression brightened and he sat up straighter. "May fifth. The party is on that Thursday night, so we'd fly out that morning. We could probably get Claire or Jeremy to take Whip for the time we're gone, and you've got vacation days you could use, right?"

I nodded, feeling a little numb.

"Then we could bop around the city on Friday and fly back Saturday." He shook my hands, smiling. "You'll get to meet some famous people."

"Oh yeah, like who?"

He slid closer to me and moved to sit behind me, hugging me to him. "I think Garrett mentioned Brad Pitt's name."

I twisted around to look at him. "Are you serious?"

He nodded. "Sure. That's the kind of circle that Garrett runs around in."

174

I jumped out of bed, shaking my head. "No. I can't go to a party like that. No way. No way!"

I headed for the bathroom and splashed cold water on my face. Charlie followed after me. He lingered in the doorway while I dried my face with a towel and perched on the edge of the tub. I stared out the window into the backyard, watched the tree swaying in the wind and once again, those doubts about my place with Charlie came back to me.

"Hey, what's wrong?" he asked. "If this is about fitting in, don't think about it."

"How can I not? We come from two different worlds. I'm just a small town high school teacher. Until you, I'd never given two thoughts about gourmet cuisine or lavish living. No way in hell would I fit in with your high-class friends out there. And your brother!" I covered my face with both hands. "Your brother will hate me."

Charlie gripped my shoulders and pulled me up. "Why should you, or I, give a crap about what my brother thinks?"

"He'll take one look at me and see a gold-digger, that's why."

"But you're not."

"He won't know that."

"Then that's his problem." He pulled me into a hug, and I let myself be pressed against his chest. "I've met your family, and that went okay. You can meet my brother."

"I just don't know."

He leaned down and rested his forehead against mine. "Please? If something goes wrong, we'll take the first flight out."

"You promise?" I asked, because I was sure something would definitely go wrong. It was a rule of my life.

"I promise."

I tapped his chest with my hands and said, "I'm holding you to that."

I waited until I was home to call Claire and tell her.

"You're going to Hollywood?" she screeched. "Oh my God, this is incredible. You'll be bumping elbows with stars!"

"That's exactly it. I'll be bumping into them and making them spill their drinks all over their designer clothes. You know what a klutz I am."

"Oh pish posh," she said.

"What the hell is that?" I cried. "Pish posh?"

She laughed and said, "We'll go shopping. Find you a gorgeous dress to wear to the party. You'll knock 'em dead."

"That's what I'm afraid of. Don't you understand? Me. At a fancy party. With Brad Pitt."

I nearly went deaf at that point and almost gave up talking to my sister. She'd had a thing for Brad Pitt ever since he flexed his muscles in *Thelma and Louise*.

"Will you get me his autograph? No, a picture. No wait. An autograph *on* a picture! And his phone number."

I rolled my eyes and crawled into bed. "You're not helping me."

She took a moment to calm down. "Okay. So what's the real problem here? You still don't think you're good enough to be with Charlie?"

"That's not quite it. I'm not good enough to hang out in his circle of rich, snobby, Hollywood stars."

"And why is that? Just because you don't have a close, personal relationship with Donatella Versace?"

"Who?"

I heard her sigh.

"Okay, here's what we're going to do. This weekend, you, Piper, and I are hitting the cities. She needs to find a Prom dress anyway. We'll make a day of it."

And she was off. Claire adores shopping, especially for me. She's been my personal fashion consultant since I was five years old. After I talked with her for an hour about clothes and makeup, okay, she did most of the talking, I called Jeremy. I needed someone's opinion that didn't have anything to do with the latest fashion.

"Do you want to go?" he asked me.

"I don't know."

"Do you think you'd have fun?"

"Maybe. You think it's a big mistake, don't you?"

"I didn't say that."

"Okay, *I* think it's a big mistake," I moaned.

He was quiet, and I started burying myself under the covers. "He said he loves me," I said. "He says if anything goes wrong, we'll leave."

"And I believe it, Mel. I think he's a great guy, and I'm happy for you."

"But should I go?"

"I'm not going to tell you what to do, even though I know that's why you called."

"Bastard, you know me too well."

"Hey, I'm the best friend for a reason, brat."

I sighed, collecting my thoughts. "I guess a part of me has always known I'd have to meet Garrett sometime."

"Aha, now we're getting somewhere. This is about his brother."

"What?"

"You're afraid of what he'll think of you."

"Well, yes, I suppose. Just the impression I get of him from Brandon and Charlie, it makes me wonder what kind of person he really is. I don't think it's the nice guy he plays on the big screen. He treats Brandon like crap, and even though I'm glad he has Charlie looking out for him now, I still don't think it's good to be estranged from his own father."

"You're gonna hoof Garrett in the nuts, aren't you?" Jeremy asked.

I laughed. "I'll try to restrain myself, but you know me."

"Uh huh. Look, Mel, I know you can be civil to people you don't like. I've seen you at parent teacher conferences. And with this trip, you just have to go with what your heart tells you, and not with what your brain says, because we all know how disastrous that is."

"If I could reach through the phone and slap you, I so would."

"I know. So what are you going to do?"

"I know that Charlie asked me to go because he loves me, and he wants to show me off," I said.

"Wow, you've become quite vain," Jeremy teased.

I ignored him and continued. "But I foresee much humiliation in my future if I go."

"All right. Think of it this way. Would you rather meet Garrett Archer in a private setting with just you, Brandon and Charlie, or in a room full of people? Where do you think that you'll be safest?"

I frowned. "Me?"

"Yes, you. This is about your comfort zone."

"I guess in a room full of people."

"Why?"

"Because then…because then I could walk away from him if I don't like him."

"Guess you've got your answer then."

I felt a little better, but still unsure of myself.

"Don't worry about it. Claire will take you shopping, and all will be well. You do clean up quite nicely, Mel. You'll show them what a real person looks like."

And that is why I love Jeremy so much.

On Wednesday night, Claire came over for our usual *Smallville* viewing, armed with two pints of Cherry Garcia ice cream and a stack of magazines. She dumped everything on my kitchen table as Jeremy struggled to open a bottle of wine.

"What's all this for?" I asked, sifting through the magazines.

She had the latest issues of *Cosmopolitan*, *Vogue*, *US Weekly*, *People* and *Star*.

"Research," she said, swiping the wine bottle from Jeremy and expertly removing the cork. He stuck his tongue out at her. "We need to find out what everyone's wearing so we can search for a dress. And, you'll need to know who's hot in Hollywood right now."

"Uh, why?"

"This is Garrett Archer we're talking about. He's not just some schmo in a Gucci suit."

"Nope, he's some schmo in a Prada suit," Jeremy muttered.

"Will I sound like a complete moron if I say I wouldn't be able to tell the difference?" I asked.

Jeremy shrugged and poured three glasses of wine. We moved to the living room and settled in front of the TV, but we only paid partial attention to what was going on. Claire was tearing out magazine pages and asking me if I liked this dress or that one, and Jeremy was mimicking her from his place on the floor, until she whacked him over the head with a rolled up magazine. Then he stopped.

When Saturday morning rolled around, I tried to get out of the shopping trip by claiming I had a massive headache, maybe even a brain tumor, but Claire wouldn't hear of it. We drove into Davenport and stopped at the mall. Before we even got out of the car, Claire and Piper went through their mall transformation that to this day, freaks me out. They checked themselves out in the mirrors, refreshed their lipstick and fluff their hair, then dumped their purses out onto their laps and weeded out the non-essential items. They carried with them their wallets, full of credit cards and cash and IDs, a comb, a brush, a pocket mirror, a lipstick, a bottle of ibuprofen, packs of gum and Tic Tac's, and hand sanitizer. Then they tightened the laces on their running shoes and we headed in. It was like they were preparing for a marathon shopping spree, and as I was hurtled through the glass doors of JC Penney, I realized that's what this was. They took shopping for clothes very seriously.

I, on the other hand, am happy if I walk out without being attacked by a perfume spritzer or someone who thinks I need twenty pairs of fake designer sunglasses. Most of what's in my closet are jeans and T-shirts, sweaters and sweatshirts, and black or khaki pants. I like to think of my style as classic, but Claire tells me it's boring. It doesn't stop her from borrowing stuff from me though. My underwear, on the other hand, is all Victoria's Secret. I do like some frilly stuff.

For the first two hours, I was happy to browse through the racks and watch Claire and Piper gush over the prom dresses. Piper tried on all of them, and it was hard to pick just one for her to buy. As Piper was in the dressing room for the tenth time, Claire brought over a short, sleeveless black dress with an asymmetrical neckline.

"That's not her style," I said, examining the dress.

"No, but it's yours," Claire said to me. "It's simple, yet elegant, and it's not a big poofy ball gown with tons of netting underneath. I know that would make you crazy."

"True." I looked the dress over and tilted my head. "It's nothing designer, will anyone notice?"

Claire looked at me. "There is no way I will ever be able to get you to buy a $9000 dress to wear for one evening."

"That's how much a designer dress costs?" I asked in shock.

"That's how much a *cheap* designer dress costs. So here, try this one."

"Is it fancy enough? Should I have a train or something?"

"You would trip and kill yourself if you had a train. You're going to a birthday party, not the Oscars. It's a low key event."

She shoved me toward a dressing room. I had to admit, I liked the dress, but it seemed rather dull compared to some of the ones I'd seen in the pages of *US Weekly*. I put it on and stepped out, facing the full-length mirror. Piper was already there, frowning over a pink satin sheath.

"It makes my butt look huge," she murmured, turning around.

"Yeah, and mine's tiny," I said.

She paused and stared at my reflection. "Mel, that dress looks great on you."

"My boobs look like they're ready to fall out. I can't wear this without a bra," I said, trying to push my chest back into the dress.

"So you wear a strapless bra, or get cups sewn in," Claire said. She stopped behind me and smoothed the fabric over my hips, sighing. "Your hips haven't started to spread yet, lucky you."

"What is this spreading you speak of?" I asked, alarmed now.

She ignored me and said, "With the right shoes, a handbag and some jewelry, I think this is the one for you."

"The first dress I tried on? Isn't there some sort of rule that says I have to check out more than one?"

"Suit yourself. But I bet you twenty bucks you end up buying this one. It's very flattering on you."

I turned back to the mirror and checked myself out. The dress was form fitting on top and flared out at the waist, stopping a couple of inches above my knees. It clung to all the right curves, covered my butt, and hid the pudge at my belly, for which I was grateful. I didn't want to spend the entire night at Garrett's party sucking it in.

"We'll see," I said with a sniff. "I may find something else though."

"Twenty bucks, sis," Claire said with a grin.

We left JC Penney and went in search of shoes. Piper had it down to two dresses, and finding perfect shoes would help her decide. I didn't want to admit that I liked the black dress and was probably going to lose twenty dollars to Claire, so I tried to discreetly find a pair of heels to go with it. My problem was, I wasn't sure if I should go with black or silver, stiletto or kitten heel.

So I broke down, waved two ten dollar bills at Claire and admitted defeat. She took over, chose black strappy heels that laced up my ankles, and made me put them on. I hobbled around for a bit, trying to get my bearings.

"They look good, and they're not too uncomfortable," I said, "but I don't know if I'll be able to get them laced up right."

"You've got a point there. Knowing you, you're bound to tie them together," Claire said.

I couldn't be mad at her because I knew she was right. Piper found some black open-toed shoes and passed me the box.

"Two banded sling backs," she said. "These won't crush your toes, and with the straps, you won't walk out of them."

I hugged her and tried them on. "These are great!"

"Now all you need is a pedicure," Claire said. "And a manicure. And maybe you should have your teeth bleached."

"Whoa, back up there. It's one party. One night."

"Yes, but your reputation will be made at this one party. Do you want to be remembered or not?"

I shrugged. "Not. I'm only going because it means so much to Charlie and Brandon. I'm not going to try and start a new career or anything."

"But you want to impress them right?"

"Not if I have to have major work done to do it. It's not worth it, Claire."

She pouted for a moment. "I think I'm jealous. You always get to have all the fun."

"If I could send you in my place to this shindig, I would. I'd much rather be camped out on my couch with ice cream and the remote control."

"And Charlie," Piper added.

"Of course. He would be feeding me the ice cream."

Claire rolled her eyes, and I went to purchase the shoes. Then it was back to JC Penney to buy the black dress. Piper also found her prom outfit, and then we went on the hunt for jewelry. After a couple more hours, Piper and I were set. We carried our stuff to the car, and I was all ready to go home when Claire stopped me.

"Wait, we have more shopping to do," she said.

"What for?"

"You need traveling clothes, and something to wear on Friday when you go sightseeing."

"I have jeans."

Claire grabbed my arm and escorted me back inside the mall. I was so sick of the place, but she insisted on helping me find new things. This time, I just held out my arms while she and Piper stacked skirts, tops, pants, shorts, and tons of accessories for me to try on.

It was dark by the time we got out of there, and I was exhausted.

"Never again," I said as I climbed into the car. They just smiled at me.

Piper drove us back to Cody, and I asked her if Brandon had secured a limo for prom night.

"Nah, we decided not to. He didn't want the other kids to think he was snobby or something."

"He is the least snobby person I've ever met," I said, "but I can understand why he'd say no to the limo."

"He's excited, and so am I. I think I'm going to have fun this year."

I was glad for her and glad for Brandon. Fun was something that he'd been missing out on before he moved in with Charlie.

Charlie was stressing out more and more each day over the restaurant. Things were going smoothly, he was just anxious to get it all together and have the opening. He was working later at night, so I had started showing up at his house with food. Simple stuff that I was learning to make. Meatloaf, lasagna, and homemade pizza. I kind of messed up with the pizza though, substituting baking soda for baking powder. I hadn't known there was a difference. He appreciated the gesture though. I think.

# Chapter Fifteen

"Piper, he's here!" I yelled, jumping away from the front window.

Claire came down the steps, camera in hand. "This is so sad," she sniffed.

"What is?"

"It's her last prom."

I handed her a tissue and hugged her. She wiped at her eyes and went to answer the door. Brandon and Charlie stood on the porch, Brandon looking quite handsome in his black tuxedo and holding a corsage. Charlie beamed at us from behind Brandon.

"Hello, Mrs. Nichols," he said politely.

"Come in, come in, no need to be so formal," Claire said. "Piper will be down in a minute."

She ushered them into the living room and flitted around like an anxious mother. Charlie put his arm around me and whispered in my ear.

"Brandon's a little nervous. His first prom."

He did look a bit jittery as he tugged at his tie. Even though he couldn't drive on his own yet, and Piper would be behind the wheel tonight, he still insisted on meeting her at her own house.

"So she can still have her grand entrance," he'd explained to me, blushing.

Piper appeared at the top of the stairs, a vision in a strapless navy blue formal dress. Her long hair was curled and pinned to perfection. She looked stunning, and I heard Brandon suck in his breath as she met him at the bottom.

"Wow," he whispered.

Piper smiled. "That's good, right?"

"Huh? Oh yes. Definitely good. Um, I brought your corsage."

He fumbled with the plastic box, and I had to swallow a giggle as he became all thumbs. The corsage was one that needed to be pinned on instead of a wrist corsage, and Brandon hesitated. The only place to pin it

189

was right above Piper's breast. If there was one thing she'd inherited from the Martin women, other than her temper and sarcastic nature, it was cleavage.

"How about I let my mom do it?" she asked, and Brandon nodded.

Claire pinned on both their corsages, then got to business taking pictures. She posed them in front of the living room fireplace, in the backyard by the wooden fence, and by the car before they left.

Finally, Piper said they had to go. Their dinner reservations were in an hour, and they had to drive to the cities. Piper hugged her mother and Brandon opened her car door. Then Charlie straightened Brandon's bow tie and slipped some money into his jacket pocket before patting him on the back.

"Too bad your restaurant isn't open yet," Claire said as they drove away. "You'd be making a killing tonight."

"Speaking of that, I have a ton of paperwork to get through if I want to open by graduation," Charlie said. He kissed my forehead. "What do you two have planned for the evening?"

"Well, at ten we were gonna go spy on the kids," Claire said.

"What?"

"At ten, parents and relatives can go up to the balcony and watch the dance for the last hour," I explained. "A lot of parents do it. Wanna go?"

"I'll pass. I'd hate for him to be embarrassed by my presence."

"They don't even know you're there. Not until the lights come up at the end."

Charlie laughed. "You two have fun."

Claire and I had a mini *Smallville* marathon and ordered pizza. At nine-thirty we headed for the high school. There was already a group of people waiting to get in, but Claire and I had a plan.

Jeremy was working the cake and punch table, and he let us in through the back door. We headed up to the announcer's box and huddled there with two pieces of filched cake from Jeremy. This gave us an unobstructed view and allowed us to judge the formal wear of other people's kids without their parents hearing us.

"Do you see them?" Claire asked.

I squinted and scanned the gym floor. With the lights so dim, it was difficult to make out who was who until the strobe lights flashed over faces. I spotted them dancing near the stage.

"He dances like Charlie," I said, pointing them out. "No rhythm."

At 10:10, the principal walked onstage to announce Prom King and Queen. Smithson called for quiet and opened the envelope for king. His face broke into a grin and he puffed out his chest as he read his son's name.

Ray Smithson accepted his crown with a pompous smile and hugged his dad. Claire and I made booing and hissing noises.

"And this year's Prom Queen is..."

Claire grabbed my hand.

"Piper Nichols!"

Claire and I squealed like teenagers. Brandon kissed her cheek, and she walked up to the stage. Her crown was pinned to her hair, and she smiled and waved. Ray Smithson moved closer, putting an arm around her waist, and Piper scooted away.

"And now the King and Queen will share a dance," Smithson announced.

The floor cleared and the music started. Piper allowed Ray to lead her onto the floor, and when he tried to place his hand on her rear, she swatted him.

"Back off, Grabby Hands," Claire growled.

The song ended and everyone clapped as another one started. Other couples came out to dance, and Piper turned to head back to Brandon. And that's when things got ugly.

Ray wouldn't let go of Piper's hand and tried to keep her close to him. She shoved at him, shaking her head and clearly saying no. Then Ray's date came over, yelling at him. He yelled back and tried to hang onto Piper. Brandon wedged himself between them, removing Ray's hand from Piper's arm, and suddenly, all eyes were on them.

The music was still playing, but no one danced. Brandon was taller by a couple of inches, but Ray was stockier, built like a brick house and with force like a MAC truck. Everyone knew how rough he could be, judging by his plays during football games.

Claire and I couldn't hear what was being said by Ray, but it was pissing Brandon off. We left the booth and pushed our way downstairs. Jeremy was already on the floor, trying to keep a fight from starting. Claire and I made it to the gym entrance in time to see Ray lob a beefy fist at Brandon's face. Piper screamed, Brandon dodged, and Ray went flying to the floor.

The principal pulled his son to his feet and dragged him out. Jeremy checked on Brandon, who was unhurt.

Then Piper and Brandon left, heading toward where Claire and I stood.

"Mom!" Piper exclaimed, surprised to see us.

"What happened?" I asked.

Brandon just shook his head. "I don't want to talk about it."

"We're going to take off. We'll be okay," Piper said.

She and Brandon made off to the exit. Jeremy joined us a moment later, shaking his head.

"I don't know what happened," he said before either of us could ask. "Ray was shooting his mouth off about Brandon not being man enough to handle Piper, and that's all I could make out before the punch was thrown. Where did they go?"

I shrugged. "They left. Brandon looked upset."

Jeremy sighed and checked his watch. "Well, my job for the evening is done. You guys hungry?"

We nodded and walked out together. I was worried about Brandon, but Piper was with him, so I knew he'd be all right for the evening. We headed for Kitty's, a small diner that was open all night. I called Charlie and asked him to meet us, but he said he couldn't. He was too busy.

"But it's almost eleven," I whined.

"You're so cute when you're like this," he said, and I could hear the smile in his voice. "How was the dance?"

I hesitated for a moment and then told him what had happened.

"Wow, Brandon doesn't usually get angry about anything," Charlie said. "I wonder what Ray said to set him off."

We agreed to call each other if we hadn't heard from Brandon or Piper by morning. We weren't sure if they'd decide to go to the after-prom party or not. Ray Smithson was bound to be there, causing trouble.

The three of us stayed at the diner until almost one, just talking and eating, what we do best. As we were leaving, Piper called Claire to let her know they were okay and would be home soon.

I stopped out at Charlie's place to see Brandon, and while he appeared to be in a better mood, there was a slight difference in his attitude. I couldn't lay a finger on what it was though. He had changed from his tuxedo into jeans and a T-shirt, and he seemed quieter than usual, as if he was deep in thought about something. I stuck around until two, when Charlie stumbled in the door, carrying a huge stack of papers. We helped him dump everything on the dining room table.

"I hate paperwork," he muttered, hugging me. Then he straightened and clapped Brandon on the shoulder. "So do you want to talk about what happened tonight?" he asked.

Brandon shrugged. "Not right now."

Charlie nodded and said, "All right. I'm here whenever you're ready."

Brandon smiled a little and headed upstairs to his room, Whip following close behind.

"I can't imagine what the other boy could have said to him," Charlie said, shaking his head. "I wonder if it had something to do with his dad."

"I don't know. Ray's kind of a jerk anyway. He thinks he can get away with anything because he's the principal's son. He's not the brightest crayon in the box, and neither is his dad. I'm surprised he's graduating on time."

"You're harsh, Mel," Charlie said, poking me in the side.

"I call 'em like I see 'em."

"Well, if Brandon doesn't want to talk about it, I have to respect his wishes."

I raised a brow. "You catch onto this parenting stuff pretty quick. Brandon must be the luckiest kid in the world to have you looking out for him. Garrett could take a few lessons from you."

"Speaking of Garrett, are you ready for the party?"

"I have been primped and prepared to within an inch of my life," I groaned. "Claire has been quizzing me daily on who's who in Hollywood. My brain feels like it's going to explode, and I had a nightmare the other night about the Civil War, only it was between the Kardashian sisters. After this, I never want to see another celebrity."

Charlie just laughed at me. "You'll be fine," he said.

I didn't tell him that I was praying he was right.

# Chapter Sixteen

"Can I get a drink now?" I asked, gripping the armrest. "I'm in first class. We get drinks, right?"

Charlie patted my hand and shook his head. "We haven't even taken off yet, and you need one already? I thought you liked flying."

"Yeah, I do. But not when I'm on my way to LA, to Hollywood, to a big-shot party with movie stars and celebrities," I said, my voice rising with each word.

"It's going to be fine. You'll dazzle everyone," Charlie said. He did ask the flight attendant for two glasses of wine, and I gulped mine down.

"I'm a high school teacher from Iowa," I said, inhaling sharply as the plane left the ground. "I'm out of your league, Charlie."

"All right, that's enough. Now you're just being absurd. Just because you're not a celebrity doesn't mean I shouldn't be with you. I love you, Mel, for the very reason that you're not a celebrity. You're human, with flaws, and quirks, and I love them all."

"I have flaws?" I exclaimed.

"Oh God, Mel, just shut up."

I turned to him to say something scathing back, and he surprised me by kissing me senseless. I was much calmer when he pulled away, but I wanted another drink.

For the rest of the flight, I tried to nap, tried to read, and tried to drown myself in alcohol. I was stopped by Charlie on the last one. I couldn't get over my nervousness, and I began to think I'd made a big mistake in agreeing to go along on this trip. It was almost guaranteed I was going to make a fool of myself in front of Charlie's brother and high society friends and embarrass him and Brandon.

Somewhere over Denver, I was ticking off all the reasons why I should have stayed at home. I was clumsy and unsophisticated. I didn't spend countless hours working on my tan or exercising in some fancy gym with a personal trainer. I didn't have regular spa treatments, or even spend a lot of money on clothes or fancy jewelry.

"I love you, Melinda," Charlie whispered, breaking into my doubtful thoughts. "Don't forget that." He squeezed my hand and calmed me with his smile.

We landed at LAX, and he held onto my hand as we made our way through the busy airport. Brandon bounced along beside me, excited to be back in LA. We collected our luggage and were greeted by a uniformed man holding a sign with ARCHER written on it.

"That's us," Charlie said, and the man nodded.

"Your limousine is this way, sir."

"A limo?" I asked, following Charlie.

"You should travel in style," Brandon said.

I gaped at the sleek, black stretch limo that was parked at the curb. The chauffer held the door open for us, and I crawled in, tripping over the edge and falling inside with a loud "Oof!"

I hit my face against the seat and lay there on the floor, mortified. My black and white skirt with its pretty chevron stripes, which Claire had said made me look so Californian, was now up around my hips, giving everyone a horrendous view of my butt. Charlie helped me up.

"Are you all right?" he asked, running his hands over my face.

"I'd like to die now, please."

Brandon got in with us, the door closed and we were on our way to Charlie's apartment. I sat there with my head down, not even caring about the scenery whizzing by. If this was how the rest of the trip was going to be, I should just get on a plane back to Iowa right now.

"It's okay," Charlie said.

"No, it's not. I'm a complete klutz."

Brandon looked at me and said, "You're just nervous. It'll pass once we get to the party. This is going to be so awesome, just wait until you see the restaurant."

"The party is tonight, and you'll meet Garrett and some other celebrities, and we'll have a great time. Tomorrow, I'll take you on a tour of the city, and then Saturday, we head back to Cody. You'll survive this," Charlie said.

"I need a cigarette," I said, digging around in my bag.

"I thought you quit," Charlie said.

"I did. I just want to sniff it."

Brandon and Charlie shrugged at each other as I found one and rolled it around in my hand. They both thought I was overreacting, but they were from here. They were wealthy. I was neither of these things, and it was playing tricks with my self-esteem.

We arrived at an enormous building and a doorman escorted us inside.

"It's wonderful to have you back, Mr. Archer," he said, nodding at us.

"William, you remember Brandon," Charlie said, "and this is my girlfriend Melinda." He pulled me close and I tried not to stumble along the thick carpet.

William's smile widened and he took my hand and kissed it. "Welcome, Miss Melinda."

We rode the lavishly decorated elevator to his apartment on the 47th floor. The place was as big as three of my houses, and looked very expensive with white leather furniture, glass end tables, and framed artwork. I blinked at some of the sculptures though. Charlie had said they scared him, and I could see why. One was nothing but silver and glass, all shiny and sharp points. It looked dangerous.

The kitchen was stainless steel, and I was surprised to see it fully stocked. Brandon explained that even though they weren't living there at the moment, Charlie still employed a cleaning lady. She had made sure to buy a few days worth of groceries for us. The view was spectacular though, and I stood at the tall picture windows for a few minutes while Charlie took care of our bags. Brandon called his dad to let him know we had made it.

"I'm heading out to the restaurant for a little bit," Charlie said. "I'll be back in a couple of hours. You and Brandon can relax here. Garrett's stopping by later so we can all go to the party together."

"Wait, you're leaving me here?" I asked, waving my arms around.

Brandon was already planted on the couch, channel surfing and eating Cheetos. He had settled in and was unconcerned about anything. I, on the other hand, was a mess.

"You'll be fine. Eat something, take a bath. Unwind," Charlie said, hugging me. "If you come with me now, I won't be able to pay much attention to you, and that's a very bad thing."

I grinned. "Yes, that is."

Charlie lowered his voice and said, "But tonight, tonight you're all mine. I'll give you all of my attention, every inch of your luscious body."

"Oh, Jesus, take me now," I breathed.

Brandon tossed a Cheeto at us. "Take it to the bedroom, please."

Charlie laughed, kissed my nose and turned to go. "I'll be back later. The number for the restaurant is on the fridge, and you have my cell number. I love you."

"I love you too."

Charlie ruffled Brandon's hair on his way out. "Be good."

Brandon waved goodbye. As soon as Charlie was gone, Brandon stood up and joined me at the window.

"Whip would be scared of the height," he said.

"Whip is scared of his own shadow," I said.

"It was nice of your sister to take him while we're gone, although I think Piper had more to do with it."

"Oh, I'm sure Piper did. Claire isn't big on dogs."

"Good thing he's not a big dog."

I smiled and put my arm around Brandon's shoulders.

"By the way," he said, "these windows don't open. The ones in the bathroom do. You can smoke in there if you need to, but you know you shouldn't. Down the hall, second door on your left."

I shook my head. "No, I've been doing so well. I won't let this weekend throw me off."

"Good," Brandon said.

"I'm going downstairs," I said. "I need some air."

Brandon nodded and sat down again to watch TV. I took the elevator down to the lobby and stepped outside. William tipped his hat at me, and I stood away from the doors to people watch. Everyone that walked by was dressed in designer clothes and the women were all perfect.

"Is anyone here for real?" I asked, and William looked at me with a confused expression.

I stayed outside, enjoying the sunshine. Just as I was about to go back in, a gorgeous, leggy blonde wearing a pink sundress and three inch stilettos passed me and stopped to talk with William. I was trying to imagine walking in those shoes without killing myself when I heard her say Charlie's name.

William shook his head and said, "I'm sorry, ma'am, he's already gone."

"Do you know when he'll be back?" the blonde asked. "I'm a very close friend of his."

Something about the way she said that made me snap to attention. She was practically purring at William, who appeared rather uncomfortable.

"I'm sorry, I don't know," he said.

"Well, can I go up to his apartment, leave him a message?"

"I can't allow that, ma'am. We have strict rules."

"I know the rules, but Charlie would be all right with me going up to his apartment."

I chose that moment to walk up to them. I wanted to know who this chick was.

"Excuse me," I said politely, and was greeted with a cold stare. "Are you a friend of Charlie's?"

She stepped back and I could feel her appraising me and dismissing me with a flick of her icy blue eyes. "I'm his girlfriend, who the hell are you?"

William coughed and stepped away to open the door for a nicely dressed older couple.

"His girlfriend?" I asked, my eyebrows rising.

The blonde flipped her perfect hair over her shoulder. "Charity Crandall."

"Uh huh," I said. "That's funny. He's never mentioned you before."

"And who would you be?" she asked.

"Melinda Martin, and I'm his girlfriend."

Charity blinked and her mouth opened, but no sound came out. I turned to William and said, "I'll be going up to Charlie's apartment now."

"Of course, miss."

I hurried upstairs and attacked Brandon for information.

"Who is Charity Crandall?"

Brandon spit Cheetos all over the white leather couch. "Is she here? She's not coming up here, is she?"

"Who is she? She was downstairs trying to schmooze with William to let her in."

Brandon turned off the television and faced me. "She's a psycho that Charlie dated about five years ago. Total whacko, scared the shit out of everyone."

"You shouldn't swear."

Brandon rolled his eyes. "He was only with her for a few months, but she got super serious, started looking for wedding dresses and invitations. She tried to move in, but Charlie resisted. He broke up with her, and she went nuts."

I slid onto the couch. "How nuts?"

"Calls in the middle of the night," Brandon said. "Showing up at the restaurant, following him around town. I heard about it from my dad, and he said Charlie should get a restraining order, but since she never did anything dangerous, he didn't. Plus, he didn't think he could get one. Her dad's a federal judge."

I crossed my arms and leaned back against the pillows. "She told William she was Charlie's girlfriend."

"Whoa. You should tell Charlie."

"Oh, I plan to. I'm the only psycho girlfriend he can have right now."

Brandon laughed.

I was soaking in the whirlpool tub when Charlie got back. He came into the bathroom, tugging at his tie. He perched at the edge of the tub and kissed me.

"Care if I join you?"

I shook my head. "Please do. How's the restaurant?"

"It's all set. Garrett's party is going to be quite extravagant, which is expected. He can never do anything without making it a huge event."

He stripped off the rest of his clothes and slid into the tub behind me, sloshing water over the side.

"You feel good," he murmured, running his hands up my arms.

"We can always skip the party," I said, sounding a little too hopeful.

"Sorry, I've got to be there to host."

"I thought Garrett was throwing this shindig."

"He is, but I'm in charge. It'll run smoother if I'm there."

He massaged my neck and while it felt wonderful, I was dying to ask him about Charity.

"So, uh, there was a woman who was trying to get up to the apartment," I said, rubbing soap up and down my arms. "Charity Crandall."

Charlie's hands paused. "Are you serious?" He sighed and I turned around to face him. "Did she talk to you?"

"She told me she was your girlfriend."

"Jesus."

Charlie took off his glasses, rubbed his eyes and leaned back against the tub.

"Brandon already told me a little about her. Is she as crazy as he said?"

"I made a huge mistake in ever going out with her, but she seemed normal when I met her. I knew something was wrong when she showed me a pre-printed wedding invitation."

"How did you meet?"

"She runs in Garrett's circle, and she was at a party. It was all downhill from there."

I stood up, letting water drip down my body, and grabbed a fluffy white towel.

"Hey, where are you going?" he asked, putting his glasses back on.

"Well, Charity kind of spoiled the mood, and I have to get ready for a party."

"You're such a tease."

"Damn right."

I left Charlie in the bathroom and headed to the bedroom to get dressed. Charlie came in just as I was slipping the straps of my black silk dress onto my shoulders.

"I think we may be late," he said, looking at me with raw lust in his eyes.

We forgot about Charity.

# Chapter Seventeen

Brandon hollered at us to hurry up. Garrett was waiting downstairs with a limo. Charlie and I went out to the living room and Brandon whistled.

"You look gorgeous, Mel," he said.

"Thanks, kiddo."

Charlie adjusted his tie and smoothed the cuffs of his jacket.

"Did you bring a gift?" he asked, and panic seized me.

"Oh my God, I didn't. What do I do now? What do you even get for someone like him? He's going to think I'm a complete loser!"

Charlie and Brandon started laughing, and I glared at them.

"What's so funny?" I demanded.

"Charlie was just teasing. You didn't have to get him anything," Brandon said. "Dad would just give it to one of his assistants anyway."

"Well that's kind of rude, isn't it?"

"It's Hollywood," Brandon said with a shrug.

We rode the elevator to the lobby, and I came face to face with Oscar-nominated actor Garrett Archer. He was as good-looking in person as he was on film, and I felt my knees knock together as he came toward us. Even though I wasn't impressed with his acting, it was still strange to be in his presence.

"You must be Melinda," he said. "I've heard so much about you, but no one said you were a goddess."

Okay, now that was cheesy.

"It's a pleasure to meet you," I said.

"Ah, the pleasure is mine."

Charlie rolled his eyes and clapped his brother on the shoulder. "Laying it on pretty thick," he said.

Garrett chuckled, which sounded fake and hollow to me, and put an arm around Brandon. "Good to see you, son. How's Iowa treating you?"

Brandon shrugged. "I like it. Charlie takes good care of me."

Garrett made a noise low in his throat and stepped back.

"Well, let's get going, shall we? I don't want to be late to my own party."

The guest list for the night's event was strictly A-list, with only the hottest stars and most important Hollywood bigwigs invited. Huge guards stood at the front doors, and fans lined up across the street to watch the spectacle. A line of limos was dropping people off at the entrance of Cinema, and it was all being photographed by paparazzi with huge lenses that were very likely to see the pores on my face.

"Holy shit," I blurted out as our limo neared the front of the line. "That's Sandra Bullock!"

I was a mess by the time it was our turn to walk the red carpet and into the restaurant. My hands were shaking, and I craved a cigarette, but even if I caved and had one, I wasn't about to light up in front of the cameras. Instead, I tucked one down the front of my dress, for emergency purposes only.

Our door opened, and Garrett stepped out. He waved to the public, air-kissing the screaming fans, and smiling broadly for the cameras. He made his way to the doors, stopping to pose and chat with reporters.

Brandon followed and made a beeline for his father. Charlie got out next and held his hand out to me.

"I can't," I said, shaking my head.

"Yes, you can."

"It's a circus out there."

"I know. I'll take you straight in. You can do this, Mel."

I extended my hand, and Charlie gave a gentle tug. I stepped onto the red carpet and was immediately blinded by the flashes going off. Charlie hooked his arm through mine and we started walking.

"Just smile," he whispered.

I pasted a smile on my face and stayed close to Charlie. Finally, *finally*, we made it inside. Cinema was a two story restaurant with crystal chandeliers hanging from the ceiling. Each table was covered in white linen with silver candelabras in the center. A magnificent oak bar took up one corner, and in another, a huge table that held a three-tiered cake and a chocolate fountain. Uniformed servers circled the room holding trays with sparkling glasses of champagne. I snagged a glass as a server passed and downed it in one gulp.

"That was insane," I gasped.

"It can get pretty crazy," Charlie said.

I grabbed another glass and was sipping this one when Brad Pitt strolled by. I choked, and Charlie had to smack me on the back.

"Oh my God, Jeremy and Claire would be dying."

Charlie grinned. "Do you want to meet him?"

"Are you kidding?"

211

"No. Come on."

It was like a dream. Charlie introduced me to Brad Pitt, and I managed to not make a fool of myself. Brad even hugged me. Garrett came over to pose for some pictures, and I prayed that I didn't look like a fool in them. He introduced me to another actor, a guy named Wendell Benton. The two chatted easily, but I could feel some tension between them.

"Nice party," Wendell said, tilting his head toward the crowd.

"It was nice of you to come all the way from New York. I expect you've been busy. Wendell owns and operates a media company," he said to me. "He used to act, was even fairly good at it."

Wendell Benton grinned and said, "Good enough to actually win the Oscar, Garrett. How's that coming along for you?" He winked at me and took a drink of champagne before excusing himself. I liked this guy.

Charlie was called away to take care of a crisis in the kitchen, and I was left alone. I examined the birthday cake, resisting the urge to stick my finger in the frosting and write "HI!" like I used to do when I was kid.

I looked around for Brandon and spotted him with Garrett at the other end of the room. I was about to make my way over there when a familiar blonde stepped in front of me.

"So what are you? A model?" Charity asked. Of course, she looked stunning and perfect, and I just wanted to rip her hair out.

"I'm flattered you think so, but no," I said. "I'm a teacher. Melinda Martin, nice to meet you."

Charity snorted. "You'll never last. Charlie needs a woman who's used to all of this."

"Someone like you?"

"He's just on the rebound, that's all. He'll come back to me."

"Wow, you're more delusional than I was told."

Her eyes widened, and her nostrils flared. "Excuse me?"

"He dumped you five years ago, get over it." I caught Brandon's eye and he waved me over. "Nice chatting with you, Charity."

"You bitch," she hissed as I stepped away from her. Then she grabbed my hair and tugged.

I screamed, and we went down hard. She was howling, pulling at my hair, and I was swatting at her, trying to get her to let go. We rolled around on the floor, knocking into a passing waiter, who dropped his tray of champagne all over us. Charity scratched at my face with her nails, trying to gouge me in the eyes.

I was screaming and squealing, and Charity was spitting and cursing me out left and right. Then there was a huge thump and the elaborate table that held Garrett's birthday cake collapsed and fell on top of us. Charity roared with rage and smashed a handful on my head. I picked up a chunk and smashed it right in her face, twisting my hand. I know some of it got up her nose, and I laughed.

"Charity, stop it!" Charlie yelled, pulling her off me. She took a handful of my hair with her.

Garrett helped me up, while Charlie dragged Charity away. I was pissed as hell, and my head hurt, and there were three long scratches down my right cheek, along with sugary frosting and bits of cake stuck to my eyelashes.

Charlie returned, his jaw twitching with tension. Without saying a word, he guided me toward the back to the kitchen. I left a trail of cake behind me as we went.

"That woman is fucking nuts!" I declared, grabbing a nearby dishtowel and wiping my face.

The chefs and servers paused in what they were doing to stare at us until Charlie waved at them to get back to work.

"I am so sorry, Melinda," Charlie said. "I didn't know she would be here. She wasn't on the guest list."

I leaned against the stainless steel counter and shook my head. "She's got a serious problem."

Charlie began pacing, his shoes squeaking against the linoleum. I stood there and pulled the cigarette from my dress, picking bits of cake from my hair. Brandon came in with a smile on his face that he was trying to hide behind a frown. It didn't work, and he snorted out a laugh.

"Dad's got everything under control out there," Brandon said. "The party's going on as if two women haven't just had a cat fight in the middle of it."

I tasted the frosting on my fingers. Buttercream, my favorite.

Charlie stopped pacing and leaned on the table. "I'm so sorry," he said again. "I just don't know what else to say."

I shrugged, and a lump of cake plopped on the floor. "Not your fault."

"This is your first time in LA, and I wanted it to be nice. Instead, you get attacked."

I gave up on the cigarette, realizing I'd forgotten to stuff a lighter in along with it, and it was soggy anyway. I straightened, going up behind him and wrapping my arms around his waist, which smeared cake along the back of his jacket.

"It's been great fun," I said, trying to sound cheerful. "Where else but Hollywood would I be able to have a champagne and cake fight with a judge's daughter?"

Brandon snickered and leaned against the counter. "I don't think she was expecting you to fight back. You really whooped her."

"Brandon," Charlie admonished. "Fighting isn't the answer."

"Right," I said. "Fighting isn't a way to solve problems." I wiggled my eyebrows behind Charlie's back. "Well, I'm calm now, and I want to party."

215

"You want to go back out there?" Charlie asked, surprised.

I stepped back and smoothed my hair, effectively smashing a frosted flower onto my head.

"Sure. You don't think I flew all the way out here to sit in the kitchen, do you?"

Charlie looked at me, dirty and covered in sticky sweet champagne and rich frosting and burst out laughing.

"You are amazing, Mel," he said, hugging me. Then he licked my ear and said, "You taste wonderful."

"Oh geez," Brandon muttered and headed for the door, just as Garrett came in.

"You can go out the back way," he said, his voice like ice. "No one has to see you leave."

"What are you talking about?" Charlie asked.

"Well, obviously she can't stay. She's caused an embarrassing scene in the middle of my birthday party, and it's been photographed and videotaped. It'll be on TMZ and all over Twitter in a matter of minutes."

I didn't know what either of those things were, but I felt my stomach flutter, and I shrank a little behind Charlie.

"So what? It wasn't her fault," he said.

"You know, I was hesitant when you told me you were bringing her," Garrett said, and I detected a slight snarl curling on his lips. "I just never thought she'd be such a hick in public."

216

Charlie walked right up to his brother and stared down at him. "You'd better watch your damn mouth."

"There's no need for that kind of language, Charlie."

"Then you better watch what you say about Melinda."

Garrett stood up straight and pointed a finger in my direction. "Get her out of here. Now."

The door swung open and Brandon burst in. "Then I'm going too."

Garrett turned to face his son. "You're staying here. I need you by my side for the rest of the night. The press loves you."

"But, Dad —"

"Just shut up and do as I say," Garrett spat.

Brandon clamped his mouth shut and cast his eyes downward. I'd been quiet up till then, but hearing Garrett speak to Brandon like that made my blood boil. I stepped around Charlie, who was clenching his hands into fists at his sides, and got in Garrett's face.

"Don't you ever talk to him like that again, or I will make it my life's mission to see to it that you regret it," I said. Garrett backed up a bit, and I went over and took Brandon's hand. "We're leaving, and we're going out the front door, so you'll just have to deal with it."

Charlie followed me out and we left Garrett standing in the kitchen, his face red with rage. I marched through the crowd, ignoring the stares and whispers and the flashes as photographers took my picture. Once I was outside of the restaurant, I took a deep breath and looked around.

"How the hell do we get home?" I asked to no one in particular.

Charlie caught up with us. "Mel, I've got a car for you. Take Brandon home," he said, passing me his apartment keys. "I've got to stay here."

"Why?" I asked. "Why can't you leave with us? I'm sorry to say it, but your brother is an ass." Brandon winced beside me, and I instantly felt bad. "Oh, honey, I'm sorry."

"No, he was a jerk to you. It wasn't your fault that Charity crashed the party," he said.

Charlie put his hands on my shoulders. "I'll be home as soon as the party winds down. I can't leave it like this."

"You left it just fine when you moved to Iowa. Why can't you leave it now?"

He pursed his lips and looked at me. "Don't make this any more difficult than it already is. Just go home. I'll be there later."

A limo pulled up behind me, and Charlie moved to open the door. I blinked away tears and got in. Brandon slipped in beside me, and the door closed. I stared at my hands as the car pulled away, wondering where the hell the night had gone wrong. I could blame Charity, after all, she was the one who came uninvited. Even though I didn't want to believe that the night was a disaster because I was there, I couldn't hold my own with these people, and I knew it.

Just as I was about to give in and cry, Brandon took my hands in his and squeezed. I raised my head and looked at him, and I felt a little better.

"We're just a couple of misfits, I guess," I sniffed.

Brandon gave a sad smile. "I've always been one, at least to my dad. But, Mel, you're better than all of those snobby people put together."

Then he scooted over and hugged me tight.

The limo stopped and we got out at Charlie's building. A different doorman was standing outside, but he recognized Brandon, and we went right up. I caught a glimpse of us in the mirrored panels of the elevator. We looked like a couple of bakery war rejects.

Once inside the apartment, I slipped out of my shoes and headed straight for the master bathroom. Brandon went to his room and closed the door. I could only imagine how he felt. I wanted to believe that there was some small part of Garrett Archer that loved his son, but it was difficult. Charlie had been right when he said Garrett treated Brandon as an accessory.

I ran a hot bath, dropping in some of the lavender scented bubble bath, and stripped off my clothes. I tried running a comb through my hair. It got stuck on dried frosting, and some of the teeth snapped off. I was bone tired as I slid into the steaming water. Clumps of sugary frosting fell from my hair and dissolved. Using a washcloth, I scrubbed myself clean, wincing when I touched the scratches on my cheek. That bitch Charity had some nails on her. She must have sharpened them to points in hopes of running into me at the party.

I drained the tub and washed my hair, then filled it up again. My mother would have been appalled at my wasteful nature that night, but I didn't care. Charlie had been angry with me when I left, I could tell from the way he spoke to me. It hurt to hear that tone, and I wondered if I'd somehow ruined us.

Then I got annoyed with my pity-party and splashed like a little kid, trying to cheer myself up. The water began to cool, and I felt clean and ready to go to bed. I slipped right under the water for one last dip in this marvelous tub. I stayed there for a few seconds and resurfaced, pushing hair from my face and blinking water from my eyelids. Then I looked up and shrieked my damn head off.

"Charlie!"

He was sitting at the edge of the tub, looking as tired as I felt. He wasn't wearing his suit jacket anymore, the top buttons of his shirt undone and the sleeves rolled up past his elbows.

"Sorry, didn't mean to scare you," he said softly. He sighed and pushed his glasses up his nose.

I sat up and put my hands on his knee, leaving wet spots. At this point, neither of us cared.

"Is the party over? What time is it?"

He shook his head. "No, but I couldn't stay, not with him out there grinning like an idiot and the two most important people in my life not there. So I left my manager in charge, and I left." He paused. "I went to see Charity."

The water cooled around me a few more degrees at the mention of her name, and I drew my knees up to my chest and wrapped my arms around them.

"I wanted to tell her something."

"Oh?"

He dropped down to his knees, resting his head in his hands on the tub's edge. "I wanted to tell her to her face that I wasn't in love with her. I never was." He reached out and tipped my chin up so I was looking at him. "I told her I am in love with you."

I blinked back tears and moved toward him, hugging him. He chuckled a little as he got soaked. Then he stood up, pulling me up with him, and lifted me out. He grabbed a towel from the nearby warming rack and wrapped it around me.

"I have got to get me one of those," I murmured against his chest.

"I'll get you one when we get back to Iowa tomorrow."

"We're leaving early?"

He looked down at me. "Do you want to stay?"

I stared up into his dark blue eyes, feeling their heat and seeing the sadness there, and I shook my head.

221

"No. Let's go home."

He smiled. "Home. I like the sound of that. Cody has become my home, Mel. With you and Brandon. LA is just too frigid for us."

I shivered against him. "Speaking of frigid…"

I let out a little squeal as Charlie scooped me up and carried me from the bathroom back into the bedroom. He placed me on the bed and did his best to warm me up.

# Chapter Eighteen

I whistled a cheerful tune as the sun shone through the windows of Charlie's bedroom the next morning. We had apologized to each other twice the night before, then sneaked out to the kitchen for a snack since we hadn't eaten at the party. I'd gotten a few mouthfuls of frosting and two glasses of champagne, but that was it. We found Brandon making sandwiches and decided to join him. He didn't say a word about my disheveled appearance. I caught him smirking a few times though. Since Charlie and I had jumped into bed right after my bath, my hair

223

dried all funky, and it was sticking out in places. I cringed at the thought of Charlie and me educating Brandon about sex.

Brandon made excellent sandwiches, piled high with fresh deli meats, cheeses, and vegetables. We sat on the leather furniture in the living room, eating and talking. Brandon wanted to leave as well, so Charlie made some calls and had our tickets changed for an afternoon flight on Friday instead of Saturday.

I was bopping around to some music in the master bedroom while Charlie was at the restaurant, taking care of some business. I was folding my clothes and stacking everything in my suitcase when Brandon came rushing in.

"You're on TV!"

He grabbed the remote and flipped on the 32-inch flat screen mounted on the wall. I stopped what I was doing, turned off the music and came around the bed to stand beside Brandon.

Some kind of sleazy entertainment show was on, where a bottle-blonde with legs up to her neck was jutting her hips out as she talked. Brandon turned up the volume and I heard her say, " - fight broke out between the two women in the middle of Garrett Archer's forty-second birthday party last night at Cinema, the restaurant owned by his younger brother Charlie."

A video clip was played, and there we were, scuffling around in the cake like a couple of pigs in the mud. And then I watched myself shove a handful in Charity's face and cackle.

"Oh my God," I moaned, burying my face in my hands.

"Apparently, Charlie Archer's former and present girlfriends decided to wrestle. Charity Crandall, daughter of California federal judge, Jeremiah Crandall, the ex, was escorted off the premises, after it was learned that she had not been on the guest list. Her $15,000 Dolce and Gabbana dress was in tatters, while the winner, identified by others at the party as Melinda Martin, a schoolteacher from Iowa, continued to enjoy the evening in a cake-covered dress from Sears." The blonde gave a smirk of contempt.

"Hey!" I exclaimed, startling Brandon. "That dress did not come from Sears. It came from JC Penney, bitch. Get it right."

Brandon laughed and turned off the show.

"You're famous, Mel," he said with a smile.

"More like infamous." I rolled my eyes and turned back to packing. "They'll forget all about me when someone else does something ridiculous."

"It wasn't ridiculous. Charity attacked you and you defended yourself."

I hugged Brandon. "You're awesome, you know that?"

I felt him tense in my arms, and he said, "My dad doesn't think so."

I held him at arms length and stared at him. He wouldn't meet my eyes, so I just waited. Finally, he let out a deep breath and raised his head.

"He called this morning, before you were up," he said.

"What did he say?"

"That hanging out with you was an insult to the name of Archer. That my grandfather is rolling in his grave at the thought of me living in the middle of nowhere."

"Cody isn't in the middle of nowhere."

"Any place that isn't LA or New York City is nowhere to my dad."

"Then he needs to get out more."

Brandon's smile was small, yet sad. "He's going to want me to come and live with him again. He didn't say it, but I know he's got a new movie coming out, and the press tour will start up soon."

I blinked. "I'm sorry, I have no idea what that means."

"It means he'll want me to go with him, to interviews and public appearances. He thinks having me with him makes him seem more approachable and maintains his image of the good, hard-working family man."

I snorted. "Whoops, sorry."

Brandon shook his head. "Nah, you're okay. I hate doing that shit."

"Brandon -"

"I know, I know. I shouldn't swear." He rolled his eyes. "But it's true."

I opened my mouth to say something, stopping when I heard the front door open and close. Anyway, what else was there to say about the subject?

We walked out into the living room to see Charlie collapse on the couch. The white T-shirt he wore stretched nicely across his chest. He splayed his arms along the back and closed his eyes. That was a truly hot image burned on my retinas. I settled down beside him and snuggled under his arm.

"How's the restaurant?"

"Smells like expensive cake and champagne. Just a tad stale."

"Oooh." I wrinkled my nose.

He tapped it with his index finger. "Don't worry. I have an excellent cleaning company, and I heard you were on TV. I got about a dozen calls."

I blushed and ducked my head. Brandon laughed and told him all about it.

"I bet you make all the tabloids," Charlie said.

"What?"

"With all the photographers there? Oh yeah. You're probably on all the gossip websites already."

"Shit."

Brandon clucked his tongue at me and went to finish packing. Charlie turned to face me and kissed my forehead.

"I promise, the next time we're here, it'll be better. This wasn't a good idea, and I take full responsibility for it."

I shrugged. "Kiss me for real, and all is forgiven."

He grinned and gladly obliged.

\* \* \*

The Monday after we arrived back in Cody, Claire called me during my lunch hour nearly hysterical. It took me five minutes to get her to calm down enough to speak coherently, and even then, I could only make out a few words.

"Paparazzi! Tabloid! Front cover!" she squealed.

"What the hell are you talking about?"

She took a deep breath and said, "You're on the front cover of the tabloids, you and that Charity Crandall."

"What?!"

"I was at the grocery store in the checkout line, and there you were, covered in cake. There are pictures of the fight and a full page article. Melinda! Everyone's talking about it!"

I sank into my desk chair and dropped my head to the desk and moaned. Thanks to the good old Internet, my family knew about the entire embarrassing incident approximately five seconds after it happened. My mother was mortified that I'd gotten into a fight, while my sister was pissed I didn't get her Brad Pitt's number. Jeremy had just been shocked into silence, and then he laughed for ten straight minutes.

When I arrived at school that morning, I ignored the stares from students and teachers and had to close the door in Gloria Milner's face as she squawked about seeing me on television and asked if Garrett Archer was as tall as he seemed.

"Mel? Are you there? Mel!"

I put the phone to my mouth. "I'm here."

"Mom bought every magazine."

"Why?"

"She's so proud of you! Taking on that rich bitch and showing her who's boss. She says you get that from her."

"I thought I had shamed her hiding inside her house for the next month."

"Nah, you knew that wouldn't last. If she actually followed through on that threat after all of your shenanigans, she'd never step outside. You know you've got to be the reason she began dying her hair so early."

I couldn't even be offended by what my sister said. Mom had started going gray right after I was born. That couldn't have been a coincidence.

"I bought copies for you. I'll drop by after school and give them to you!" Claire said.

"Thank you," I said, although I wasn't sure if that was the right thing to say.

I called Charlie as soon as school let out, and he insisted on taking me out for ice cream to celebrate my making it into the tabloids. We met at my house, after I changed clothes and got the magazines from Claire. She was waiting for me inside, hopping around the living room like a little kid that had to pee. She was too excited for her own good.

We checked out the magazines, and she even offered to make me a special scrapbook to commemorate my first trip to LA. I turned her down and shooed her out the door just as Charlie arrived.

He took me to McDonald's, and we ordered sundaes. We were halfway through them when a sleek, black Porsche pulled into the parking lot and a tall, leggy blonde got out. I squinted out the window, watched her walk up to Charlie's truck and run a hand along the hood. Then I dropped my spoon.

Charlie bent to retrieve it. "I'll grab you another one, klutz," he said with a smile.

I could only point stupidly, and Charlie frowned and looked outside.

"Sonofabitch," he muttered.

"So I'm not hallucinating."

He shook his head. "What the hell is she doing here?"

Charity Crandall looked  stunning in faded skinny jeans, a cute pink baby tee, and a black leather jacket. She raised her sunglasses, leaving them perched at the top of her head as she came inside. Of course she was ogled by every eye in the place, including the women.

She spotted Charlie and her face broke into a brightly bleached smile. Then her gaze slid to me, and the tiniest frown appeared, but vanished after a second. After all, frowning caused wrinkles. She came right over to our little booth and beamed down at Charlie.

I wished I hadn't just thrown on jeans and a sweatshirt. I hadn't even refreshed my makeup, and my hair was pulled back in a messy ponytail. Compared to Charity, I looked like a complete slob.

Charlie stood up, and Charity gave him a hug and a kiss on the cheek.

"What are you doing here?" he asked, and in a not too kind voice.

Her smile faltered for a moment, and she glanced at me. She blinked, resembling an innocent doe, and I shoved a spoonful of ice cream in my mouth to keep from breaking off the end and stabbing her with it.

"Well, you told me to come," Charity said, and I choked.

"Where the hell did you get that idea?" Charlie asked, patting me on the back without even looking.

Sadly, this was becoming a routine for us. I seemed to have forgotten how to eat correctly since meeting Charlie.

"When you came to see me after Garrett's party. You said I should move out here after you. So here I am. I'm house hunting. Do you want to come along?"

Charlie's expression turned to one of horror.

"I told you to move *on*, Charity. To get over me because we weren't going out anymore," he said. He turned to me and said, "You ready to go?"

I nodded and jumped up. Charlie took care of our trash and then put his arm around me as we left. I could feel everyone staring, and in my head they were all comparing Charity to me, and I was losing. In reality, they were probably hoping for another cat fight in front of Ronald McDonald himself.

Charity trailed after us, babbling about how the distance was what hurt them, that she wasn't supportive of him enough when he had to travel for business because she just missed him so much.

"But I'm here now, and we can be together," she said as I climbed into the truck. Charlie closed my door and walked around the front to get to the driver's side, but Charity blocked him. I rolled down my window to hear her say, "I'm here, and I can put all my attention on you, and you can stop playing around with *her!*" she cried, jerking her head in my direction. "Garrett said you were done with her anyway –"

My ears perked up, and Charlie stopped cold.

"What did Garrett say?" he asked.

"That she had embarrassed you so bad that you were breaking it off with her and that I should comfort you –"

"And you believed him?"

"Of course. Garrett wouldn't lie to me."

"Garrett lies to everyone," Charlie said. "Go home, Charity. I don't want your attention or your little games. I'm with Melinda, and we're not playing."

He stepped around her and got in the truck. We sped away, and I had to turn around and look behind me. She was still standing there, her head down. A part of me felt bad for her, but not for long.

Charlie stopped at a red light and called his brother. When Garrett's assistant told him Garret was in a meeting, Charlie hissed, "I don't care if he's in a meeting with the damn President of the United States. Get him now. Tell him it's about his son."

The light turned green, and Charlie floored it. I gripped the armrest to keep from sliding into the door when he took a hard left turn. A moment later, Garrett came on the line, surrounding us with just the right amount of concern in his voice. It was smarmy as hell, and I wanted to smack him.

"Charlie? What's happened to Brandon, is he hurt?"

"I want you to stop giving Charity bright ideas."

"What on earth are you talking about?"

"You told Charity she should come out here and comfort me?"

A pause and then, "Charlie, whatever it is you're talking about, I have no idea."

"Cut the crap, Garrett. I know you hate me, but can we just agree to stay out of each other's lives?"

"That's harsh."

"She's here, you idiot. You lied to her, and she misunderstood me, and now she's here!"

I twisted the seatbelt between my fingers and listened. I'd never seen Charlie so upset.

"You've lost me," Garrett said. I heard a slight smugness now, and it pissed me off.

Charlie ended the call and pounded the steering wheel. There was silence as he drove us back to my house. He parked in the driveway and turned to face me.

"She won't leave right away," he said, and he sounded so dejected I just wanted to hug him.

"But you told her to."

"And look how well she listens," he said, smiling a little. "I just want you to promise me to you'll stay away from her."

"I thought she wasn't dangerous," I said, feeling a little afraid now.

"I don't think she is. But look at what she's doing. She's moving out here, to be with a man that doesn't want her. I'm going to call her father."

"The judge?"

"He'll make her see reason. For now, just don't invite trouble."

"You think I would do that?"

Charlie grinned. "Honey, trouble seems to follow you around." Then he kissed me.

# Chapter Nineteen

If trouble had a name, it was Charity Crandall. It seemed she was bound and determined to win Charlie back, all while making my life hell as she went along. She rented a house in the fancy neighborhood where Charlie and Brandon lived, just a block over.

"She tries to give me rides to school," Brandon told me. "She's outside waiting for me in the morning, and when I say no, she follows the bus. She's creepy as hell."

I agreed, so I couldn't scold him for swearing. Her black Porsche was spotted everywhere, and I received hourly reports from my mother, because everyone told her the gossip.

"What's wrong with her?" Mom asked with annoyance. "She can't find a man in Hollywood?"

My thoughts exactly. Charlie was special, I'd give her that, but is any man worth going after when he doesn't want anything to do with you?

Brandon started to get jumpy again while we drove. He was always looking for her, wondering if we were being followed. I tried to assure him everything was fine, that Charlie was taking care of her, and then one day I did spot her a few cars behind us as we made our way through the downtown area.

I had Brandon pull into a parking space in front of BeBe's Sweet Shop, told everyone to stay put and got out myself. Charity parked a few spaces down and got out of the Porsche.

She saw me coming at her and froze, all blue eyed innocence. I hated how good she looked and wanted to scuff her expensive Italian leather boots.

"Melinda, what are you doing here?" she asked, flipping her hair over her shoulder. "Aren't you supposed to be teaching?"

"I am. Driver's Education. See that car down there?" I pointed. "Brandon is with me, and your following us is making him nervous."

Her eyes fluttered in confusion, and the tiniest frown allowed by Botox creased her forehead.

"Following? I'm just here to buy some brownies," she said, motioning to the candy shop. "I hear they're the best in town."

"Yeah sure, brownies," I said. "Like you would eat anything containing calories."

Her shoulders straightened. "I'm offended to think you believe I'm doing something wrong. I'm just trying to get acquainted with the town." She folded her arms and glared at me. "So far, people haven't been very welcoming. I suspect this has something to do with you."

"No, it's all you, Charity. Just what do you think you're doing here anyway? Besides pissing off Charlie. He doesn't want you, don't you get it?"

"Of course he does. He's just blinded by your Midwestern looks for now."

I blinked, unsure if that was a compliment or an insult. I decided to take it as a compliment to save myself from having to slap her.

"He'll come back to me. He just needs to see me," she continued. "He'll realize what he left is better than what he has."

She motioned to her body, and I ground my teeth together until they hurt. I blew hair from my eyes and sighed.

"Stop following Brandon around," I said, and she opened her mouth to object, but I stopped her by adding, "Charlie wouldn't want Brandon upset."

That seemed to have an effect. She snapped her mouth closed and spun around toward the bakery. I turned to go back to the car, and that's when I noticed we'd attracted a crowd. I swore under my breath and ducked my head.

"Drive!" I said once I was in my seat.

Brandon took us to school, and I dismissed them. A student office worker was waiting for us. He handed me a note from the principal. I was to report immediately to Smithson's office upon receiving the note.

Damn it. What could he want? I went right to Smithson's door and knocked. He was frowning when I stepped inside.

"I've just received a complaint from a concerned parent about you," he said, staring at me with his squirrel-like eyes.

"About what?"

"You had a public altercation with a citizen on the sidewalk in front of Bebe's," he said, "while on a drive with students in a school car."

I blinked hard and frowned back at him. "What the hell?" I cried.

He stood up and hurried to shut his office door. "There's no need to curse," he said.

"Someone just called to tell you that?"

"A few minutes ago. She seemed very upset that you were throwing a tantrum in front of students."

"She?"

"Yes."

Charity. It had to be her.

"Why were you out driving with students in a school car?" he asked, tilting his head.

"Please tell me your stupidity is just an act," I said, my voice dry with disbelief.

"Melinda, there's no need —"

"I'm a Driver's Ed teacher, you dumbass!" I shouted in his face. "I was in the Driver's Ed car with three of my Driver's Ed students!"

Smithson's face flamed, and he shrank away from me, hitting the desk behind him.

"I didn't realize —" he stammered.

"I'm sure the person who called you was Charity Crandall, a woman that's obsessed with my boyfriend, Charlie Archer, Brandon's uncle. She's following us all around, causing trouble. I confronted her yes, but there was no fighting."

"Really, Melinda. Fighting? That's a bit unprofessional," he said, then circled his desk in haste as I whirled on him, claws out.

"Are you deaf? I didn't fight with her. I just told her to stop following us. I'm protecting my students. They come first, as they should with you as well."

"Of course they do. I just wanted to know what happened. You can go now." He sat down and folded his hands. I could still see they were shaking.

I let out a sharp breath and yanked open the door. Everyone in the main office was staring with wide eyes.

"Oh for Pete's sake," I muttered and left.

I went right outside and took several deep breaths to try and calm down. Whatever game Charity was playing, it was wearing down on my patience. I yanked a cigarette from my pocket and shoved it between my lips. I struck a match and was a breath away from lighting up when a hand touched my shoulder and I jumped, making stabbing motions with my lit match.

"Whoa, whoa!" Jeremy cried, ducking. "Are you okay?" Concern, and maybe a bit of fear, was written all over his face.

I shook my head, tears threatening to fall, and he pulled me into a hug, but after he tossed aside both the match and the cigarette.

"I heard about your shouting match with Smithson. Did his head explode?" Jeremy asked hopefully.

I giggled, feeling a little better.

"I had a verbal argument with Charity. She called to complain."

"Was there cake and champagne involved?" Jeremy held me at arm's length and looked me over.

"Not this time. But we were out front of Bebe's. I suppose I could have run inside and grabbed a cupcake or something."

"What does Charlie say about her?"

I stuck my hands in my jacket pockets.

"He's annoyed, but not overly concerned. So far, she's been in town for three days, and she hasn't done much more than be a bother to Brandon and me."

"I thought Charlie was going to call her father?"

I nodded. "He can't get through. Personally, I think her dad knows she's a real nut and wants nothing to do with her."

"You and Brandon need to have a serious talk with Charlie," Jeremy said.

"He's so busy right now. He wants the restaurant open by graduation so he can give the seniors a party."

"But you and Brandon and your safety are more important."

"I know."

"So will you talk with him?"

I nodded. "I'm seeing him tonight. I'll bring it up then."

"Okay. And tell him that if he doesn't take care of her, I'll have no problem stepping in," Jeremy said.

"Aww, that's so sweet of you," I said, feeling loved.

"Sure thing. She's hot."

I froze and gaped at him.

"Kidding, kidding," Jeremy teased, backing away from me.

He ran back inside before I could smack him.

* * *

Charlie was instructing a crew of decorators in the dining room when I arrived at the restaurant that afternoon. He nodded at me and I went to wait in his office while he finished. I sat in his chair behind the big desk and spun around a few times, but I soon grew bored of that and found a deck of cards in his top drawer. I was building a house with them when he came in.

"Good, I'm glad you're here," he said.

I wagged a finger at him. "Don't. Breathe."

He paused and watched as I finished my third level of cards.

"Uh, Mel?" he asked. "There's something important I need to tell you."

"Shhh," I instructed. "I'm almost done."

I was just putting the finishing touches on the roof when the voice of my nightmares said, "Charlie! What a fabulous place. It's even better than your other two!"

I gasped and my hand jerked, knocking the entire structure down. The cards scattered all over the desk and some even fell to the floor, where my jaw was currently resting as well.

"What the hell is she doing here?" I managed to get out as I stared at Charity standing in the office doorway.

Charity saw that I was there and her mouth twitched in anger, then fell right back into a smile.

"Melinda, I didn't know you'd be here," she said, all sweet and innocent.

"Same here."

Charlie stepped between us, his hands up. "Okay, before things turn ugly, I just want to say that having you both here at the same time is a good thing. I want us to talk about our current situation like normal, calm adults."

I almost spit, I was so mad, and my fist crashed down onto the desk with a loud thump.

"So much for calm," Charity said, flitting her eyelashes like some astonished baby deer.

Charlie grabbed my hand before I picked up the scissors from his pen cup. It was a little unnerving that he could read my mind like that.

"Uh, why don't we all sit down?" he suggested, giving me a look.

Charity perched in a chair while I stayed behind the desk. I noticed that Charlie didn't sit, probably just in case either of us lunged at the other, he could try and stop it.

"So, uh, what we have here, is uh, um," he stammered, "is a misunderstanding of sorts. I was hoping we could reach a solution that everyone is happy with."

Charity crossed her legs and smiled, leaning forward to tap him on the thigh.

"I don't see a problem, Charlie," she said. "You wanted me here, so I'm here. Melinda just needs to understand the way things are between us."

"Oh?" I asked. "And just how are things between you and Charlie?"

She smiled and said, "Wonderful. The way they've always been. Charlie and I are good together. What he had with you was nice also, but let's face it. Which of us is more suited to his lifestyle?"

"Oh my God, are you for real?" I demanded, getting to my feet. Charlie shifted position, moving in front of me. I looked him in the eye and said, "Charlie, sweetheart, I hate to say it, but you wouldn't be able to stop me if I tried to get at her."

He blinked and stepped aside.

"Melinda, you have some serious anger management issues you need to work on," Charity sniffed.

"And you are living in a state of denial," I shot back at her. "What does Charlie have to do to get you to realize he doesn't want you? He never did and he never will. Your presence here isn't accomplishing anything. You're nothing but a nuisance to us all."

Charity's expression changed so many times, so fast, I couldn't figure it out. She stood up and lifted her chin.

"All Charlie has to do is tell me to leave, and I'll leave. I'm not some idiot."

I threw Charlie a pointed look, and he wiped his palms on his jeans and turned to face her.

"Charity, it's over between us," he said. "There was never anything there in the first place. We dated for a while, we had some fun, and now it's over. I don't want you here, and I think you should go home. Whatever Garrett said to you, it was false, and if I somehow misled you, then I'm sorry. But I'm with Melinda now, and that's the way it is."

I smiled, satisfied at what Charlie had said. Although, I would have said it even slower and enunciated more, just to make sure she got it.

Charity stared, unblinking at Charlie for almost two minutes. It made my eyes water just to watch her. Then her whole body jolted, and she glared hard at us both.

"How can you possibly want her over me?" she screeched. "She's nothing compared to me. NOTHING!"

Her face became red, then purple, and her eyes were huge. My God, she looked almost rabid.

"Charity, calm down," Charlie said, reaching for her.

But she slapped his hands away and headed for the door.

"You want me gone? Fine. Your loss, Charlie," she spat. "But you'll be sorry, both of you. I promise you that. You'll be sorry!"

She was screaming obscenities as she left the restaurant. A moment later, we heard the roar of the Porsche, and the tires squealing as she tore out of the parking lot.

"Whoa," Charlie whispered, still in shock. "I've never seen her like that before."

"Should we call animal control?" I asked, trying to lighten the mood. "She was practically foaming at the mouth."

"Mel…"

"Sorry, sorry. Look, she's just upset because you laid it all out for her," I said. "She'll go back to LA, max out a credit card on some designer clothes and find another guy to latch on to. It'll be okay."

Charlie pulled me into a hug and pressed a kiss to my nose. "I hope you're right."

# Chapter Twenty

The reports from my mother over the next few days were that Charity's car stayed parked in her driveway, and there was little activity inside her house. I hoped it was because she was planning on leaving town soon. I hadn't seen or spoken to her since our brief meeting in Charlie's office.

On Saturday, Charlie spent the whole day at the restaurant. I left him alone to work, but I had plans for that evening with him.

"All work and no play makes me cranky," I told him over the phone. "I'm coming to pick you up at seven, no matter what. I don't care if I have to drag you out by the hair, but you're getting out of that building for the night."

He laughed and said, "No need to drag. I'll go willingly."

He was sitting out on the curb when I showed up.

"Will your truck be okay here?" I asked.

He hopped in my car and buckled up. "It'll be fine. Where are we going?"

I kissed his cheek and wiggled my eyebrows. "I made you a French dinner."

"Ooh la la."

"Don't be too impressed. It's French fries and duck."

"Duck? You made duck?"

"Well, Claire cooked the duck and brought it over. But I made the fries from scratch."

He looked at me in disbelief, and I had to confess.

"Okay, okay, so Ore-Ida made them from scratch. I just deep fried 'em."

We got back to my house and ate on the living room floor surrounded by candles, then cuddled together until he suggested we move up to my room. We extinguished the candles and went upstairs. Once we were in my bed, the real party started.

"Thank you," he whispered, trailing kisses along my shoulder.

"For what?"

"For making me stop working to take some time to play."

"Happy to help."

He claimed my mouth with his, and I relished the feel of his lips. After a moment, Charlie lifted his head and frowned, raising himself to balance above me.

"My kissing's that bad?" I asked, gasping for air. Charlie was such an excellent kisser, I couldn't get over it.

"Do you smell that?" he asked.

"It wasn't me," I said with a grin. "I'm serious, it wasn't."

But Charlie wasn't smiling. "No, no. It smells like..."

I sniffed and sat up. "Smoke. But we blew out all the candles."

Charlie hopped up and wiggled into his jeans. I would have appreciated that sight more if he hadn't said with great urgency, "Get dressed, I'll go check it out."

He threw on his shirt and disappeared into the hallway. I got dressed and was just about to go after him when he came running back, slamming the door shut behind him.

"Grab your cell phone. We need to get out and call the fire department," he ordered, going over to the window.

"What? Why?"

"Because the house is on fire, Mel." He opened the window and peered down. "We can get out this way."

I was frozen to the spot, my mind trying to process what he'd just said. Charlie motioned for me to hurry up.

I could smell the acrid scent of smoke as it curled its way under my bedroom door.

"We're going out the window?" I asked.

"We have to. The stairs are blocked."

I looked toward the door. "All my stuff is down there."

Charlie took a moment to look at me, his expression sad. "I'm sorry, baby, but it's gone."

I swallowed hard and nodded, following him onto the roof above the porch. He dropped me into the bushes and jumped down after me. Then he took my hand and we ran across the street.

My heart was lodged somewhere in my throat as I dialed 911 on my cell phone. I gave the dispatcher my address, then called my mom and my sister. A fire truck and an ambulance arrived, along with two squad cars. The police moved us further down the street.

My house was engulfed in flames, and all I could do was stare. Charlie got a blanket from the paramedics and wrapped it around my shaking shoulders. He held me against him while I shivered. My parents and Claire arrived with Piper, and then Jeremy. The group of us stood huddled together and watched in silence. Several hours later, the fire was out, and the remains of my house smoldered.

A crowd had gathered, including Gloria Milner's mother-in-law. I knew that if nosy Gloria said one word to me about my house, kind or otherwise, I was going to hit her. Charlie excused himself to talk with the police after making sure I was being looked after.

"What happened?" Claire asked me.

"I don't know. We had candles lit earlier, but I know we snuffed them out before we went upstairs," I said, shaking my head. "I know they were out."

"All of your memorabilia," Claire whispered.

"I know. It's all gone."

Claire hugged me tight. Charlie returned with a police officer.

"Ma'am, the fire department is about done here, and they'll investigate first thing in the morning. Is there somewhere you can stay?" the officer asked me.

"She can stay with me," Claire said.

I looked at Charlie, who nodded.

"It's probably best to be with family tonight," he said, hugging me.

Claire led me to her car and helped me inside. Piper climbed into the backseat, and Charlie buckled me in and kissed my hands.

"I'll call you tomorrow," he said.

I was numb. Everything I owned was gone. As we drove away from the burned ruins of my house, I saw a black Porsche parked at the end of my street. The windows were tinted, so I couldn't see inside, but I knew who was in it.

"That's her," I said, pointing to the car.

"Who?"

"Charlie's ex-girlfriend, the psycho one. That's her car! That bitch burned down my house!"

"You mean Charity?" Piper asked.

I twisted in my seat as we turned the corner, still glaring at the car. "Yes, Charity. She said we'd be sorry, and look what she's done!"

"You should tell the police about her," Claire said.

"Oh, I intend to." I slumped down and seethed. It felt better than giving into my sadness that my house was gone.

* * *

Claire knocked on the guest room door at eight a.m. the next morning, the cordless phone and a cup of coffee in her hands.

"This is for you," she said, passing me the coffee, "and the fire marshal is on the phone."

I took a sip first, felt it sear a path down my throat, and put the phone to my ear.

"I hope I didn't wake you," a cheery male voice said.

"No, no, I was up," I croaked, and he laughed.

"This is Adam Lock, the Cody fire marshal. I'm over at your house, and I just wanted to let you know what I've found."

"You're there right now?"

"Yes, ma'am. Been here since five. Anyway, I just wanted to tell you that I'm going to be putting the police on this. I'm afraid it looks like someone intentionally burned your house down."

My heart lurched. I was awake now. "Arson?"

"Yes, ma'am."

"Can you stay there please? I want to hear this in person."

"I'll be here."

I clicked off the phone, downed the entire cup of coffee and got dressed. Claire went with me, and I called Charlie on the way over. He was waiting for us when we arrived, chatting with the fire marshal.

"Miss Martin, nice to meet you," Adam Lock said, shaking my hand. He was shorter than Charlie, stockier, and about the same age as my dad. He pointed to the remains of my house. "An accelerant was placed at the front and back doors, as well as the bottom of the stairs and lit with a rag dipped in alcohol."

"Someone was in my house?" I asked in disbelief. Claire grabbed my arm and we shared a look.

"This is a matter for the police now," Adam said, frowning. "If the arsonist knew you were inside, this was an attempt on your life."

I went cold all over, and I felt Charlie tense beside me. My car had been parked outside where I left it after I picked up Charlie. If Charity had driven by, she wouldn't have seen his truck, since it was still at the restaurant, and assumed I was alone.

I needed to call the police right away. Charity Crandall had tried to kill me.

"Forget calling them," Claire said. "You need to go to the police station in person and talk to someone."

Charlie agreed with her and offered to drive me. I insisted we get Brandon so he could share his concerns about Charity. But first I checked on my car. It hadn't sustained any damage at all, aside from a little smoky smell inside. I drove it back to Claire's house and left it in the garage, out of sight. Not that Charity couldn't have found out her address, but I thought it best not to leave it in the driveway like a beacon.

Charlie sat beside me at the police station while we waited for a detective to talk with us. My knee was bouncing up and down in agitation, and I couldn't stop thinking that Charity was a serious mental case and running around town. Brandon came up to us carrying two cups of coffee. I took mine but didn't drink it. The last thing I needed was more caffeine in my system. He sat down on the other side of me and patted my bouncing knee.

"It'll be okay," he said.

I nodded while gritting my teeth. A woman in jeans and a yellow polo shirt headed toward us. I wouldn't have guessed she was a cop without the brown leather gun holster she wore. She was small, shorter than me, and she looked very young.

"I'm Detective Louise White," she said, shaking hands with us. "I'll be handling your case. Please, come with me. My desk is this way."

She moved another chair over so all three of us could sit, then she took her place at her desk and flipped to a fresh page in her notebook.

"I understand you believe you know who's responsible for your house fire," she said, looking at me with sympathetic eyes. "I'm sorry about that, by the way."

"Thank you," I said. A lump formed in my throat for the thousandth time, and I swallowed it away. "We think the person who did this is his ex-girlfriend. Her name is Charity Crandall."

Brandon gave her Charity's current address. Detective White wrote everything down and asked, "And why do you suspect it was her?"

Charlie and Brandon took over then, recounting our meeting in LA at Garrett's birthday party, her decision to follow us back here, and her actions.

"I do remember seeing something about the party," Detective White said with a half-smile.

"She kind of lost it the other day," Charlie said, looking at me.

"What do you mean by that?"

"I asked her to meet with myself and Melinda. I wanted to make it very clear to her that she was mistaken about my feelings for her, and she reacted badly."

"She told us we'd be sorry," I said. "That's a threat right?"

Detective White nodded. "Yes. Did anyone else hear her say this?"

"I don't know. There were workers at the restaurant who saw her leave, maybe they heard her. She wasn't happy," Charlie said.

"Can you arrest her?" Brandon asked.

"Well, since we don't have any hard evidence, all we can do is bring her in for questioning. I want to talk to her myself and see what she has to say. I'll go over to her place and have a chat with her."

"What should we do?" I asked.

"You should go back to your sister's house and stay there. If she did do this, she may be unstable, and I'd rather you weren't out and about."

"Will you let us know when you talk to her? What she has to say?" Charlie asked.

"I'll be sure to get in touch with you. In the meantime, I want you all to go home and try not to think about it. I know, that sounds stupid," she said when we all opened our mouths to protest, "but you should try."

We thanked her, shook hands again and then left. Charlie dropped Brandon and me off at Claire's.

"Are you going to your place?" I asked as I got out of the truck.

"I'm going to drive around. I just don't think Charity will be home when the police show up to question her."

"Why can't I go with you?"

"No. I want you to stay here. Get some sleep. You've got a hectic few days ahead of you, dealing with the insurance company and all."

He kissed me goodbye, and Brandon ushered me inside. He and Piper went downstairs to the rec room to hang out and watch a movie. Claire wanted me to nap, but that was impossible. I paced around the living room instead.

An hour later, Detective White called. We chatted for a few minutes, then I hung up the phone and sat down on a stool at the kitchen counter, watching while Claire made lasagna.

"Any luck?" she asked.

"The police have checked her house, but she's gone. They can't find her car anywhere, and none of the neighbors knows where she is," I snarled.

"How is that possible?"

"She didn't talk to anyone. She just twittered around town and stalked us."

"No, I mean, how can they not know where her car is? There aren't a lot of Porsches in town," Claire said.

"Oh. Well, that's true."

I slumped on the countertop and played with the cheese grater, running a chunk of mozzarella up and down until I scraped my knuckles against the blade. I cursed and hopped over to the sink, running my hands under the faucet. Claire got me a bandage and helped me.

"This isn't the time to start showing destructive behavior," she said.

"It's the perfect time. I want to find Charity and burn her car."

"Don't say that."

"Why not? Claire, I don't have anything. No clothes, no photographs, nothing. I lost all the Superman stuff I've been collecting since I was a kid. How fucking fair is that? And she gets away with it. Even if she is caught and it's proven that she did it, her dad won't let anything happen to her."

Claire patted my back and pulled me upstairs.

"Where are we going?" I asked.

"You're going to take a nap."

"I'm not tired."

Claire turned to me and gave me a stare that was very similar to Mom's. "Yes. You are."

She shoved me into the guest bedroom and pointed me toward the bed. Then she unplugged the phone and took it with her.

"Hey!" I said, trying to take it back. "What if someone calls for me?"

She danced away from me and swatted at my hands.

"Then I'll play messenger and take the call. You get some rest and stop thinking about revenge. It won't help or solve anything."

"It makes me feel better," I grumbled, as I climbed into bed. Claire tucked me in and left.

I tried to sleep, but there was something nagging at me about this whole situation. Charity had been watching us for days, shadowing our every move. She'd shown up everywhere. It wouldn't have surprised me one bit if she'd followed us from the restaurant to my house.

So if she'd tried to kill me, she would have known that Charlie was there too. Had she taken a turn for the worse? Instead of just obsessing over Charlie, she wanted us both dead?

I threw back the covers and slipped into my shoes. Then I opened the door, cringing when it creaked on a squeaky hinge. I waited a few seconds before tiptoeing out into the hallway.

I could hear Claire talking on the phone in the den. I sneaked out the back, stopping to grab my cell phone from the kitchen, and ran around to the side door of the garage, hopped in my car and backed out of the driveway. I saw the upstairs curtains move, and Claire peeked out at me. She opened the window to shout at me, but I was already squealing down the street. I called Charlie and asked if he'd seen Charity yet.

"I'm still out driving around," he said. "Haven't spotted her. Where are you? I hear traffic."

"I'm, um, out."

"I thought I left you at Claire's."

"You did?" I said, sounding stupid. Then I sighed. "Okay, I can't just sit still while she's out there. What if she tries to come after you?"

"Me?" Charlie laughed.

"Come on, think about it. Why wouldn't she know you weren't in the house with me?"

"That sounds grammatically incorrect somehow."

"Charlie, I'm being serious!" I said, even though I was going over it in my head, and it did sound kind of wrong. "Whatever. She would have known. She's unhinged."

"And you think chasing after her is a good idea?"

"I think she might be dangerous, and I want to be with you if we find her."

I knew he was thinking about it. "All right. I'm by the library right now. Meet me in front of the restaurant and we'll go from there."

"Good, yes. See you soon."

I hung up and tossed the phone on the passenger seat. I was about ten minutes away from the restaurant, and I figured I'd beat Charlie there. I was stopped at a red light, tapping my fingers on the steering wheel when it happened. A car slammed into me from behind, shoving me into the intersection and jolting my head back against the headrest.

The back of my little VW Beetle crumpled like a tin can, the glass from the rear window shattering onto the pavement. I screamed and clutched my head until I stopped moving. Then I did a quick limb count, realized everything was still there, opened my door and fell out.

"Are you all right?" a man asked me, helping me up.

"What happened?" I asked.

The man pointed to the car behind me, and I turned to see a black Porsche with a ruined front end.

"She ran right into you, didn't even try to stop," he said.

"Oh my God," I whispered.

I hurried over to the mangled Porsche. Sure enough, Charity was in the driver's seat, her head resting against the steering wheel and bleeding from a gash above her left eyebrow. She'd hit me hard enough to deploy the airbag, and it looked like it had hit her square in the nose.

An ambulance and two police cars arrived at the scene, and two paramedics made their way over.

"Ma'am, we need you to back up," the male paramedic said. "My partner will check you out."

The female took my hand and led me to the curb. She checked out my eyes and asked if I was in any pain.

"No, no. I hit my head, but that's all," I said, trying to see if Charity was all right.

"Melinda!"

I saw Charlie coming towards me, his eyes wild with worry. I jumped up and he gave me a tight hug.

"What happened, are you okay?"

"I'm fine. But Charity, she hit me, she –"

Charlie's head whipped around, and he watched as Charity was lifted from the car and placed on a stretcher.

"This is insane," I cried.

Charlie never let go of me while he called Claire so she could come and get me. Then he dialed Charity's father and got through by telling his assistant that his daughter had been in a car accident. Charlie told him he should come out here as soon as possible.

"And bring her a good lawyer," Charlie said, before ending the call.

I was told to go see a doctor if I started to experience any pain or dizziness, and I signed a medical release stating I had refused medical attention at the moment. We were told Charity was awake and responsive.

"We're taking her to St. John's Hospital," the female paramedic said.

Charlie waved at Claire, who sprinted toward us, then said to me, "I'm going to the hospital. You give your statement to the police and have Claire take you home."

"I don't have a home," I said, my voice flat.

"To her house. Get some rest and I'll be over later."

I narrowed my eyes at him. "Why can't you come over now?" I asked.

"I need to check on Charity."

"No you don't."

Charlie frowned. "Mel, she's hurt."

"So am I!" I cried, aware that I was sounding like a jealous twit and not caring. I was about one second away from stomping my foot in anger. "Okay, so I'm not bleeding, but I'll have a stiff neck tomorrow."

He put his hands on my shoulders and squeezed. "She's in big trouble, Mel. I'm pretty sure she hit you on purpose, and the police still want to question her about your house fire. I want to hear what she has to say."

Claire reached us then, took one look at us staring each other down, and backed up a few steps.

"Please don't be difficult about this," Charlie said. "Go with Claire. I promise you, I'll stop by later."

And then he walked away. He followed after the ambulance. After Charity. I was so mad I was shaking.

"Do you want to sit down?" Claire asked, her voice very soft.

"No. I want to talk to the cops and go to the hospital," I spat.

"But Charlie said —"

"I don't care what Charlie said." I could feel the tears starting. "That woman has taken my house and my car in two days. Two! I want to know how she expects to get away with it."

Claire was quiet after that. I gave my statement to the police and informed them of my current case file about the fire.

"Are these incidents connected?" one cop asked, scribbling in his notebook.

"They may be. Talk to the fire marshal Lock, and Detective Louise White. She's the one handling the investigation."

I followed Claire to her car and got in. She drove us toward the hospital, staring straight ahead the whole way.

"Claire, I'm sorry," I said, feeling like a complete ass.

She parked and turned to look at me.

"I'm just upset," I said, wringing my hands. "Things have been so tense between us ever since Charity arrived, and I'm hurt that he seems to be playing right into her hands." I sniffled and Claire handed me a tissue.

"Mel, it'll be okay," she said. "You can't take it personally that he went after her to the hospital. She had to be carried off on a stretcher. You walked away. He's a good man trying to do the right thing."

"I know," I wailed.

"Do you still want to go in?"

I took a moment to compose myself, looked up at the huge building and nodded.

"Yes."

She smiled and we walked inside together. We found Charlie sitting in the ER waiting room.

"How is she?" I asked.

"I thought I told you to go home."

I waved a hand. "I take direction about as well as she does. How is she?"

Charlie glanced at Claire, who just shook her head.

"Well, she's got a concussion, and her nose is broken. Other than that, she's okay. The doctors are fixing her up."

"When can we talk to her?"

Charlie's eyes widened a little. "You're not going to punch her in the nose, are you?"

"Nah, I'm thinking jaw."

He smiled. "The police want to talk to her first, but I doubt she'll say anything until her dad gets here."

"From LA? That's going to take a while," I said.

"Actually, no. He had just landed in Des Moines when I called him. Guess he'd had enough of her behavior. He's on his way here right now, and he's none too happy." He touched my neck. "Do you want to get checked out?"

I leaned into his touch. "No. I do want to be here when her dad arrives though."

"Judge Crandall is not a nice man," Charlie said. "He's strict, and he's known for his tough rulings."

"Good. Maybe he'll throw the book at Charity. Just not at her face," I added.

Claire groaned at my sorry attempt at a joke. Charlie chuckled. We hung around the hospital, waiting for Charity's dad to arrive. Charity was screaming to leave, and Detective White told her she could after they chatted. Charity refused to say anything more until her father got there. So she sat on a bed behind a curtain, arms crossed, and facial expression stormy. I walked by once, just to peek in at her, and I swear she hissed at me. An honest to God hiss! I was so startled I almost knocked over a nurse carrying a tray of urine samples. That would have been so gross.

Claire, Charlie, and I were sitting in the hard plastic chairs when the ER doors burst open. I was just beginning to feel a little tired, but that perked me up right away. We turned, expecting to see a real medical emergency, not the entourage of dark suited men and women. Charlie stood up as a tall distinguished looking man with gray hair came over. He was dressed in a tailored black pinstripe suit that appeared to be very soft. I resisted the urge to reach out and run my fingers up his arm.

"Where is she?" he demanded. His voice was deep and gruff. Claire and I shrank a little behind Charlie.

"She's okay," Charlie said.

"I didn't ask how she was, I asked where," the man snarled.

Holy shit. This was Charity's father?

Charlie pursed his lips and pointed. Judge Crandall walked away and we could hear Charity squeal with relief.

"Remind me never to commit a crime in California," Claire said, rubbing at the goose bumps on her arms.

The three of us edged our way over to the curtain. Detective White was trying to speak, but Judge Crandall wasn't listening, either because she was a cop or a woman, I couldn't be sure.

"I'm taking her home. You don't need anything from her."

"Sir, she's a suspect in an arson case. She's going to be placed under arrest," Detective White said.

"What kind of evidence do you have?" Judge Crandall asked. "Witnesses? Motive?"

The detective bristled. "A gas can was found in the trunk of her car, along with lighter fluid and rags. No one saw her set the fire, but her car was spotted in the neighborhood. Her motive is jealousy. She wanted her competition out of the way so she could get to Mr. Archer."

"Rubbish. You have nothing. I'm taking her home."

Someone yelled out, "I object!" and all eyes turned to me. Shit, had I spoken out loud?

"Excuse me?" the Judge asked, glaring at me.

I feared my insides were melting under that glare.

"She may have burned down my house," I said, moving forward, trying to ignore the pounding of my head. "She ran into me with her car. I want both things investigated."

"Who are you?"

"I'm Melinda Martin, Charlie's girlfriend."

"Oh yes. The woman who rolled around in the cake in the Sears dress," he sneered.

"It was from JC Penney, asshole!" I screamed, lunging for him.

Charlie tried to drag me away, but I wiggled away from him and went running back.

"Your daughter is a bad egg, a rotten nut," I said, pointing at Charity who was cowering and whimpering behind her father. "She needs help, and she also needs to admit to what she did. You're a judge. I can't believe you would condone criminal activity!"

"Are you questioning my morals?" Judge Crandall asked.

"I'm thinking you need to buy some more, instead of spending money on fancy suits." I reached out and touched his arm, feeling the softness of the material. "Ooh, this is fabulous. Who's your tailor?"

"Get her out of here!" he roared.

Charlie threw me unceremoniously over his shoulder and carried me away. He called for a doctor, and I was checked out. I was tired, hungry, and had a headache the size of a house going on. I was given some pain medication and then Charlie dumped me in the backseat of Claire's car and told her to get me home as fast as possible. My head was spinning and I passed out before we'd even left the parking lot.

# Chapter Twenty-One

I woke up a few hours later, and blinked away the fog that had invaded my brain. I raised my hand to rub at my eyes and winced. I tried to lift my head, but it felt like lead, stuck to the pillow. For a moment, I panicked. I could move my fingers, my toes, and I wiggled my hips. Was it possible to be paralyzed from the neck *up?*

"So you're awake."

I heard Jeremy's voice to the left of the bed, but I couldn't move to see him.

"I think I'm paralyzed," I croaked.

"You're such a drama queen. Your neck is stiff and sore. It happens with whiplash."

I relaxed a little and rolled so my lower half was hanging over the bed. Then I gripped my head in both hands and sat up.

"Owwww."

"You need a pain pill?"

"Yes, please."

He passed me a pill and a glass of water. I swallowed and looked at Jeremy.

"What are you doing here?" I asked.

"Claire called me, told me what happened. She needed me to carry you upstairs." He tapped my thigh. "You need to lay off the Cherry Garcia, babe."

"Oooh, if I wasn't injured, I'd kick your ass."

He laughed and moved to sit next to me on the bed. He started to massage my shoulders, which felt wonderful.

"What were you thinking, Mel? Going after her. You knew she was dangerous."

"I wasn't thinking. I don't think." I frowned. "I just wanted to know where she was and find out if she'd burned my house down."

"And now you have no car either."

"Fuck."

Jeremy patted my back. Claire knocked on the door and poked her head in.

"Do you want to talk to Charlie?" she asked.

"Yes," I said, reaching for the phone.

She didn't have one. Instead, she moved aside and Charlie walked into the room. He nodded at Jeremy and knelt in front of me.

"How are you feeling?"

"Like hell warmed over. You?"

"Tired."

Jeremy stood up and excused himself. He and Claire left us alone, closing the door behind them. Charlie climbed onto the bed and we curled up together. He rested his head on my chest.

"I love listening to your heartbeat," he whispered.

I stroked his hair and waited. But after a few minutes, he was out cold, snoring softly. I was antsy. I wanted to know what was going on. Was Charity still here? Was she in jail? I nudged him, and he rolled off of me, still asleep. I got up and walked to the window, opening it to get some fresh air, and I saw Claire and Jeremy standing in the driveway.

"We'll have to be careful now. Mel will find out otherwise," Claire said.

What? I crouched closer to the windowsill and listened. I knew eavesdropping wasn't polite, but I had kind of given up polite years ago.

"Why can't we just tell her? Why do we need to keep sneaking around?" Jeremy asked. "It's not doing either of us any good."

He sounded mad.

"I'm just not ready to tell her yet."

"When will you be ready? If ever?"

"That's not fair!" Claire said.

"You're right. It's not fair," Jeremy said. "To me." He walked away from her, toward his car. "Tell Mel I'll call her later."

He backed out and drove off. Claire stood outside for a moment, her arms crossed over her chest. Her lower lip was jutting out like it did when she was annoyed. Then she turned and came back inside. I moved away from the window.

That sounded like a lover's spat to me, and I wasn't sure what to make of it.

I sat back down on the bed and wondered when in hell my life had taken a sharp turn toward Crazyville.

Charlie woke up half an hour later and yawned. "I'm sorry," he said. "I didn't mean to fall asleep."

"It's okay," I said. I waited a beat, and then I pounced. "What happened at the hospital after I left?"

He sat up and propped a pillow behind his back.

"How's your neck?"

"Fine, don't change the subject."

"Charity finally talked."

"And?"

"She hit you on purpose," Charlie said. "She saw you driving, and decided to take you out. She was going to come after me next."

I nearly fell off the bed.

272

"Her father was very reluctant, but he shared with the police that Charity has spent some time in a psych ward in a very private hospital out in Washington state. She gets a little possessive, obsessive, and homicidal at the same time."

"Holy shit."

"She knew we were both in the house that night."

"She wanted to kill us."

"You for humiliating her in public, and me for spurning her and turning my back on her. Her dad thinks she had gotten over me, but when I showed up again for Garrett's party, and with a new girlfriend, she snapped."

"So what happens now?"

"Her dad's taking her home."

I rubbed my ears. "I'm sorry, I thought I heard you say he was taking her home. As in, leaving the state? Won't be held responsible for her actions? Getting away with it!"

Charlie grabbed my hand. "He's going to get her some help. Since she's confessed to the crimes, there won't be any kind of trial, and she can plead out. Her dad pulled some strings to get her released into his custody."

"That's complete and utter bullshit. What about my house? All my things? And my car?" I jumped up, then sat down when my head protested. "Just because her daddy's a judge, she gets away with attempted murder?"

"She's sick in the head, Mel. Mentally ill."

"So what does that say about you?" I spat at him. "You dated her."

Charlie frowned. "I know you're upset, but Judge Crandall wanted me to give this to you." He dug out his wallet and passed me an envelope.

"I hope it's the name of his tailor," I muttered, tearing into it. I pulled out a piece of paper and stared. "It's a check."

"Flip it over and see how much it's worth."

I shook my head and shoved it and the envelope back at Charlie. "I don't want it. He's trying to buy me."

"He's trying to make up for what his daughter did. At least think about it."

I hesitated, still holding the check. I flipped it over, my eyes dropping to the signature, a flowing squiggle that vaguely looked like Jeremiah Crandall's name. Then I checked out the number.

"This is a joke," I said.

"No. It's not. And trust me, he's good for it."

"That's an awful lot of zeros."

"He asked about your possessions, and I told him all about your Superman collection."

"Oh God," I moaned. "I'm sure he snorted at that."

"He didn't. Turns out he's a huge fan as well. He knows the value of some of the things you owned, and he wants to help you."

I looked at the check again. Still a lot of zeros.

"If I cash this, will Charity still have to take responsibility?"

Charlie nodded. "Oh yes. He's serious about getting her help."

My shoulders sagged a little. "Well, maybe…"

For that amount of money, I could buy a piece of Kryptonite.

\* \* \*

After Judge Crandall took Charity back with him to Los Angeles, things sort of turned back to normal. I was still technically homeless, and since my car had been totaled, I had to make do with a rental until I found something else. I wanted another blue VW Beetle, but Claire thought I should try something new.

"Something that won't fold so easily," she said, cringing.

I pouted about that for awhile. After all, the accident wasn't my fault.

I went through very little hassle with the insurance companies, and I received a nice sum of money to get myself back on my feet. With Judge Crandall's check, I could afford something nice that my dad wouldn't have to fix up for me. Since the school year was almost over, Claire said I could stay with her until I could devote all my time to house hunting. She didn't want me to stress out any further.

Charlie learned that Charity was being treated in that fancy psychiatric hospital in Washington state and wouldn't bother us anymore. Charlie and I tried not to think or talk about her too much. I was still a little bitter. When someone stopped at Claire's house asking for donations to a local charity, Claire told me I freaked out and chased the poor guy halfway down the street.

I don't remember any of this.

Charlie's restaurant was almost complete, and all he needed to do now was have fliers printed and run the spots in the newspapers and on television advertising the opening and the graduation party. Brandon was so much better at driving than when we first started, and I wasn't worried anymore about him passing the test.

After we finished our lesson one evening, I let myself into Claire's house, kicking off my shoes at the door.

"Hey, Mel," Piper said. She came out of the kitchen with a bowl of fresh popcorn.

"Hey, what are you doing home?" I asked. "Aren't you supposed to be at work?"

Piper sat down on the couch, folding her legs beneath her. "No date tonight?" she asked, sidestepping my question.

"Charlie's busy ordering food for the restaurant. So? You, dear. It's only 6:30. Dry cleaners closes at seven."

"I kind of, uh, quit."

"Kind of?" I sat down in the armchair, and she passed me the bowl. I took a handful and passed it back.

"My boss gave me the option to quit or be fired. I chose to quit."

"What happened?"

"He said he's been getting complaints about my attitude." She pushed her bangs from her eyes. "I'm flippant, rude, and I can't accommodate the customers. So I tried to explain that I can't accommodate everyone. I mean, when a lady brings in a shirt with a stain and we can't get it out, I'm sorry, but it's not my fault. And if the stain has been there for three months, there isn't a lot we can do."

Piper was on a rant, and I let her go, quietly munching on popcorn.

"And then tonight, a guy called and said to me, 'If I were a silk tie, and I needed to be dry cleaned, how much would I cost?'"

I let out a snort, and Piper laughed.

"That's what I did too!" she said. "And then I asked him if this was some kind of stupid riddle, and he got mad." She shrugged. "So that's that. I hated working there anyway."

"So what are you going to do this summer?" I asked. "Your mom will flip if you don't save up some extra money before you head off to college."

"I know. So, I was thinking about asking Charlie if I could work at the restaurant as a hostess or something."

I sat up. "Oh yeah. He'll go for that. As long as you don't dump someone's food in their lap. Give him a call tomorrow."

"Cool."

I looked around. "Where's your mom?"

"I don't know. She was gone when I got here." Piper tossed a piece of popcorn in the air and caught it in her mouth. "Maybe she's out with her secret boyfriend," she said, making air quotes on the word "secret" and rolling her eyes.

"So she is seeing someone," I said.

"Yup."

"Who is it?"

Piper gave me a curious stare. "You mean you haven't figured it out yet?"

"I'm slow. I'm still putting the pieces together."

"Who do you *think* it is?"

I tapped my chin with my index finger. "I think it's Jeremy."

Piper touched a finger to her nose, like in Charades. I leaned back in my chair.

"What a couple of sneaks," I said.

"We can confirm this," Piper said, smiling like an evil little scientist.

"I'm in."

She told me to call Jeremy's cell phone from mine. Then she would call Claire's from hers. If they were together, which we assumed they were, we may be able to hear them.

Jeremy picked up after three rings, a bit breathless, and I threw Piper a thumbs up.

"Hey, Jere, what're you doing?" I asked.

"Um, just working out."

*Yeah, right,* I thought. Jeremy wouldn't work out unless forced to at gunpoint.

"Do you wanna get together later? I'm not seeing Charlie tonight."

"Oh well, I kind of have other plans."

I saw Piper dial her mom, and I paused and listened. Sure enough, a cell phone rang on Jeremy's end, and the ring tone was Ode to Joy. There was a rustling of something – sheets? – and I could faintly make out my sister's voice.

"Oh, okay, sure. I'll call you tomorrow," I said.

Jeremy gave a shaky sigh, and we hung up. A minute later Piper hung up, looking quite smug.

"They've got to be at his place," I said. "No way would your mom meet someone at a hotel."

"They're so lame," Piper said, flopping down on the couch. "Why wouldn't they just tell us?"

I shook my head and stood up. "I'm going to find out."

"Whoa, you're going over there? Now?"

"Sure. It's the only way they'll be honest with us."

Piper nibbled on a thumbnail. "I don't know. Embarrassing them like that?" Then she looked at me and grinned. "Do you want my camera?"

# Chapter Twenty-Two

Claire's car was parked around the corner, and I tried not to growl as I climbed the steps to Jeremy's second floor apartment. Without knocking, I let myself in, using my spare key. Open Chinese food cartons sat on the coffee table, and I peered inside one. Mushu pork, Claire's favorite. Jeremy wouldn't touch that stuff if he were two bites away from death.

A pair of shoes that I knew belonged to Claire sat by the couch, along with a skirt that she'd borrowed from me and never returned. I snatched it up and tucked it in my purse. Hey, I needed clothes now.

I walked down the hall, spotting a bra, a matching pair of women's underpants, men's khaki slacks, and black socks. I paused at Jeremy's bedroom door and heard two people inside. It sounded like they were talking, for which I was grateful. The sex part was over.

I grabbed the doorknob and flung open the door, revealing my sister and my best friend naked in bed together. They shrieked and pulled the covers up to their chins. I rolled my eyes.

"Oh please. I've seen you both before," I said, and walked away.

I was in the kitchen when they emerged. Jeremy had put on his pants, and Claire was wearing one of his T-shirts. I sat on the kitchen counter, swinging my legs against the cabinet doors, poking around a box of Thai noodles I'd found unopened in the fridge.

Jeremy cleared his throat and then sighed, at a loss for words.

"We're sorry, Mel," Claire said. "We just didn't know how to tell you."

I nibbled on a noodle and shrugged. "How about, 'Mel, we're having sex'?"

Jeremy bristled. "It's more than that."

"Okay. 'Mel, we're dating' would have sufficed. I would have assumed the sex part eventually."

"We didn't want to hurt you," Claire said.

"So instead of being honest with me, you sneak around behind my back and let me find out on my own?"

Jeremy narrowed his eyes at me. "How *did* you find out?"

"I've been putting clues together for weeks, but Piper confirmed it for me."

Claire turned white. "Piper knows?"

"She's known since day one. You can't fool that kid," I said, pointing my fork at my sister. "She's smart, you know."

Claire buried her face in her hands and moaned. "Oh my God."

I hopped off the counter, closed the carton and stuck it back in the fridge. "What's the big deal? Why couldn't you tell me the truth?"

"We were afraid you'd be pissed," Jeremy said. "Because of how possessive you are."

I paused. "Excuse me? Wanna explain what you mean by that?"

"The Cody Theater? Ring any bells?" Jeremy asked. "There's still a part of you that's pissed at Charlie for changing it."

"Oh, well, that," I sniffed.

"It's always been you and me," Jeremy said, motioning with his hands, "and then when Claire got divorced, you invited her to join us, and then it was the three of us. I know you didn't think there'd be any problem, but that's because you never knew I've had a crush on Claire since I met her."

I felt a migraine coming on and rubbed my temples.

"Why the hell didn't you tell me?"

"Honest answer?"

"Well, duh."

"I was afraid you'd beat me up."

I blinked at him. "Huh?"

"I know you're protective of the people you love. If you thought for a second that I'd hurt your sister, I know you'd come after me with a sharp pair of manicure scissors or something. I heard what you said to Beau at the church on their wedding day. No way in hell was I going to voluntarily make you come after me."

"I'd choose hedge clippers, but anyway," I said.

"The truth is," Claire broke in, "Jeremy and I went out for coffee one night while you were out of town for some Driver's Ed meeting. Things just kind of clicked for us."

I gripped the sides of my head and squinted at them. "So, this is for real?"

Jeremy looked at Claire, who gazed back at him in such a sickening way that I had to grab the countertop for support.

"Oh, Jesus," I muttered. I threw my hands in the air and made a crossing motion. "All right, whatever. You have my blessing. Now no more sneaking around, okay?"

They nodded and grinned at me.

* * *

I was out of Dr Pepper.

Shit. I'd been so preoccupied with trying to get my life back together after the whole Charity incident, I'd let my little classroom fridge go empty. This meant I was going to have to make a special trip to the teacher's lounge, which I hated. I scrounged up some quarters and checked the hallway. No Gloria in sight, which was good. She had taken one look at my face after my house burned and my car was wrecked and had stayed away. I think Jeremy may have warned her that I was on the edge.

I sprinted down the hall and slipped into the teacher's lounge, surprised to find the place was empty. I briefly wondered if there was some sort of meeting I'd missed a memo on. It wouldn't be the first time. Ah well, better to get my caffeine and get the hell out.

I plunked my quarters in the machine and hit the button. A can of ice cold Dr Pepper rolled out to me. I popped the tab and downed a good portion of it. Then I checked my mailbox. I was sorting through the cards and magazines when two cool hands covered my eyes from behind.

I smiled. "Charlie, what are you doing here?"

I felt hot lips on my collarbone, working their way up my neck.

"You could get me in trouble if we're caught," I said, giggling as his breath tickled my skin.

Then he turned me around and kissed me full on. I had my eyes closed, but when he pushed his tongue in my mouth, I frowned and opened my eyes.

It wasn't Charlie kissing me. It was Garrett.

I screamed and shoved him away from me, and since he'd had his hand tangled in the front of my shirt, two buttons popped off. My chest was partially exposed, and I couldn't pull the material together fast enough. Garrett leered and licked his lips.

"I can see why my brother appreciates you so much," he said.

"What the fuck are you doing here?" I yelled. I wiped at my mouth and resisted the urge to spit. For about two seconds. Then I leaned over the sink and hacked away.

"I came to see you. I heard you'd handled the situation with Charity."

"Yes, and now I get you as a reward?" I asked, straightening. "Whose twisted idea of a joke is this? What are you doing in town? Does Charlie know you're here?"

"It's a surprise."

I searched for a stray safety pin or paper clip, anything to keep my shirt together. Finding nothing, I picked up a nearby stapler and used that. Garrett chuckled.

"You are amusing, Melinda. A lot like Pamela."

"Well, you won't succeed in stealing me away from Charlie."

"Give me time. I can do anything."

"Except win an Oscar," I said, and he glared. "But you are a bona fide ass. Congratulations on that. You still haven't answered my question. Why are you here?"

Garrett adjusted his tie and tugged at the cuffs of his suit jacket. "I'm here to take Brandon back."

"What?"

"I have a publicity tour coming up. I want him with me. I just wanted to make sure you knew. You are, after all, his teacher."

"And as his teacher, I think I have to tell you that it's a bad idea. His driving test is a week away, and the school year is almost over."

"He can finish driving in LA."

"No, he can't. He'll have to start the program all over again, and the requirements are different state to state. He's done it here," I said. "Let him finish."

Garrett shrugged. "Not my problem. The public loves it when Brandon is with me. The little girls just adore him. He'll make a terrific actor someday."

I looked at Garrett like he was crazy, because, well, he was. How could any parent be so inattentive to their child?

"Brandon wants to be a doctor. He wants to help people," I said.

"No, he'll be an actor. That's that."

"You are an arrogant jerk, aren't you?"

I picked up my can of Dr Pepper and moved to walk away from him. He hopped in front of me.

"Charlie's not worth it," he said, reaching out to run his hand down my cheek.

It made my skin crawl, and I slapped his hand away.

"He's worth ten million times more than you are."

I hurried past him and out of the lounge. I didn't stop shaking until the final bell rang, and then Brandon came up to talk to me.

"What's wrong?" he asked once the classroom was empty.

I swallowed the lump in my throat and said, "Your dad's here."

Brandon blinked. "What do you mean, here?"

"In town. He's come to take you…home," I said, hating the word. In my mind, I was screaming that home was here, in Cody with Charlie and me.

"I, um, does Charlie know?"

I shook my head. "I haven't had a chance to call him."

"I'll tell him. I'm sure Dad hasn't talked to him. He likes the element of surprise. Catching everyone off guard is a kick for him."

Brandon waited for me to close up the classroom and we walked outside together. He skipped riding the bus so I could drive him to the restaurant to see Charlie. When we got outside, there was a long black limousine waiting

288

at the curb. The window zipped down, and Garrett peered at us.

"Hello, son. Hop in."

Brandon slung his backpack over his shoulder and shook his head. "I'm going home now."

"That's correct. Home. With me. Let's go. You're done here."

"Dad, I don't want –"

"Do you think I care what you want?"

Brandon flinched, and I saw the little boy in him again. I wanted to leap through the car window at Garrett, and I even took a menacing step forward, but then remembered we weren't alone. So instead, I put my arm around Brandon and steered him to my little rental car.

Garrett got out of the limo and trailed after us. Lingering teachers and students stopped to gawk. Some screamed and rushed over for an autograph. I took advantage of the situation and got Brandon out of there.

Once we reached the restaurant, we ran inside. We found Charlie in the office, going through lists from his suppliers.

"Hey, guys," he said, smiling. "What's up? Oooh, I don't like those looks. What now?"

"Dad's here," Brandon said. He dropped into a chair, slumping down and crossing his arms over his chest.

Charlie rolled his eyes heavenward. "The hits just keep on coming. What does he want?"

"He wants to take Brandon back with him. Just pull him out of school with less than two weeks left to go. What kind of creep is he?" I asked.

"A special kind," Charlie said, scrubbing a hand over his face. "Where's he staying?"

Brandon and I shrugged.

"You don't know?" Charlie asked.

"Uh, we kind of ran away from him," Brandon said.

Charlie picked up his phone. "I'll call his cell."

Brandon and I left him to make the call and wandered around the restaurant. We found ice cream in the walk-in freezer and sat down at the stainless steel counters to dig in. As we ate, we could hear Charlie yelling.

"Oh man," Brandon murmured. Then he raised his head and looked right at me. "If you had a way to stop this forever, this fighting between Dad and Charlie, would you do it? Even if it hurt someone?"

I paused with my spoon halfway to my mouth. "That depends on who it would hurt, and how bad," I said, my eyebrows furrowing in confusion.

Before Brandon could say anything more, Charlie came into the kitchen.

"He's going to let you finish the school year, but then you have to go with him," he said.

"I don't want to. I want to stay here."

"I know, but," Charlie sighed and his voice got soft. "I have no legal say in how to take care of you."

I threw my spoon into the tub of ice cream, disgusted.

"This is horse shit," I said, slapping my hands on the counter. The sound echoed around us. "He can do that? Just swoop in and take Brandon away?"

"He's Brandon's father," Charlie said, sitting on a stool beside him.

Brandon had stopped eating. I looked at both of them. They had identical looks of defeat on their faces, and it sickened me to the core.

# Chapter Twenty-Three

Friday rolled around and Garrett was still in town, staying at one of the local hotels. It didn't take a network of Mom's gossips to tell us what he was doing because he was on the news, in the papers, smiling his cheesy grin and charming everyone in sight. Brandon was miserable, even though Charlie and I tried as hard as we could to cheer him up. All he saw in his future were unending press tours and a lifetime of being stuck in front of a camera with his father. It killed me to see him so down.

We were hanging around the restaurant's dining room, marveling at how fast the work crews had finished and what a great job they had done when Garrett showed up unannounced. Brandon had been smiling, but needless to say, our happy mood took an immediate turn for the worse.

"What's up, Garrett?" Charlie asked, trying to be civil.

"I just wanted to see the place. You've outdone yourself, little brother."

"Thanks."

"Of course, I can't say how successful it'll be, considering its location..."

Garrett let the statement hang, and I sucked in a breath at Charlie's expression.

"It'll do just fine," he said through clenched teeth. "Was there something you needed?"

Garrett tucked his hands into his pants pockets and grinned. "I've come to let you know that I've changed my mind. I'm heading back to LA tomorrow, and Brandon's going with me."

Charlie stepped forward. "You said he could stay until the end of the school year. Why change the plans now?"

"My agent called. He's pushing up the start of my press tour. We head out Sunday morning."

"I don't want to go yet, Dad," Brandon said. "I'm not done here. Melinda's worked so hard with me this semester to help me get my driver's license."

Garrett sighed, but it wasn't one of compassion. It was annoyance I heard.

"We leave on a flight out of Chicago at 3:00 tomorrow afternoon," he said, as if Brandon hadn't spoken at all. "I'll expect you to be ready to leave here by nine in the morning."

Charlie placed a hand on Brandon's shoulder. "Will you go wait in the kitchen please?" Charlie asked. "I just want to talk with your dad a minute."

Brandon nodded and turned to go. I decided to go with him, but stopped when Charlie asked me to stay. Brandon threw a questioning glance at me, and I shrugged in response.

"Let's sit down," Charlie said.

We sat at a round table, the chairs creaking beneath us. It was like the chairs could sense the tension through our butts or something. The thought made a giggle bubble up in my throat, and I coughed it away. I folded my hands in my lap and waited.

"Can't we work something out that'll keep everyone happy?" Charlie asked. "Brandon could join you somewhere along the press tour, after he's done with school. Would it be that bad to let him skip a few interviews?"

"You're missing the point," Garrett said, tapping his fingers along the linen tablecloth. "Brandon is an integral part of these kinds of tours. I need him there."

"You use him, and it's not right. Give the boy a chance to finish a school year with his peers. He's never done that before, and he may even thank you for it."

"His education is important, I'll admit. It's why he's had nothing but the finest schools and tutors. Until now. No offense, Melinda," Garrett said with a smirk.

Beneath the table, I raised both middle fingers in his direction.

Garrett stood up and smoothed his pant legs. "We're leaving tomorrow. Don't worry about it, Charlie," he said, seeing his brother's look of defeat. "Brandon got his way by asking to live with you for awhile. But now that's over. Look, if it makes you both feel better, I'll hire someone to ensure he finishes his driving education. He'll be fine."

Charlie and I just sat there and watched Garrett walk out. A few minutes later, Brandon emerged from the kitchen and plunked a huge carton of chocolate and marshmallow ice cream on the table, along with three spoons. Without a word, we dug in.

* * *

Charlie paced around his living room, running his hands through his hair, removing and replacing his glasses again and again. Brandon was upstairs in his bedroom with Whip, packing.

"What do I do?" he asked. "I can't let Garrett take him, not now. He's almost done with the school year.

295

He's better here, and he doesn't want to go. But I'm not his father."

I tried to reach out to him, to get him to just stop and sit down, but he jerked away from me.

"Charlie. Charlie!" I cried, finally catching his attention.

He spun to a stop and looked at me. I took a deep breath and grabbed his hands. He gave a shaky sigh and said, "Maybe, maybe I need to let him go. I know it isn't what you want to hear," he continued, even as my eyes widened and my mouth opened. "But maybe he needs to stand up to his father on his own. Like I did."

"You're just going to let him go? Let Garrett ruin his life by dragging him around on publicity tours. Damn it, Charlie, Brandon's adjusted here. He has friends, a real life. You want to just give all that up?"

"No, of course not. I've worked hard to help Brandon, and so have you. I don't want to see that work go down the drain any more than you do. I'm just saying that maybe this is the time for Brandon to show his father the kind of person he is."

I pulled away and shook my head. "No. Garrett's being his usual selfish bastard self, and he's dragging his son down with him."

He followed me as I circled around the couch. "I know you love Brandon. I do too. But I'm not his father, and I can't save everyone."

I whirled around so fast that I stumbled and knocked into him.

"You're not even trying! You could save him," I said, my voice sharp. "If you cared about him, you wouldn't let Garrett take him. You'd go to court and fight for him."

"On what grounds? Just because my brother is an asshole doesn't mean he doesn't love his son. And he's always been cared for. That's not enough for me to get involved in a custody battle that I wouldn't even win. If anything, Garrett would use this crap with Charity against me and say that my personal life is plagued with issues. He might even drag you through the mud."

"Me? What could he say about me?"

"Have you forgotten about your one-on-one match in his birthday cake?"

My mouth dropped open as I realized he was right. Garrett could make Charlie look really bad.

"I'm not a superhero, Mel," he said. "I can't just swoop in and take him away. I'm not his father."

"You're more of his father than Garrett. You should at least give a damn! If not about me or us as a couple, at least about Brandon."

Charlie stared at me, his eyes flashing. "You think I don't?"

"What?"

He leaned on the arm of the couch. "You're still mad at me for the theater, aren't you?"

I blinked and frowned. "No, I —"

"And for taking you out to LA in the first place, and for letting Charity burn your house down."

"What? Charlie –?"

"And wrecking your car," he said, his voice rising. "I couldn't save you from any of that, and now you think I can't help my own nephew. Is that it?"

I backed away from him. "Stop it, you're talking crazy. You're upset."

"I have every right to be upset. There's a boy upstairs that's about to have his life completely fucked up by his father, and there's nothing I can do about it!"

I didn't blink as I said, "Like your father did to you."

Charlie's jaw was rigid, and then it started twitching with anger.

"This has nothing to do with my father."

"Bullshit. He screwed up by not accepting you for what you were. He didn't like that you weren't following in his footsteps, and he made you very aware of that fact. Just like Garrett does with Brandon."

I felt a wave of dizziness wash over me as I looked at Charlie. He was so angry, and I knew I had pushed the limits of our relationship by mentioning his father.

The doorbell rang, causing us both to jerk our heads toward the door. Charlie opened it and in walked Garrett.

Great, just great. Exactly what we needed at this moment.

"I could hear your conversation halfway down the driveway," Garrett said with a smile.

"What are you doing here?" I demanded.

"I just stopped by to see how my son was doing. Is he ready to leave tomorrow?"

Charlie closed the door and came to stand in front of his brother.

"No."

"Excuse me?"

"I said no. Brandon's not ready to leave with you tomorrow. He's wants to stay here, with me."

Garrett pursed his lips. "Why would he want to do that?"

"Because he doesn't want to be used anymore. He's through being your pawn," Charlie said.

"Oh? He hasn't said anything to me about this."

Charlie straightened. "He's tried. You just refuse to hear him."

"You think so?"

"I know so. Let him stay, Garrett. If you have any heart in you at all, you'll leave him with me."

"Well, baby brother," Garrett said, flicking lint from his suit jacket, "you don't have any say here. He's not your son."

I shivered at the cruel way Garrett's lips twisted as he said those last four words, at the way Charlie's shoulders slumped in defeat.

Garrett turned to me. "And what does the lovely teacher have to say?"

I looked to Charlie who remained motionless, then focused my attention on Garrett. I squared my shoulders and glared at him.

"I think you're an asshole for using your own kid like this, for publicity purposes. It's not right, and you know it."

Garrett tilted his head. "You seem to think you know a lot about us. One trip to Hollywood and you're an expert." He leered at me and moved closer. "Have you told him about us yet?" Garrett asked, slipping an arm around my waist. He looked at Charlie and smirked. "She's got a great mouth."

I reared back and slapped him with all my might. He staggered a bit, holding his cheek.

"She's so feisty," he said.

Charlie stood frozen to the spot, his face contorted in anger and betrayal.

"Nothing happened," I said, feeling my stomach give a violent flip. "I swear, Charlie."

"What's he talking about then?" Charlie's voice was just above a whisper and his eyes were glittering with fury.

"He caught me alone in the teacher's lounge at school," I explained. "He sneaked up behind me, I thought he was you!"

"You kissed him?"

I shook my head and took a step toward Charlie, but he backed away.

"No! He kissed me. I pushed him off –"

300

"She's a wildcat," Garrett threw in.

I screamed at him, "Shut the fuck up!"

But to my horror, Garrett continued. "Nice birthmark on her left breast too."

I could only stare in shock. Charlie was shaking, his hands curled into fists at his sides. Garrett straightened his tie and cleared his throat.

"I'll be at my hotel. I expect Brandon there in the morning by nine," he said. Then he smiled at his brother, nodded at me, and left. The front door closed with a definite click, and I thought my knees would give out.

I swallowed hard, trying to speak.

"Charlie, I -"

"Just go."

"What?"

"Get out."

"Please, let me explain -"

Charlie blinked several times and glared at me. "You've said enough. Please go," he said, his voice firm and leaving no room for discussion.

I thought everyone who ever claimed to be able to feel their heart breaking was full of crap, but at that moment, I knew it was true. The pain in my chest was like someone was tearing my insides apart as I gathered my coat and purse. I paused at the door and said, "I'm sorry."

Charlie remained silent.

Once I was in my car, the floodgates opened. I cried harder than ever before and wondered what the hell had just happened. I drove around for about a half hour, not sure where to go. My house was gone, Claire and Piper were away on a college visit, and Jeremy was with them, and I was in no mood to face my parents like this. I headed back to my sister's, after stopping for a fresh pint of Cherry Garcia.

The house seemed so empty with everyone gone, which didn't help my mood. I checked my cell phone, but no one had called. I took it as a sign that Charlie and I were really over.

I tried to see the bright side by thinking at least I would have the whole summer to get over him. But who was I kidding? It was going to take a lot more than a summer to get over Charlie Archer. I dished out the ice cream and settled onto the living room couch. I was just about to turn on the TV when I heard the distinctive creak of the porch steps. My heart rate kicked up a notch, thinking it was Charlie.

I left the ice cream on the coffee table and went to see. I could tell it was a man, and judging by the black hooded sweatshirt, it wasn't Charlie outside, and it wasn't Garrett either, thank God. When the figure looked up, I gasped and flung open the door.

"Brandon! What are you doing here?"

"Can I come in please?"

I stepped aside and he hurried past me.

"Does Charlie know you're here?" I asked.

Brandon shook his head, his dark hair falling over his eyes, just like Charlie's.

"I sneaked out. Please don't call him. I needed to talk to you."

I nibbled on my thumbnail, torn between letting Charlie know his nephew was with me and wanting to hear what Brandon had to say. "He'll be worried when he realizes you're gone."

"This is important," he said, pulling an envelope from his back pocket. "I don't want to go back with Garrett. I want to stay here, with you and Charlie."

"Right now, I'm not too sure about Charlie and me," I sighed. "But come on, I've got ice cream."

After he had his own bowl, Brandon handed me an envelope. It was long, worn around the edges and bent, and may have once been a bright white.

"What is this?" I asked.

He swallowed a bite of ice cream, looked me square in the eye and said, "My future."

Something about that made me shiver.

"Just open it," Brandon urged.

I stared at the envelope, afraid of what it held. "Are you sure you don't want Charlie to be here?"

"It's about Charlie."

Slowly, I pulled the contents out and placed them in my lap. There were three items: a photocopied birth certificate, a gold cross pendant, and a three page letter to

Brandon. I glanced up and saw him sitting on the edge of the couch, wringing his hands together. Our ice cream sat and melted in their bowls.

"This came to me a year ago, at the end of last February. I had just turned fifteen. It's from my mom," he said, his voice soft. "Do you know about her?"

"A little," I said. "Charlie told me she died not long after you were born."

Brandon nodded. "That's what I believed too."

I looked at him. "What are you saying?"

"My mom didn't die when I was a baby. She didn't die until over a year ago. Everything about my life is a lie."

I rubbed my temples, wishing for some alcohol. "I think you need to start at the beginning," I said.

Brandon took a deep breath. "My mom, Pamela, was Charlie's girlfriend first. They were together for awhile, and Charlie liked her a lot. He brought her home for a visit, and she met Garrett. He seduced her, stole her away from Charlie. Garrett was always jealous of his brother."

I noticed him not calling Garrett "Dad" and a funny feeling started in the pit of my stomach. I must have had a strange expression on my face, because Brandon gave me a sad smile.

"You see where this is going," he said. He picked up the birth certificate and pointed to the date. "Everyone always said I was born premature, but still a healthy baby. My mom was already pregnant before she left Charlie."

"Oh my God," I breathed.

"My grandfather was still alive then, still a major name in Hollywood, and Garrett's acting career was just starting to take off," Brandon said. "Grandpa thought she'd make a perfect trophy wife, and having a kid would boost Garrett's popularity. He suggested they keep this to themselves, even though they all knew Charlie was the real father. Garrett convinced her that Charlie would never be able to take care of her and a baby, so she agreed to go along with the lie, even letting Garrett put his name on the birth certificate. But after I was born, she changed her mind. She wanted to come clean, tell Charlie the truth, but Garrett wouldn't let her. So he paid her off. He paid someone else to fake her death certificate and moved her out of the country. She'd been living in Paris, and he was still paying her a monthly stipend up until she really did die of cancer. She was never brave enough to tell Charlie the truth, but when she found out she was sick, she wrote a letter and left it with her lawyer to give to me after she was gone. Everything I just told you was explained in that letter."

I stared at the pages, turning them over and over in my hands.

"The pendant was my mother's," Brandon said. "Charlie gave it to her, and she kept it."

I swallowed past the lump in my throat and asked, "Why haven't you said anything to Charlie? To Garrett?" My mind was racing. Nothing made sense anymore.

"I didn't know Charlie. I only ever saw him at Thanksgiving and Christmas, maybe my birthday. Grandpa and Garrett didn't like it when Charlie was around, even after he became successful with his restaurants. But I wanted to know him after this came to me."

"Garrett's been tormenting Charlie for years, using you. How awful!" I said. My opinion of Garrett Archer dropped from *Pond Scum* to *Crap That Pond Scum Wouldn't Even Stick To.*

"But see?" Brandon said, getting excited. "I don't have to go back with Garrett. I can stay with Charlie. My real dad. And you can move in with us, and we can be a family."

Tears sprang to my eyes as I looked at the earnest expression on his face.

"Brandon, I don't think Charlie wants to see me right now."

"I know you had a fight. I could hear most of it, but you can forgive him, right?"

I lurched forward and pulled him into a hug.

"You can make this right, can't you?" Brandon asked.

I cried as I held him. I didn't know what I could do at that moment.

# Chapter Twenty-Four

I moved away from the window when I saw Charlie's black truck pull up in front of the house. He had been civil on the phone when I called him to tell him Brandon was with me, but I could tell he wasn't pleased.

"He's here," I said.

Brandon rose from the couch and shoved his hands in his jeans pockets.

"Are you sure you don't want to be with me when I tell him?" he asked.

I shook my head. "This is something you need to do in private."

He nodded and hugged me. Charlie rang the doorbell, which just didn't feel right to me. I opened the door, and we stared at each other for a long minute, not speaking.

Then he sighed and said, "Let's go, Brandon."

That was it. Brandon slipped past me and followed Charlie to the truck. Once seated in the passenger seat, Brandon waved at me. I waved back as Charlie roared away.

After they were gone, I didn't know what to do. I had no one to turn to, and I didn't want to stop and think about what had happened to my relationship.

So I started cleaning. I decided to organize Claire's collection of CDs and DVDs. I was busy working, alphabetizing the CDs when my phone rang an hour later. I jumped up and grabbed it, stabbing at the buttons to answer it.

"Hello?" I asked, out of breath.

"Melinda," Charlie whispered, his voice shaking. "I-I don't know what to do."

It seemed to be the emotion of the evening. I slid to the floor and leaned against the wall. "I know. I don't either."

"What if it's true? What if Brandon is my son?"

"Then you continue to care for him, and love him, and protect him," I said, cradling the phone close to my ear. "What changes is that he calls you Dad instead of Garrett."

"That slimy sonofabitch," Charlie spat. "He robbed me of all these years with Brandon. And my dad! He made me feel stupid and used because Pamela dumped me for Garrett, when he knew all along that I was Brandon's father. If he were still alive, I could kill him for that. Garrett too."

"Just stay away from Garrett," I said, sitting up. "Get a paternity test done first, just to prove that Brandon is 100% yours. Then Garrett has nothing to threaten you with."

"I'll schedule one first thing tomorrow," Charlie said.

We were quiet for a moment, until Charlie said, "Melinda, I'm sorry."

I let out the breath I'd been holding. "I am too. I should have told you about Garrett."

"What happened? How did he know about your birthmark?"

I gulped and said, "He pulled open my shirt."

"He attacked you? God, I will kill him," Charlie growled.

"Please, just let it go. It didn't go any further, and I didn't want to tell you because I knew you'd be angry. Just leave it alone."

"Melinda, about us," Charlie said, sounding hesitant. "I don't know if we, if I can do this. I think we need to, to just hold off for a bit. I need to get this straightened out with Brandon…"

His voice trailed off and I felt tears slip down my cheeks. "I know, it's okay. Take your time."

"I do love you."

"I know, and I love you too. And Brandon. I'll be here if you need me."

I could hear Charlie's ragged breathing on the other end and knew he was crying, just like me. And that was the end of our conversation. I clicked off the phone, buried my head in my hands and sobbed.

* * *

I was still in bed when my cell phone rang at 9:05 the next morning. I'd dragged myself there after falling asleep on the living room floor. I grabbed at the phone and pulled it under the blankets with me.

"Hello?" I asked, sounding croaky and sick.

"Would you mind telling me where the hell my son is?"

I threw off the blankets and sat up.

"Garrett? How did you get my number?"

"Yes, it's me," he said, his voice harsh and loud. "It's not like information is hard to get, especially when you're a celebrity. Now where the hell is my son? I wanted him here at nine." I gulped hard and Garrett yelled, "Is he with you? Is Brandon there?"

I held the phone away from my ear, trying to think. Should I tell him what I knew?

"Melinda? Are you listening to me?" Garrett continued. "You better find my brother and tell him to deliver Brandon to me in thirty minutes or I'll have him arrested for kidnapping."

Something inside me snapped. I got out of bed and began pacing around the room, gearing up to rip Garrett Archer a well-deserved and long-awaited new one.

"Listen up," I hissed. "Brandon is not some accessory to be brought to you whenever you bellow. He's a human being, a much better one than you, I might add."

"Spare me your drama," Garrett broke in, which pissed me off even more. "Just because you're fucking my brother doesn't give you any right to lecture me."

"Oh? Well then," I said, punching the air as I spoke. "Just because you're jealous of your brother doesn't give you any right to steal his son and pretend he's yours!"

I was out of breath and dizzy from yelling, so I sat down on the bed. There was silence for a full sixty seconds from Garrett. I know because I counted, and suddenly I knew everything Brandon had told me was true.

"What the hell did you just say?" Garrett growled.

"I think you heard me just fine," I said, calmness settling down around me like a warm blanket. I examined my nails and decided I'd go get a manicure today, treat myself.

"I don't know what kind of nonsense Charlie has been telling you -"

"It was Brandon. Something about his mother not dying when he was a baby and living in Paris."

He stopped talking again, and I had to slap a hand over my mouth to stop from giggling. I was giddy over my ability to render this man speechless.

"Where are they?" he asked a moment later.

"I'm not sure. Charlie said they were going to get tested. You know, tested for paternity?"

I was swinging my legs over the side of the bed, bouncing. I knew it was wrong to take such pleasure in what I was doing, my mother would have called it "sadistic" but I was enjoying making Garrett squirm.

"Fuck!" he exclaimed and hung up.

I called Charlie's cell phone.

"Melinda, what's up?" he asked, his voice soft and tired.

"Garrett just called looking for Brandon."

"Yeah, he's already called us too, but we're not answering."

"Where are you?"

"In a clinic in Des Moines. We're next."

My heart beat faster. "How's Brandon?"

"A little freaked. He won't sit still."

"Tell him I love him," I said. "And you too."

"I know. We love you too."

I swallowed the lump forming in my throat and said, "I kind of let Garrett know what you were doing."

"You did?"

"I kind of, uh, rubbed it in," I said, sounding sheepish, but Charlie just laughed.

"I can just imagine how excited you were. I can almost see your impish smile."

"Yeah, well, I'll let you go now. Good luck."

"Thanks."

He paused, and I could sense that he wanted to say something more, but he didn't.

We disconnected and I rubbed at my eyes, feeling an overwhelming urge to get out of the house. The results of the test wouldn't be in for at least a day, and since today was Saturday, it was likely nothing would be known for sure until Monday. If I stayed home, I'd drive myself insane.

So I showered and dressed and headed out in my little rental car, hating every minute of it. I was worried about Charlie and Brandon, and about Charlie and me. I wasn't sure we could recover from this. We had apologized, but I could tell there was still some tension between us, there had been for weeks, ever since we came back from LA. I didn't want to admit that part of our problem was me and my stubborn streak.

I doubted that I was good enough for Charlie, and I wasn't sure he had shown me that I was. Or maybe he had, and I was just too stupid to realize it. It was all messed up, and it pissed me off.

I spent $300 on new clothes and useless crap that I didn't need, and it didn't make me feel any better. I skipped lunch and drove back to Claire's house. Claire, Piper and Jeremy were home by then. I walked inside, dropped all of my bags on the floor and stared at them.

Claire took one look at my face, my disheveled appearance and circles under my puffy eyes, and took my hand and pulled me to the living room. She sat me down on the couch and asked, "What's wrong?"

"Everything," I said, feeling my lower lip start to tremble.

Jeremy retreated to the kitchen and brought back some ice cream and spoons. Piper hovered in the arched doorway and bit her lip, watching us.

"Garrett wants Brandon to go back to LA with him for a publicity tour," I began.

"Oh, that's bad. Why can't Garrett let him finish the school year?" Jeremy asked.

"Because he's an asshole," Claire threw in, then she patted my hand. "Go on."

"Brandon doesn't want to go. He doesn't want to go with Garrett ever. And he might not have to." I took a deep breath. "Garrett may not be Brandon's father."

Jeremy dropped a spoon full of ice cream onto the carpet. "What? Then who is?"

Claire gasped and covered her mouth with her hands. "Charlie?"

I nodded.

"How?" Jeremy asked.

"Long story short, Charlie's ex-girlfriend left him for Garrett, but she was already pregnant. She told Garrett the truth, but he paid her to keep her quiet. She recently died in Paris. Brandon just found out, and he's been waiting for the right moment to say something."

"Where are they?" Piper asked.

I looked over my shoulder at her. She was hunched over, almost curled in on herself, her face pale and her hands shaking.

"Piper, did you know?" I asked.

Claire whirled around. "Piper!"

My niece nodded and came over to sit by us.

"Brandon told me a few weeks ago, on prom night. When Ray was trying to dance with me and Brandon stepped in, Ray started saying awful stuff about how his dad didn't want him, and how even Charlie was embarrassed by him. It hurt him, and he confided in me. He made me promise not to tell. He didn't know how to tell Charlie, and he wanted to make sure Charlie wouldn't reject him."

"How could you keep that a secret?" Claire asked.

"Because Brandon is my friend and he asked me to."

Simple as that. If only everything were that easy.

"Where are they?" Piper asked again.

315

"In Des Moines, getting a paternity test done."

"Oh God," Claire said. "This is like a soap opera."

"And it gets better. Or worse, depending on which way you want to look at it," I said, shrugging. "I think Charlie and I broke up."

Complete and total silence. Not what I was hoping for.

"What the hell happened? What did you do?" Jeremy asked, and he sounded so mad that all of us jumped.

"You're going to blame me?" I asked in disbelief.

"Well?" he prompted.

I looked around at everyone and said, "It wasn't entirely my fault. We both said things that we didn't mean, and it went very wrong."

Even as I said it, it sounded lame.

"Look, it's done. I don't know if we'll be able to fix it. So please, just let it go."

Claire shushed Jeremy with a look and turned to me. "So when do we find out for sure if Brandon is Charlie's son?"

"Probably by Monday. I don't know if the clinic is open on Sundays."

"What if it's true?" Piper asked.

"Then he gets to stay here, and Garrett can stop using him as a prop to make himself look better to the public," I said.

Piper nodded. "That is the best thing that could happen to Brandon."

I reached over and gave her a hug. I couldn't have agreed more.

Sunday was the slowest day of my life, and I drove Claire nuts with my mindless pacing. Brandon texted Piper, telling her they were staying in Des Moines until they received the results. They hadn't heard anything more from Garrett.

Monday morning, I went to school, and I wasn't at all surprised to see that Brandon was absent. I worried about his driving test on Wednesday, but there wasn't much I could do about it.

Charlie called me during my lunch hour. I took my cell phone and sat in the corner of my classroom, cupping it close to my mouth.

"He's mine," Charlie whispered, and then he broke down and cried.

I wanted to reach through the phone and hug him, but since I couldn't, I said supportive things, trying to calm him down.

"God, Mel, I have a son. Brandon is my son," he said, trying out the word.

"What about Garrett? Have you told him?"

Charlie took a deep breath. "I did. He didn't apologize or anything. Just hung up on me."

"How's he going to explain this to the public?"

"I don't know, but I'm sure he's had a plan since day one. He'll spin it somehow so he still ends up looking good."

Silence dropped between us.

"Well, I have to go. Brandon will be in school tomorrow," Charlie said.

"Okay. Give him a hug for me," I said.

"I will."

He disconnected, and I held the phone to my ear for a full minute after that, not wanting to think that much more had been ended than just a phone call.

After school was out for the day, I drove home in a state of confusion. My mind was just too full of thoughts and feelings about my life over the past few months. I'd known it was going to be different the second I laid eyes on Charlie, but I hadn't known how.

With Charlie, I'd found something special. I'd learned that I could give someone my love and not expect anything in return. And I'd also learned the benefits of good house and car insurance.

I hadn't realized it, but I'd turned toward the theater. I was surprised to see Charlie's truck outside, but no work crew anymore. Even though Charlie had called me at school earlier, I still wanted to talk to him in person. Brandon was probably there too, and he deserved a serious hug. So I pushed aside my jumbled thoughts and stopped to say hi.

I knocked on the door and poked my head in. The lights were on, and I gawked at what had been finished so far. The walls were painted a rich green and framed artwork hung from brass hooks. The hostess stand was a dark oak, and stood just in front of and to the left of the bar. The bar itself was half stocked with a long mirror reflecting the pristine bottles and glasses.

I heard voices coming from the main dining room, so I headed in that direction. Brandon and Charlie were sitting on the steps having a serious conversation. I didn't want to interrupt, so I backed away.

Brandon saw me though, and jumped up.

"Mel!" He hurried towards me and I grabbed him in a hug. "Isn't it great news?"

"It's wonderful," I said.

Brandon stepped back, and I nodded at Charlie who'd followed.

"Hi," I said, feeling very shy and out of place. "I didn't mean to barge in."

"You know you're welcome anytime," he said.

I didn't move to touch him, and he didn't move toward me either. I watched Brandon's expression of joy disappear. I rocked back and forth on my heels, trying to come up with something intelligent or witty to say, and I got nothing.

"Okay, well, I'll just, uh, go now," I said, turning to leave.

Then I froze. Standing in the doorway was Garrett, dressed in a designer suit and shiny Italian shoes. He looked just as poised and in control as ever, although I knew he had to be seething just below the surface.

*Hmm, maybe he's a decent actor after all,* I thought.

319

"Well isn't this a happy little scene," he said.

"What do you want?" Charlie asked.

"Can't I drop in and see how my brother and my son are doing?" Garrett asked, holding his hands out.

"You mean *my* son?"

Garrett's smile faltered a bit. "All right, all right. So where do we go from here?"

I glanced between the three, feeling even more out of place than usual. I knew I didn't belong there; this was a family matter.

"You're going back to LA, and you're going to leave Brandon alone," Charlie said. "I can't expect you to apologize for what you and Dad have done, so you can't expect me to forgive you."

"Let's be reasonable here. I did what I did because I didn't think you could handle the truth," Garrett said, and Charlie laughed.

"This isn't some fucking Jack Nicholson movie. It's real life. And if we're going to be honest here, you lied to me and used Pamela to benefit your own pathetic movie career. Let's face it, Gare," Charlie said, tilting his head as he spoke. "Before you got Brandon, you were doing crappy bit parts. You wanted to be a leading man, gain the sympathy of the public. What better way to do that than to suddenly be a widowed father?"

"That's not fair. I care about Brandon."

"You're such a self-centered ass —" Charlie started, but was stopped by Brandon's hand on his shoulder.

Brandon stepped forward, his jaw set.

"You always said I should stand up for myself and be a man," he said, looking straight at Garrett.

"Finally, you're listening to me," Garrett said, nodding.

I thought I would puke, so I took a step back, grabbing the wall for support.

"Yes, I am. So hear me when I say this," Brandon said. "I don't want you in my life. If you leave right now, we won't tell the press about what you've done."

"What?"

"Can you imagine the scandal that would cause?" Brandon continued, stepping forward. "It would ruin the good name of Archer."

"You can't —"

"Why can't I? Which tabloid rag would be best for me to call first?"

Garrett balled his hands into fists. "You wouldn't do that. You hate the spotlight so you wouldn't jump right in front of the cameras with this."

"Garrett, I'll do anything I can to make sure you don't hurt us anymore," Brandon said.

He sounded very tired, yet brave, and I couldn't have been more proud of him.

Garrett glared at Brandon and Charlie. Then his gaze slid to me and stayed there. I shivered.

"This is not her fault," Charlie said, stepping in front of me. "This started almost seventeen years ago when you decided to seduce Pamela. The only person here that's at fault is you, Garrett."

"I can't believe you'd want to stay here," he said to Brandon. "I can give you so much more, so much opportunity. What can he give you?"

Brandon looked to Charlie and smiled. "A home."

I let out a little cry and covered my mouth with my hands. Garrett swore under his breath and turned to leave, hopefully walking out of our lives forever.

# Chapter Twenty-Five

Wednesday morning. Time for Brandon's driving test. He was calm, joking around with the girls and laughing. He seemed settled, somehow, and that made me happy.

What made me unhappy was the fact that Charlie and I hadn't seemed to connect again. I knew there were still feelings there, but it was as if we had run out of things to say to each other. Every thought I had of him somehow led back to the bad stuff that had happened. Maybe we had made a mistake in trying to be together.

Brandon drove with ease through town and even pulled off a perfect parallel parking downtown. He passed with flying colors, and I was so proud of him.

At the end of the day, he waited to talk with me.

"Garrett's releasing a statement," he said.

"Wow. How's he spinning it?"

Brandon smiled. "Something about a question about our medical history, and him finding out that I wasn't his son. His publicist faxed Charlie a copy. It's pretty slick. Makes him look like a wounded puppy. I'm sure he'll gain a lot of sympathy points."

"Is Charlie going to do anything?"

"He issued his own statement. He's going to go along with Garrett's story, and he asked that the press be considerate of this difficult time for the Archer family," Brandon quoted. "Except it's not so difficult. Not for us at least."

"So things are going well," I said, picking up an eraser.

Brandon grabbed another and we began cleaning off the board. "Yeah, things are great."

"Has he, uh, mentioned me?" I asked.

Brandon was quiet for a minute as he ran his eraser in perfect lines across the whiteboard. "He hasn't," he finally answered. "I think he's doing some serious thinking."

I sighed. "He's probably wishing he'd never gotten involved with me."

"No, he's thinking about whether or not to stay in Cody."

This alarmed me. "What? You're moving?"

"I don't want to, and I've told him that. I want to stay, but he's not sure if it's a good idea."

My heart banged against my ribcage. Charlie didn't want to even be around me. I couldn't blame him though, and I reasoned that it might be better for me as well. It would be easier to get over him if he wasn't so close.

Brandon was disappointed. He wanted a family so bad, and he'd been close to getting it. But the way things were between Charlie and me, I just couldn't figure out a way for us to work.

I went home that night and camped out on my couch to watch the celebrity gossip shows. It was all over the place about the "Shocking secret revealed!" about the Archer family. I snorted. They didn't know the half of it.

I couldn't help but applaud Charlie's decision to be the bigger man and not drag the situation under the microscope of the press, but a part of me wanted to see Garrett suffer. Just because he was a rat, and I didn't like him.

On Friday, Brandon showed me the card he'd received in the mail from Garrett, congratulating him on passing his driving test. Inside the card was a picture of a silver Mercedes and a key.

Brandon wrote a polite letter back, thanking Garrett for the gesture, and declining to accept the car. He was going to proudly drive around in Charlie's car until it died or he earned enough money to buy himself something else. He also informed me that Charlie had decided to stay in Cody, at least until Brandon finished high school.

This was great news for Brandon, but I feared it may drive me insane.

* * *

Claire was shaking as we entered the high school gymnasium. I could feel her excitement and sadness as she gripped my hand.

"My baby is all grown up," she sniffed.

"I know. I'm so proud of her," I said.

Claire nodded and dabbed at her eyes with a tissue. We found our parents saving seats for us and sat down. Jeremy was helping to line up the students for their grand entrance and wouldn't be able to sit with us.

"Is Beau coming?" I asked.

Claire shrugged. "I called him, twice. The first time he said he was coming for sure, then the second time he said he wasn't certain anymore he could make it." Her eyes narrowed a little. "I could hear Sharon in the background. I think she was nagging at him to get off the phone. You know? At times, I almost feel sorry for him. She's a real bitch."

"And he deserves her. He's a prick."

"I know you've always hated him, but he was a decent father to Piper," she said.

I held my tongue. Twenty minutes later, when the music had started and the students had started filing in, Beau had still not shown up. Claire growled.

"I take back what I said about him being a decent father," she said.

I patted her hand.

The ceremony was pompous and long, and in a gym with no air conditioning, it didn't take long for the natives to become restless. The guest speaker wouldn't shut up, and was boring as hell. Finally, someone in the crowd of students made loud snoring noises, and the speaker took the hint and cut it short. The principal moved up to the microphone and began reading the names of the graduating students. When it was Piper's turn to walk across the stage, Claire, our parents, and I stood up to shout her name, but we were drowned out by two male voices in the balcony hooting and hollering. I turned around and saw Brandon and Charlie hanging over the railing, waving their arms in the air, and my heart seemed to lodge itself in my throat.

I faced the stage again and sat down, taking deep breaths to stop the dizziness that threatened to knock me over. I blinked back tears and tried to focus on Piper getting her diploma, but my vision was blurred.

"Shit," I whispered, sniffling.

Claire passed me a tissue, and I tried to discreetly blow my nose. It was hard with my mother staring down at me. I knew she liked Charlie and was disappointed we weren't together anymore, but it was like she was blaming me for the entire thing. Her unsettling stare could make a 400 pound gorilla back away.

The ceremony ended and everyone rushed out to meet their graduate. Claire grabbed Piper in a bear hug and swung her around.

"Mom!" Piper laughed. "I'm in public!"

Claire kissed her cheek. "I don't care. And now I'm going to pass you off to your family to embarrass you further."

Piper rolled her eyes, even though I could tell she was happy. Her cheeks were flushed and her eyes were shining as I hugged her.

"Where's Dad? Is he here?" she asked, clutching her diploma to her chest.

A silence settled around us all as we exchanged sideways glances. Claire cleared her throat.

"Baby, he couldn't make it. I'm sorry," she said.

Piper's shoulder slumped a bit. Then she shook her head and said, "Oh, okay."

"Piper!" Brandon flew past me and hugged her hard. "You're so awesome, congratulations."

I didn't have to turn to know that Charlie was now standing beside me. I could smell his cologne, and I had to resist the urge to grovel at his feet and beg him to take me back.

"Hi," he said.

I nodded at him, trying to ignore the fluttering of my stomach.

"Claire invited us."

"Hey, that's fine," I said quickly, forcing a smile to my face. "How's Brandon?"

Charlie grinned. "He's adjusting faster than I am. The idea of me being his real father seems very natural to him."

My heart relaxed a little as I watched Charlie's expression change. He was talking about his son, and I could hear the pride in his voice. I pictured this day two years in the future, Brandon's graduation. I knew Charlie would be the proudest parent in the entire school. If they were still here.

I gulped and tapped Claire on the shoulder. "I'll, uh, I'll go get the car," I said.

She nodded at me and passed me her keys without blinking. I said hello and goodbye to Brandon and made a hasty exit, running outside and straight for Claire's car. I knew this was the coward in me making an appearance, but I couldn't stop it.

I pulled up to the front of the building and parked, staring straight ahead until Claire and Jeremy came out.

"Nice exit there, Mel," Jeremy said, climbing in the back seat.

"Bite me," I snarled.

Claire frowned at Jeremy and shook her head at him. I drove us back to Claire's house to finish setting up for Piper's party. Since the backyard was so tiny, the food was being laid out inside the living room, and the tables and chairs were out in the garage and the driveway. Piper stayed behind at the school to take pictures with friends and teachers. I knew she was upset that her father hadn't come, and Claire was beyond pissed. She stomped around the kitchen, slamming cupboards and drawers, muttering under her breath. I told Jeremy to keep working and pulled her aside, locking us both in the bathroom where I handed her a cigarette. Then I lit one myself.

"Mel, I quit years ago," she said, staring at it in her fingers. "And you quit too."

I pushed open the window above the toilet and turned on the fan. "I know. But sometimes bad habits are the ones that save your sanity."

She took a puff and exhaled out the window. "Why can't we do this outside?"

"You don't want Mom to show up and see us smoking. She'd kill us both."

I took a big puff and began coughing. It had been so long since I'd last had one, and it tasted terrible. I ground it out in the sink and tossed it in the trash.

Claire giggled and continued sucking down her cigarette. She seemed to relax and sat on the lid of the tank, tapping her feet against the closed toilet seat.

"I can't believe he didn't come. His own daughter graduates high school and he doesn't even bother," she said, but without venom. Now she was just sad.

"You both are better off without him. He's such a scum sucking pig." I smacked the bathroom counter, wishing it were Beau's damn head.

Claire gave a little cough and said, "It was nice of Charlie and Brandon to come."

My whole body jerked at the mention of Charlie.

"Yeah, it was," I said. "He likes Piper, and he's grateful for her help with Brandon."

Claire finished the cigarette and stood up, lifting the toilet seat and dropping in the butt. She flushed and came over to the sink to wash her hands and brush her teeth.

"Is it really over between you?" she asked, squeezing toothpaste onto her brush.

"I think so. I don't see how we can recover. He's right. I'm too stubborn for my own good."

Claire rinsed and spat. "And that's what's going to keep you apart."

I crossed my arms and frowned. "He's stubborn too. If I'm going to apologize, he has to as well."

"For what?"

"Well, for, for…" I paused trying to remember. "For turning my theater into a hoity-toity restaurant."

Claire rolled her eyes. "That's been over and done with for months."

"For bringing Charity here to burn down my house and wreck my car."

"Not his fault she's nuts. And he didn't bring her here. She followed him."

I turned and yanked open the bathroom door. "See if I ever give you another cigarette again," I said and stalked off.

People had started to arrive, and Piper was there, greeting everyone with a warm smile and a hug. Jeremy came over and asked how Claire was.

"Fine for now, but if you were any kind of boyfriend you'd make sure Beau's body was never found," I said.

"That's mature, Mel," Jeremy said. "What's happened to you?"

I shrugged and spotted Charlie and Brandon coming up the driveway. "I'm reverting back to childhood. Maturity hasn't gotten me diddly."

I left him and retreated to the kitchen to make sure all the food was getting put out on the tables, and to hide from Charlie. My mom was already in there, arranging sandwiches on a tray. She spotted me before I could spin around and leave.

"Is Charlie here?" she asked, her voice soft.

I sighed and pulled the vegetable tray from the fridge.

"I guess it's your turn," I said. "Are you going to tell me I'm stupid too? Everyone else has."

"Melinda, I have never said you were stupid," Mom said, and she sounded a little hurt so I shut up. "I do think that Charlie is the best man you've ever been with though, and that maybe you reacted a little too harshly. He loves you. I can see it in his eyes every time he looks at you." She paused and wiped her hands on a dishtowel. "It's the same way your father looks at me."

I glanced up at her. "Dad?" I asked.

She nodded. "In case you haven't noticed, you inherited my stubborn streak."

I couldn't help but snort in agreement.

"It's caused problems between your dad and me, but we work through them. *Together*," she said.

She picked up the tray and started for the door. I mangled a celery stalk between my fingers for a moment before asking, "How?"

Mom stopped and looked over her shoulder at me. "Compromise," she said, then she took the sandwiches out to the living room.

I stared after her, that one word echoing in my head. I shook myself and went to the kitchen door and peeked out.

Mom was checking out the table, talking with an aunt, when I saw Dad glide up behind her and reach around to swipe a sandwich. Mom jumped, then whirled around and swatted him on the arm. He pulled her close and kissed her nose, then offered her a bite. She was grinning as she chewed.

I slipped out to the backyard and sat on the cement step. My parents had been married for thirty-eight years, and while I had memories of them arguing, they always made up, even smiling and hugging when it was all over, because they each agreed to compromise.

Dear God, I was admitting that my mom may have actually had a point. Hell would be freezing over any minute. My head hurt.

And then Beau rounded the corner of the house and I had a sudden urge to kill.

He was carrying a plate of food and looked as dumb as ever. Since the divorce, he'd let his hair grow longer and his stomach wider. I had hated him on sight when I first met him twenty years ago, and now I simply loathed him.

He spotted me and came to a startled halt; his face slack jawed with surprise. I knew I was glaring at him with a murderous glint in my eye.

"Uh, hi, Melinda," he said, turning, getting ready to run.

"Hey, Beau," I said, my voice dripping with malevolence. "Missed you at the ceremony this morning."

He turned an interesting shade of red and swallowed audibly. I knew he was scared of me, Claire's little sister that held big, ugly grudges. On the day he married Claire, I cornered him in the church and threatened to slice off his jewels with a cheese grater if he did anything to hurt her.

I had yet to follow through on that, probably because I didn't own a cheese grater. I perked up a little though, remembering that Claire had one.

"Yeah, well, uh, I was busy," he stammered.

"Uh huh. People out front not thrilled to see you?"

His blush darkened to crimson.

"Where're your wife and kids?"

"She didn't think it was best to come."

"To the graduation itself or the party?"

He didn't speak. I stretched and stood up. He took a step back, almost tripping over an errant garden hose.

"So she didn't want you to see your own daughter get her diploma, and you rolled. Wow. That's sad, Beau," I said.

"Are you gonna kick my ass now?" he asked. "I've been waiting for it for a long time."

I stopped right in front of him, and he tried to stand tall, but I saw the fear in his eyes and wondered if I was that scary.

"No, I'm not going to kick your ass. I'm not even going to tell you to leave."

"Why not?" he asked, his eyes narrowing with suspicion.

I gave a heavy sigh. "Because even if I do think you're the biggest walking asshole on the planet, you are still Piper's father. And I know she loves you, so I wouldn't hurt her by telling you to get lost."

I walked past him to join the rest of the party. Piper was talking and laughing with Brandon, and Charlie was chatting with Jeremy and Claire. My parents were circling the crowd of friends and relatives, arm in arm.

I stood there and watched, thinking there was something very right about the scene. This was how I wanted my life to be. I just didn't know how to get it back now.

Charlie looked up and caught my eye. We held gazes for a moment, until I broke it and ran inside the house. I busied myself setting out fresh salads and more napkins, when I felt a hand at my back.

"Melinda?" Charlie asked, his voice gliding over me.

I felt tingly as I turned around to face him. His eyes were bright blue and sad as he stared at me through his glasses. I didn't know what to say. "I'm sorry" seemed too little too late, and I just couldn't be near him. It hurt to see that look on his face.

"I have to go," I said, and tried to step around him, swallowing the lump in my throat.

He reached out and grabbed my hand, but I pulled away, and he didn't follow. I ran upstairs and locked myself in my room until I saw him and Brandon leave. Then I let myself cry for what I'd let slip through my fingers.

# Chapter Twenty-Six

Another episode of *Fear Factor* had just started when Jeremy arrived. There was a marathon happening on one of the cable channels that showed nothing but cancelled shows. *"Watch surgically enhanced people ingest things that no one in their right mind should ever put in their mouths for 12 straight hours!"* I was already four hours in. Jeremy let himself inside and appraised me with a critical. I was sprawled on the couch, surrounded by junk food and comfortable in my pajamas.

"What?" I asked around a mouthful of ice cream. Some of it dripped down my chin, and I swiped at it with my sleeve.

"You're a mess, Mel," Jeremy said, shaking his head and sitting down next to my feet.

"Hey, I showered today. These are clean jammies."

"You're not going to the opening?"

I growled under my breath. "For the millionth time, no, I'm not going. We broke up, remember?"

"You had some differences in opinion."

"Can you blame me? He defended that crazy ex of his and told me I was overreacting. My house and everything in it is gone, and my car is totaled. I think I have the right to overreact if I want to. I've earned it, damn it!"

I jammed my spoon into the carton of ice cream so hard it broke through the bottom. I got up and carried the container to the kitchen sink before it melted all over me. Jeremy followed.

"This isn't about the house and the car, and you know it. You could give him another chance. You love him, don't you? And what about Brandon?"

I turned on the water and drowned out Jeremy's voice. He gave up and went upstairs to find Claire. I shuffled back to the couch and plopped myself down. I resumed my face stuffing and television watching and didn't speak when they came back. Claire looked nice in a simple red dress with thin straps. She seemed a lot happier in general now, ever since she and Jeremy had admitted they were seeing each other.

"Mel," she started.

I grunted and she sighed and turned to Jeremy, who shrugged.

"Okay, fine. We're going," she said. "If you change your mind though, we can come back and get you."

I gave no response. They left, and I buried myself under a blanket and sulked.

Yes, tonight was the grand opening of the newest restaurant in town, and Charlie owned it. Everyone was going to be there because it was a combination grand opening and graduation party for the seniors, and I would admit to being curious about how it turned out.

I rolled over, ignoring the people on TV eating pig parts that were not bacon or pork chops, and pulled a pillow over my head. No, I didn't care, I tried to tell myself. So what? So what if I missed Charlie and Brandon, and I had nothing to do for the next three months except eat everything in sight? I knew I had to find a new place to live. Claire was my sister, and she loved me, but I couldn't stay with her forever. Besides, she had Jeremy now. I'd heard them talking about moving Jeremy in after Piper left for college.

That was still taking some getting used to, but I'd get over it.

Charlie on the other hand...

For a moment, I sympathized with Charity. Charlie was turning out to be a hard guy to forget about. However, I was not about to turn psycho if he started dating someone else. And living in Cody, I would hear about it.

Okay, so maybe I was going to have to move out of state.

I flipped off the TV and continued to hold the couch down. If I kept this up, by the time school started again, I'd weigh a lot more, but at the moment, I didn't care. I was giving up dating. Also, the idea that I could find a man like Clark Kent. Jeremy had been right. My ideal had been skewed from the time I was five years old.

I sat up and reached for the bowl of popcorn, glancing at the clock on the wall. The party was just starting. I could picture Charlie out on the floor, greeting guests, chatting with reporters, and being as charming as ever. Every unattached woman in town was probably there, dressed in quarter inches of fabric, hoping to attract the newly single millionaire. Brandon would be there too, beaming over the success of his father. No one would miss me. Melinda Martin, the crazy teacher that drove Charlie Archer away.

I paused at the thought. Had I driven him away? I had pushed, that's for sure. And why?

Because he'd wanted me to calm down, to realize this wasn't some movie, and he wasn't a superhero, but he loved me like one.

Dear God, he did love me. And I loved him.

"What have I done?" I asked aloud.

Whatever it was, I needed to fix it, even it just meant we could be friends. If it wasn't too late.

I jumped up and ran to my room, tossing off my pajamas as I went. I dressed as fast as I could, at the same time dragging a brush through my hair. I dabbed on some makeup, grabbed my purse and car keys, and was hurtling toward downtown in my rented car that I hated with a passion because it wasn't my Beetle.

I was still a few miles away when the stupid car sputtered and slowed. I stared in absolute disbelief as the gas gauge slipped down past E and then stopped altogether. I managed to steer the car into a public parking lot before it died on me.

I was in shock. How could I be out of gas? What kind of cruel joke was this? I was on a mission, damn it!

I called Jeremy's cell phone, then Claire's, and then my mom's. No one picked up, and I screamed in frustration. The city buses stopped running at seven, and it was after nine now.

I could walk it, I decided. It wasn't that far; I could do it. It would burn off some calories as well. Bonus! So I took off, then cursed myself after a few blocks. Walking in heels was a bad, bad, stupid idea.

I hobbled to the corner of Main Street and 2nd Avenue and sat down on the bench at the bus stop. I pulled off my shoes and wiggled my toes. I still had a long way to go, and I didn't want to arrive gross, sweaty, and with blisters on my feet. Just when I was about to give up and crawl home, a familiar black truck roared to a stop in front of me.

And then Charlie was kneeling in front of me, looking gorgeous and strong in jeans, a crisp white shirt, and a dark brown suede blazer. Just the sight of him caused me to burst into tears. Charlie wrapped his arms around me, pulling me close, and I inhaled the sweet scent of leather and his cologne mixed together. He always smelled so rugged.

"Mel, are you all right?" he asked, nudging me with his shoulder. "How did you get out here?"

I hiccupped and raised my eyes to meet his. He was concerned, and he loved me, I could see it in his gaze, and I knew I'd made a huge mistake in not doing this sooner.

"I'm so sorry," I said, swiping at my eyes and smearing mascara down my cheeks.

"For what?"

"For being selfish and stupid. I knew you cared about me, and that you wouldn't do anything to hurt me."

"I never will, Mel. I love you."

"I know!" I wailed, crying harder. "Can you forgive me? I know I was awful. I know you're not a superhero, but, but –"

"Shh, it's okay," Charlie said as he leaned in to kiss me.

But I shook my head. "No wait, let me finish." I took a deep breath and said, "I know you're not a superhero, you can't save the world. But you're *my* superhero, and you can save me."

Charlie leaned back on his heels and tilted his head. "What am I supposed to save you from, Melinda?"

I gulped hard. "Myself. Save me from myself. I'm a mess. You've seen it for yourself. I expect too much of people, and when they let me down, I push them away. I'm selfish about stuff. I didn't want you to change the theater because I thought it was mine. I have to let go of the past and see the future. And I want you in it, Charlie, I do. I love you."

"Sometimes holding onto the past is good," he said softly. He cupped my face in his strong hands and rubbed away my mascara streaks with his thumbs.

"What?"

"I want to show you something," he said, standing up and pulling me with him. He guided me to the truck.

"Wait a sec, I just made a huge declaration of my feelings here, and you want to show me something?"

Charlie looked at me funny, and I frowned.

"Sorry, sorry. There I go being selfish again. I'll try to change that," I said, climbing into the passenger seat.

"Don't change too much," Charlie said.

I was confused. As soon as Charlie was behind the steering wheel, I turned to him and asked, "Hey, don't you have a restaurant opening tonight?"

"I do."

"So why aren't you there?"

He gave me that look, the one that made my knees go weak and my heart beat faster.

"I looked around the room and I knew that the person I wanted there most, wasn't there because I couldn't get past my own stupid feelings of inadequacy and let her know just how much she means to me."

"Oh," I whispered, and then Charlie kissed me, and all thoughts left my mind.

Charlie started the truck and headed north, away from downtown. I was feeling warm all over, and didn't notice right away, until we took the turn that would lead us to his house.

"What are we doing?" I asked.

"What I need to show you is at my place."

"You want to have sex?"

"What? No, I mean, I do, but no, not right now," he said.

We pulled into the driveway and Charlie took the keys from the ignition.

"Okay, I don't get it," I said, throwing up my hands.

"Just follow me. You'll understand."

He took my hand and we walked around the house to the massive shed in the backyard. Charlie pushed aside the sliding door and flipped on the lights, and I blinked against the sudden brightness. When my eyes adjusted, I saw what was there. Piled into neat stacks and glowing at

344

me in all their red velvet beauty were twelve of the original theater seats.

"What is this?" I asked. I stepped forward and ran my hand along the material of one of the chairs.

"I was saving this for after I asked you to marry me," he said, and my eyes widened. "Oh yes. I want to marry you. Even though I might go completely gray in two years." He ran a hand through his hair.

"You'll look distinguished," I said. "I'm still confused though."

"About getting married?"

"Oh, God no. Let's do that right away."

Charlie laughed, and I had to refrain from jumping over the seats and throwing myself on top of him.

"These are for your theater," he said.

"What theater?"

"The one I was going to build into our house, just for you. A small home theater with your favorite seats."

"Oh my God," I said. "You kept these for me?"

"I've had them for you all along. I want you to hold onto the things you cherish most." He moved close to me and ran his hand down my face, stopping to cup my chin.

I melted against him. "You're included in that list, you know."

He nodded and dipped his head to kiss me. I was left breathless and very hot.

"Can we make this work?" he asked when we broke apart.

I nodded and hugged him to me. "I'm going to try. I've been miserable without you, Charlie. I love you, and I'm sorry for the way I acted."

"I am too. I should have been more sympathetic to your situation. You lost everything in the house fire, and I didn't see how much that hurt you."

"It was just possessions. The most important things in my life are you and Brandon. I want to make this work between us. I want us to be a family."

Charlie grinned. "Brandon will love to hear you say that. Do you want to go to the party now?"

"Yes. I want to see all your hard work."

We walked hand and hand outside and he drove us downtown. The parking lot was full, and people were lined up waiting to get inside. A huge white banner hung from the upstairs windows. *Congratulations Seniors!*

We walked inside, and Claire let out a scream when she saw us and ran right over.

"Does this mean you're together again?" she asked, pulling at my arm.

Charlie laughed. "For as long as she'll have me."

"Finally, you see reason," Claire said to me.

"We compromised," I said. My mom winked at me and laced her fingers with Dad's.

Brandon came over and gave me a huge hug and a kiss on the cheek. "We missed you," he said. "Now, are you ready to party?"

The food was excellent, and everyone kept complimenting Charlie on a job well done. Claire interviewed him for a feature article in a gourmet magazine, and he posed for plenty of pictures. Brandon showed me how quickly they were posted onto social media. The opening night at Cinema III was a success.

I hung back a little and watched from the balcony. Jeremy and Claire came up to stand on either side of me.

"Some dreams do come true," Jeremy said, nudging me with his arm. "The theater isn't the way you remembered it, and that's okay. You can make new memories."

"With the man of your dreams," Claire said. She smiled at me, then at Jeremy.

I couldn't help but smile back. "He is, and I will."

I hugged them both and excused myself to join Charlie. He spotted me coming and came to the bottom of the steps, placing his hand on the rail and looking up at me in a way that I never imagined a man could look at a woman. Walking down the carpeted stairs, I felt like a princess. When I reached the bottom, he extended his arm, and I looped mine through his.

Life isn't a movie. A superhero isn't likely to show up and sweep you off your feet, but when a real good man does come along, be prepared for bumps and curves in the road that you have to take in stride. Don't slam the brakes, or you'll hurt yourself by getting whiplash, and don't stop, otherwise you'll never reach your destination.

I'd learned all this with Charlie, and I was intent on making sure that he stayed my hero.

www.ingramcontent.com/pod-product-compliance
Lightning Source LLC
Chambersburg PA
CBHW071847220626
47052CB00002B/3